NATALIE BLANK

Evernight Teen ®

www.evernightteen.com

Copyright© 2024

Natalie Blank

ISBN: 978-0-3695-0529-3

Cover Artist: Jay Aheer

Editor: Melissa Hosack

NATALIE BLANK

DEDICATION

To my son, Gareth.

.

NATALIE BLANK

Natalie Blank

Copyright © 2024

Part One: Happiness
Daniel

This is the last funeral.

Total: 19

Death count: 20

The last one was a suicide. There is no service for him. No one would go, even if there was one.

Usually, at the end of May, the seniors prepare to graduate. Instead, a dozen are buried alongside seven would-have-been seniors had they lived just a few weeks more. Every parent wanted their own ceremony for their son. So it was arranged there would be two to three a day for however long it took. Two were held at the synagogue, six at the cathedral, nine at the funeral home, and one on a farm.

This last one is at the Baptist church. It's for Charlie Woodman, one of my best friends. We always joked about his last name, mainly out of jealousy. During ninth grade initiation for football, we all had to drop our pants and run across the field. The last one to reach the end zone got smacked on the ass with a wooden paddle. Charlie, being 6'5" and three hundred pounds, was the last to finish. For all the speed he lacked, he made up for it in girth. The guy had no problem impressing the ladies but mostly with his charm and good old-fashioned manners. He was humble to the extreme, a legit listener, and a loyal friend.

Gracie, his younger sister, sings Amazing Grace as they lower Charlie's casket into the Earth. She's *only* 6'1", the tallest girl in school. She's fifteen and dreams of becoming a country-pop singer, the next Taylor Swift but the black version. Even though Charlie is gone, her voice is flawless.

I focus on Gracie rather than Charlie. He's going into the ground and never coming back. But Gracie will endure. Gracie has to deal with tomorrow and the day after. Everyone has to deal with the aftermath. The rest of the world grieves with us, prays for us, and sends us kindness and support with their tweets and riots against the White House and NRA, but how long will it last? A month? Two months? Will we just be another statistic by mid-summer? Or whenever another attack happens? It could be today. Or tomorrow.

But the loss stays with us forever.

Gracie is beautiful. Most people notice the endless legs before anything, but I'm watching her lips, the pull of her chocolate brown skin as she stretches her mouth for a long note. Her eyes close, but now and then, she opens them and gazes at the sky. She won't look at Charlie's casket either. Besides their skin color and kinky short hair, they don't hold much in common, look-wise. Charlie had big, bold features, a squashed nose, and a massive jaw. Gracie's features are softer and more angelic.

I give her major props for today. She's the only singer so far to hit every note without shedding a single tear. Has she cried? Has she grieved at all? She doesn't look tired or pained like everyone else.

Everyone grieves in their own way. So they say.

Everyone grieves.

At least they should. Can I? Have I?

Toward the end of the service, Coach Colebrook puts his hand on my shoulder. I didn't realize he was standing behind me the whole time. He whispers uncomfortably too close to my ear, "You'll be the one they all look up to now."

Little does he know, I'm not playing football next year. Or any year.

He sniffles back a tear and squeezes my shoulder, even though his body is still weak from the bullet wound. "We need you to be strong."

I nod, appeasing him as I do with anyone these days. I can't tell you how many parents have hugged me, sobbing their eyes out, saying what a good teammate I was to their sons, how I led the team to victory with all my game-saving kicks, and how I'll do it all again when I play for Notre Dame.

But I can't. I won't.

This is the last funeral. This is the last time I'll nod my head and be appeasing.

Tomorrow, I will move on.

How? No clue.

Where? No idea.

But it has to happen. I can't live like this for much longer.

The funeral ends. People linger. I'm not one of them. I take one final look at Gracie, who can't disappear from view no matter how hard she tries, and silently say my last goodbyes to Charlie. I take the long route to the parking lot to avoid the parents. I'll scream if one more crying mom tries to hug me.

I get inside my car, an old Honda Civic with a lot of mileage but a load of heart, and gaze across the town. Morville, Pennsylvania, nicknamed Moo-town, has an area of 8.5 miles and a population that floats between six and seven thousand. We are known for grass-fed ice cream, cows, too many churches, and our state-winning football team. Or at least that's what Wikipedia says. We are a safe, mom-and-pop kind of town. Franchisees don't have crap on Mary's Diner or Hillbill's bacon-flavored ice cream. We're the "it" place to raise kids, eat good food, and be able to get from one side of town to the other without a sweat. Sure, it's a thirty-minute drive to the nearest mall or highway, but you can't beat our view of the stars.

But that was Morville two weeks ago. Wikipedia needs to be updated, and no one has the guts to suggest an edit. Not yet. Not when people like Coach Colebrook, the only other person to cheat death that day, still have hope that things will return to "normal".

Two minutes later, I'm at my house. I change out of my suit and pet Jojo, our ancient old cocker spaniel who sleeps most of the day. Then I drive to the animal hospital where my dad works. He's an award-winning, animal-saving surgeon. During the off-season, I work for him, learning what I can about animals and medicine. My dad never expected me to show much interest, but after Mom left, being around animals has become second nature. Typically, I work from three to five, but since the shooting, I've expanded my hours. I don't even care if I get paid for working overtime. I need a safe place, away from my mourning town.

Hallie, the secretary, greets me with apologetic eyes. She's nearing seventy but has no plans to retire anytime soon. "Hi, Daniel. How are you?" She immediately offers me candy from her bone-shaped bowl.

I take a mint. "I'm alright, Hal. How are you?"

She takes one as well. "Just fine. It hasn't been too busy today."

"Hasn't been busy in a while."

Almost everyone on the team had a dog. I wonder how all those dogs are doing. Dogs grieve too. Would Jojo mourn for me?

"How was the funeral?" she asks, her eyes making that *I'm so sorry* look again. "Or do you hate me for asking?"

"It was long. Baptists sing a lot. Where's my dad?"

"He ran out for a few minutes, but he should be back soon. He left some paperwork for you to do."

"Is that all?"

"And Samantha needs her walk."

Samantha is the vet's foster dog. We always have one or two fosters we care for until they're adopted out. Samantha is a four-year-old St. Bernard. She came to us coated in fleas and matted hair, with several ingrown nails and a swollen eye. After three months of care, she's now the best-looking dog in town, but no one is in the mood to adopt right now.

If Charlie were a dog, he'd be a St. Bernard. Maybe that's why Samantha and I get along so well. She looks forward to her afternoon walks with me, wagging her fluffy tail and slobbering with joy. I zone out on my phone, pulling up random YouTube videos and reading reviews of movies I will never see. Toward the end of our walk, I check my email. I have over two hundred unopened messages, and the number will continue to grow. I'm a huge target for journalists, all curious about how I'm "handling" the loss of my team. I don't know why people use the word "handle" when it comes to grief. A simple "how are you doing?" is way more humane-sounding than "how are you *handling* things?" But who am I to dictate what is humane in a world where an angry young man can buy an assault rifle and gun down an entire football team?

But was he *just* angry?

I hate thinking about it and lead Samantha back to the hospital. There are two ladies in the waiting room, each holding purse-sized dogs that growl at harmless Samantha. The women immediately recognize me, even though I don't know them, and whisper amongst themselves.

"Yes, that's him."

I don't want to be known as *him*. The kid who got away. It's not like I ran away. I wasn't even there. I was home with strep throat all thanks to my cheating ex-girlfriend. Had I been healthy, I'd have been there. Gunned down like everyone else and buried in the ground.

I walk Samantha back to her colossal crate and give her a few treats. Dad has returned, but he's on the phone with someone, talking about treatment plans for an anorexic cat. I didn't know such a thing existed. I take a seat in the back office to start on the paperwork.

A few minutes later, Dad sticks his head in. He has short, black hair and such white skin, one would think he was Count Dracula. I thankfully only inherited his hair color. My mother is Puerto Rican, so I'm blessed with tan skin for life. When I let my hair grow out, I look like Aladdin. But I shave it down for football season, so nothing blocks my view of the goalposts. I won't have to do that this year, so maybe I'll see how long I can grow it.

"Thanks for walking Samantha," Dad says.

"No problem."

"I'm sorry I couldn't make it to the funeral."

"You came to most of them."

"Yes, but Charlie was a good friend of yours."

"They all were."

Dad nods, silently taking that in. Lately, communication between us has been awkward or nearly non-existent, but it's not his fault. He's trying to be a good father, but he has a business to run. He wants to help, but he has no idea how. He can fix broken bones and prescribe medications, but he doesn't know how to deal with grief. When Mom left, the man went to work the next day as though everything was normal. He didn't drink heavily or burn through cash. He focused on getting things done. I must be following in his footsteps, taking the productive route. But it feels more like the isolation route.

I tap my finger against the computer.

"Why don't you assist me with the next patient?" he suggests instead.

I shrug my shoulders. "I'd rather just do the paperwork."

He sighs and rubs the sides of his long, slender nose. "Look. I know you don't want to talk about it, but have you considered seeing someone?"

"I'm not down for the whole therapy thing. I'm just gonna take it day by day if that's all right."

"Whatever you need. I just..." He takes a deep breath. "What about a support group? There's one at St. Matthew's."

"I don't want to talk to anyone. Especially to people in town."

"There are also a lot of support groups online. You could talk anonymously with someone."

"Someone...?"

"Someone who's been through what you've been through. Someone who could relate to having survivor's guilt."

"I don't have that." I don't know what I have.

"You'd never have to meet them. But you could at least talk."

I nod, considering his advice, but also so he'll leave me alone about it. The conversation ends a few seconds later, the purse dogs needing his attention.

Dad closes the door to give me privacy, not that I need it to enter and update patient info.

After a dozen or so forms, I take a break to watch another YouTube video, a preview for the next James Bond movie. I only get through three seconds before the first gun fires off, and I almost throw my phone.

Is this how it's going to be for the rest of my life? Will everything remind me of what I've lost? How does anyone move on from this?

I've never been one to spill my thoughts and feelings, even to my closest friends. I'm an introvert. I distrust most people. And I don't believe in God or any form of religion. I do believe in happiness though. I believe that life should be joyful, pleasurable, and productive. That's what football was for me. Now it's just a memory. Something I can never get back. Even if I somehow mustered up the confidence and courage to play in college, I don't think I'll ever make another field goal as long as I live.

Not wanting to watch any more videos or do any more paperwork, I check out this "online support group". After some Googling, I come across a site that looks like one of the brochures being passed around town. All about loss and grief, how connecting with others is the best thing to do, and to never give up on humanity. There's a blog where people can post their stories, but everything is so depressing to read. But it has a private chat room, just as my dad said. A place to talk anonymously with someone.

I rub my forehead. Why am I doing this? To appease my father? Or to deal with the grief? Perhaps it's the survivor's guilt. Maybe deep down I feel like I should have died with my team. Sometimes I wish I could sob and lament like everyone else, but I'm not like everyone else. I *was* the quiet, observant one on the team. I didn't leap for joy after every field goal. I smiled and nodded, knowing I did my job. And whenever we lost a game, I didn't beat myself up over it or sulk. Instead, I thought about what I could do better the next time.

Will talking to someone help me to move forward? To see things in a new light?

I create a screen name: Kicked123. Not *kicker* because that's not what I am anymore. Once I complete my profile, which is optional, I enter the chat room. Only eight other people are signed in—all with depressing screen names like OrphanChild72 and Widow4Life. Only one screen name seems to register any sort of optimism. In fact, it nearly makes me laugh.

LookingForMyLostSock.

Kicked123: **Have you found your lost sock?**

I sit back and wait.

A minute later, I receive a reply.

LookingForMyLostSock: **stuck behind the dryer**

Kicked123: **That's a bummer. Was it a special sock?**

LookingForMyLostSock: **no just thought the sn would make people laugh**

Kicked123: **It made me laugh.**

LookingForMyLostSock: **u r the first**

This isn't so bad. Sock person has a sense of humor. But will sock person be helpful?

Kicked123: **Are people super serious on this site?**

LookingForMyLostSock: **extremely**

Kicked123: **Have you talked to many people?**

LookingForMyLostSock: **a million**

Kicked123: **That's quite a large number. Has it helped at all?**

LookingForMyLostSock: **in what way?**

Kicked123: **Helped you to move on?**

LookingForMyLostSock: **nope**

Kicked123: **Then why are you here?**

LookingForMyLostSock: **hoping someone will make me laugh**

I can't help but think I might learn something from this sock person. But he or she could assimilate a thing or two about capitalization and punctuation.

Kicked123: **What's your name?**

LookingForMyLostSock: **i dont tell people my name**

Kicked123: **I only ask cause right now you are "sock person" in my head.**

LookingForMyLostSock: **im a girl**

Kicked123: **Now you'll be "sock girl" in my head.**

LookingForMyLostSock: **that doesnt sound right**

Kicked123: **Do you like soccer? Maybe you can be "soccer girl" instead?**

LookingForMyLostSock: **my name is maya**

Kicked123: **It's nice to meet you, Maya. I'm Daniel.**

LookingForMyLostSock: **dont start digging not gonna share much else**

Kicked123: **I don't need to know your street address or phone number. I'm a private person too.**

LookingForMyLostSock: **privacy is important**

Kicked123: **Why did you tell me your name then?**

LookingForMyLostSock: **cause u laughed at my sn**

Someone knocks on the door, nearly jerking me out of my chair. I minimize the chat page. "Come in."

Dad peeks his head in. "Hey, sorry to bother you, but there's someone here to see you."

"Someone as in…?"

"Gracie."

"I'll be right out."

I sign off and rush out the door. If there's one person in town I'll talk to, it's Gracie Woodman.

Maya

He signed off.

I guess I wasn't so funny after all.

Neither was he.

Now I can add Kicked123 to the giant list of people who refuse to chat with me after one session. People get pissed because I don't sympathize with their sob stories, and I don't share my own. It's not like I make fun of them. I just don't give them the kind of attention they're looking for. Because, honestly, I don't know what they need. Who knows what they *really* need after they lose a loved one or get their leg shattered by a bullet? It's the trauma we're talking about, not so much the grief. But everyone focuses on what or who they lost. Not what has become of themselves. It takes guts to look in the mirror and be okay with what you're left with.

I close my laptop and take a swig of Jack Daniel's. I don't even feel the burn anymore. Alcohol and I have a BFF kind of status, and the only thing that ticks it off is not adding in some carbs. My diet consists of 90% potato chips, and 10% pita bread, peanut butter, and dessert cherries. I also take iron supplements since I don't eat red meat and Tylenol for the occasional leg pain.

My phone buzzes. I fall back onto my unmade bed to check it. It's Nicole, asking if I want to hook up again. That sounds like a good idea, but Nicole is starting to get clingy. I made it clear from the start I don't do relationships, dating, or anything remotely romantic. Everyone knows I'm bi, and I love to fool around, but I don't mess with any particular person for long.

I text her back.

Me: **right now?**

She answers almost instantly.

Nicole: **Sure. Your apartment?**

I look around my room. It's always a mess. But Grams doesn't care, so I take advantage of the space, decorating it with random things like empty bottles, retro figurines, and black thrift store curtains. I burn incense to mask any questionable smells, like the pile of laundry flooding in and around my closet. Nicole doesn't mind the clutter, so long as the bed is relatively clean. The sheets smell fine, but I spray some perfume just to be safe.

After five minutes of making her wait, I text her back.

Me: **hurry up**

I smile and grab a bag of chips from my stash under the bed. Gotta fuel up.

Fifteen minutes later, the doorbell rings. I step over dirty clothes and empty chip bags to get out of my room, then it's another four or five steps to the front door. When I open it, Nicole is standing there with a dozen red roses. She's got it bad for me.

"Wow." I scratch the back of my ponytail. The skin is itchy cause I haven't washed my hair in several days. "Are those for me?"

"They're obviously for your grandmother." Nicole laughs and steps inside, holding onto the bouquet. She's wearing a skintight pink dress, black heels, and lots of makeup. Her blonde hair falls to her shoulders, perfectly straight and smelling like Crispy Cream donuts. Why she uses a product that makes her smell like a pastry is beyond me. "Where is the old maid anyway?" Nicole looks around the living room, expecting Grams to be sitting in front of the TV.

"She went to Chicago for the weekend. Somebody's getting married."

"How come you didn't go?"

"Nothing to wear." I slap my hands against my black T-shirt and purple sweat shorts.

Nicole laughs and runs her teeth across her big bottom lip. "Where should I put these?" she asks. "Do you have a vase?"

"Uh, yeah, somewhere." I have no idea.

"They'll be fine for now." Nicole sets them on the kitchen counter then stretches her arms around my waist. She presses her lips softly against mine, smiling between each kiss like this is meant to be romantic or sweet. I slide my tongue into her mouth and squeeze her bottom, taking things up a notch. Nicole always likes to go slow, savoring every touch, every moment, whereas I just want to throw her on my bed and get to it.

Plus, the more time she spends with me, the harder it is for her to leave.

Taking the tempo into my own hands, I pick her up and carry her into my room. I'm considered small to most people, but Nicole is rail-thin because, unlike me, she doesn't eat any carbs. I throw her on top of my bed and immediately shed my shirt and shorts. I have nothing on underneath. Nicole lifts her dress, taking her good sweet time, smirking like senior-citizen speed is supposed to be sexy. For a moment, I consider ending this, but if I just imagine it's someone else, someone less ridiculous, I'm more than willing to keep going.

She tries to kiss me, but I push her back and remove her underwear since that will take at least thirty more seconds if she does it herself. Her eyes go wide, excited from my aggression but also a little nervous. I like it when she lets me be the dominant one.

There's no foreplay, no intense make-out session, no eye contact. Even though Nicole fights for that, I don't let her win. I pinch my eyes shut and do exactly what I need to do to please myself. Since Nicole takes forever, she often doesn't reach my level in time. In which case, she pleasures herself.

But today, she wants me to do it for her.

I step away to put my shorts back on. She remains on the bed, panting, reaching toward me, begging me to come back with those pretty blue eyes. I don't want to touch her anymore. I'm done.

She sits up, her eyes on fire, and grabs me by the arm, pulling me toward her. She kisses my stomach and then my hip. Any lower and she'll hit my—

"Stop!" I jerk back.

Her eyes blink a mile a minute. "What?"

"Don't kiss me there." My hands hover protectively over my thigh.

"What? It's not like it hurts anymore."

"It doesn't matter. Don't fucking kiss me there."

Her eyes swell with tears. "You can be so cruel sometimes." And now she ugly-cries. "Don't you care about me at all?"

Do I care? It's hard to care about someone when the people who created me never gave a shit about me. But I don't want to think about my gene pool. I want to be alone.

I pull my ponytail loose. Black hair falls to my waist. I'm going to take a shower as soon as she leaves. I don't want to smell like Crispy Cream the rest of the day.

"You should go," I say.

She wipes the snot from her face and stands, pulling down her dress and using whatever she can find on the floor to wipe between her legs. "What did I do wrong? I'm sorry I tried to kiss your scar. I wasn't thinking."

I roll my eyes and try to take somewhat of a pleasant tone. "Nicole, I don't want to be your girlfriend, okay? I just want to have sex with you. And that's it."

"I can't do that anymore. I need more."

"Then look elsewhere."

She snatches her underwear off the ground and kicks an empty bottle of Jack. It bounces off the wall but does not break. "Screw you, Maya! You're a selfish, hollow bitch! And you smell like fucking potato chips. I hope you die!"

So dramatic. I chuckle. Finally, someone has made me laugh today!

"Why is this funny to you?" she screams, nearly tripping into her underwear.

"You sound so ridiculous right now."

"Because I have an actual heart? You don't!"

"Oh, no. Too bad." I wave my hands like I'm scared. My sarcasm turns Nicole's cheeks bright red. She might destroy something if I'm not careful.

But instead, she storms out of my room and into the kitchen to retrieve the roses.

I follow at a safe distance.

"You don't deserve flowers from anyone. Not even on your gravestone!"

"It's a good thing I plan to be cremated."

"Burn in hell!" Finally, she gets through the front door, slamming it shut.

Good riddance. She's out of her mind if she thinks any of her insults will affect me, other than making me laugh. In one ear and out the other.

I return to my room, take another swig of Jack, and check the time. 4:15 PM. It's too early to go out yet. But it gives me time to consider my options. Diego sent a text a while ago.

Diego: **Clubbing tonight?**

Diego is my favorite person to go clubbing with and my drug dealer, but he wants me, and I don't want him, so I send him a sad face and tell him I can't. I also have an invite from my 21-year-old cousin to go to Dave & Buster's. That's a much better idea. She gets an ecstatic emoji and a yes.

Even though I desperately need to shower, I open my laptop and look over my chat with Kicked123. It's been over forty-five minutes since he signed off. I don't know why I think he'll return. To talk more about socks?

Grams' apartment is tiny, but we have our own washer and dryer, nestled between the kitchen and second bathroom. I gather all the clothing in my room and hurl it into the washing machine. As I pour the detergent, I notice the lost sock, now covered in dust. I reach my hand as far as it'll stretch, but the stupid sock is just too far away. Screw it. I close the lid of the washing machine and return to my room.

After my shower, I do my monthly shave and tweeze, put on some lotion, and brush out my hair. It's always been long and thick. My coaches wanted me to cut it, convinced it would hinder my performance, but I never had issues with the extra weight around my head. It looked beautiful, up or down. Connor would call me Princess Jasmine.

I don't linger on that thought for too long.

It's almost five o'clock now. I eat another bag of chips and return to my laptop. I fool around on YouTube, watch a couple of stupid videos and previews for shit movies but eventually get back to the chat room. I've disappointed and offended hundreds of people on this site, but what about Kicked123? Was he just not interested? Or was my humor too much?

My phone buzzes again. This time it's my Aunt Meg.

Aunt Meg: **Have you applied for the internship yet?**

The woman is always trying to get me to "do

something with my life" even though I don't need to do anything. When I turn eighteen in three days, I'll cash in on my inheritance. I won't need to live with Grams anymore. Won't need to depend on anyone. I'll finally be able to leave this horrid place and make a name for myself somewhere else.

There's just one problem with that whole plan.

I don't have a plan.

Because I don't know what I want to do or where I want to go. The only place that ever made me happy was Fantasy Land, but that was years ago.

Procrastination. Or poor life skills? I can't decide, so I type about something else.

LookingForMyLostSock: **i tried rescuing my sock but failed its all covered in dust now really gross needs to be thrown away thats what you do when something is old and gross right? why try to fix it? there r plenty of other socks out there why should this sock matter so much? why should i give this sock another chance? what did this sock ever do for me? other than protect my feet from dirt? have I taken the sock for granted?**

I sound like a lunatic. Thank God he's not online because if I were to send this to him, he'd freak out. He'd probably—

Kicked123: **Hey, sorry! I didn't mean to leave like that. Are you still up for chatting?**

He signed back on! And apologized? Why would he do that?

"Daniel," I say his name finally. For the first time in a very long time, I want to communicate with another human being. I want to make a connection.

So I send him my sock paragraph and open another bag of chips.

Daniel

The doorbell rings, but I don't answer until I finish reading Maya's eccentric paragraph about socks. I laugh several times, but then I wonder if it's something deep and personal she's trying to share with me. An analogy of some sort. Is the sock supposed to represent someone in her life? Or a memory?

Dominos for dinner again. Dad can't cook to save his life, and while I can, I haven't felt the need or desire. I pay the delivery guy with cash and carry the pizza back to my bedroom. Dad is staying late at the hospital to do emergency surgery, but I'll leave him a few slices.

Jojo follows me to my desk, awakened by the smell. The dog will sleep through a tornado but always wake up for food.

I type a response before eating.

Kicked123: **What kind of sock is it? Adidas? Nike?**

LookingForMyLostSock: **bombas**

Kicked123: **I've never heard of that brand.**

LookingForMyLostSock: **most comfortable socks on the planet**

Kicked123: **They must be special.**

She doesn't respond right away, so I dive into my food. Pepperoni, green peppers, and mushrooms.

Jojo growls, demanding a slice.

I toss her a pepperoni.

LookingForMyLostSock: **did someone kick u?**

Kicked123: **I play football.**

Used to. But I don't say that. She's avoiding the sock subject now, so maybe it's a sensitive topic.

LookingForMyLostSock: **r u the kicker?**

Kicked123: **Yes.**

LookingForMyLostSock: **u must have long legs**

Kicked123: **Yes. But proportional to my body.**

LookingForMyLostSock: **im not tall**

Kicked123: **I'm not either. For football that is. I'm 5'9".**

LookingForMyLostSock: **im 5'3"**

Even though I have no idea what she looks like or how old she is, our height difference sounds ideal. I used to fantasize about dating someone tall like Gracie Woodman, but after my encounter with her this afternoon, that fantasy is long gone.

LookingForMyLostSock: **how old are u?**

Kicked123: **I thought we weren't going to do the personal questions.**

LookingForMyLostSock: **i changed my mind**

Kicked123: **Because of the sock?**

LookingForMyLostSock: **no**

Kicked123: **Then let's do it the old fashion way.**

LookingForMyLostSock: **???**

Kicked123: **asl?**

LookingForMyLostSock: **what does that mean?**

Kicked123: **Age. Sex. Location. It's what our parents did in the 90s when they chatted online.**

LookingForMyLostSock: **ha glad I wasnt around then but ok**

LookingForMyLostSock: **almost 18**

LookingForMyLostSock: **not sure if i want to have sex with u**

LookingForMyLostSock: **location is somewhere in the US**

LookingForMyLostSock: **or r u asking me where i want to have sex?**

Is she for real? I laugh again, nearly choking on pizza. Is it wrong for me to be enjoying this conversation? Aren't I supposed to be sharing my guilt and grief?

Kicked123: **Sex is referring to your gender, not if you want to have sex.**

LookingForMyLostSock: **my bad**

Kicked123: **You made me laugh again.**

LookingForMyLostSock: **good**

Kicked123: **I'll answer your way. I'm eighteen. I'm not sure if I want to have sex with you until I figure out the message behind your sock story. And my location is somewhere in Pennsylvania.**

LookingForMyLostSock: **u live in morville**

Kicked123: **How'd you figure that out? Are you a computer hacker?**

LookingForMyLostSock: **google   twitter   facebook**

Kicked123: **We're the top story right now.**

LookingForMyLostSock: **u r a newbie**

Kicked123: **I'm guessing you're not a newbie? Since you've talked to millions of people. And this site has been around for a while.**

LookingForMyLostSock: **i joined a year ago**

Kicked123: **How come? If not to move on, then why?**

As I wait for her reply, I think about my motive. Maybe I want a distraction, a way to escape from all this. It would be easier to have an outlet than to dig through my trapped emotions.

LookingForMyLostSock: **its easier to be myself online**

LookingForMyLostSock: **if i offend someone they just block me or stop talking to me but in real life they try to send me to a shrink**

So there is some guilt or grief she's dealing with, but it's not something she wants to open up about. I can relate to that.

Kicked123: **My dad wants me to see a shrink.**
LookingForMyLostSock: **wont help**
Kicked123: **He's worried I'm holding it all in.**
LookingForMyLostSock: **take a laxative**
Kicked123: **LMAO. You're funny.**
LookingForMyLostSock: **im blunt**
Kicked123: **Have you told anyone your story?**
LookingForMyLostSock: **the sock story?**
Kicked123: **The story everyone has on this site.**

I no longer care about the sock. I want to know what happened to Maya. And why she uses humor to avoid talking about her feelings. What is she hiding?

I toss my crust to Jojo. Maya is taking an extra-long time to respond, so I slaughter another piece of pizza. Three minutes go by.

And then Maya signs off.

"Damn."

I can't get upset. I did the same thing to Maya earlier today. All because of Gracie Woodman, which turned out to be a crap show.

****

Two Hours Earlier

Before venturing to the waiting room, I stopped in the bathroom to wash my hands. After touching so many pieces of paper, I felt too gross and contaminated to be around someone as refined as Gracie. I even patted water over my hair, taming the ends from spiraling into my face.

Once clean, I took three deep breaths and went to the front lobby.

Hallie was with a customer, while Gracie loitered by the window, reading a brochure about adoption.

"Are you interested in getting another dog?" I asked, hoping to start the convo on a brighter note than, "hey, how are you handling things?"

"Oh, no," Gracie said, putting the brochure back. A bit of color rushed to her brown cheeks. "Two is enough."

"Sorry, I was working."

"I know. I didn't want to take up too much of your time. I just ... I wanted to talk to you about something important, in private, if you have a few minutes."

"Sure, not a problem." I turned to Hallie. "I'll be back in a little bit."

"Take your time," Hallie said, winking.

I held the door open for Gracie.

She smiled and lowered her head as she slinked outside. The bottom of her black funeral dress flurried as she sat on the Dalmatian-spotted bench. It wasn't exactly the most comfortable place to sit, but I gave her as much space as possible, which ended up being about an inch.

She clasped her hands together and stared at the sidewalk. "What I'm going to ask is hard, especially since I don't know you that well. You were close to my brother, but not with me, which is fine. You're going to college soon, and I still have three more years of high school. And we really have nothing in common." She laughed nervously.

"Except for Charlie."

She ran her teeth across her bottom lip. "Right."

"Is this about Charlie?"

"It's *for* him."

"Tell me."

I figured she'd want me to take some of his personal items or ask for comfort. But instead, she pinched her eyes shut and said, "I want you to go to D.C. with me."

"To...?"

"To protest." She opened her eyes and looked me dead on. Suddenly, that inch between us felt demolished, and Gracie had all the space to herself. I could barely breathe, and before I could even think to open my mouth, Gracie went on a rampage. "This has to stop. It happens way too often, and it's just going to get worse and worse. We have to do something. We need better gun control laws *everywhere*. If we go to D.C., we can march in front of the White House and demand change."

"Oh." I didn't think I'd be traveling that far anytime soon.

"Don't you think it's time the government does something?"

"I don't know if you're going to get that kind of change right now. Students marched and protested back in March, and nothing really changed."

"That's not an excuse not to try."

"I'm not trying to make excuses. I just ... I don't know what I think about all this."

"You don't?" Gracie blinked several times, and her nostrils flared in disgust. "All your friends are dead. Because some monster drove to Texas, walked into a gun store, and walked out with a semi-automatic."

"We don't know his whole story yet."

"Are *you* sympathizing with him?"

"I just like to have all the facts before I make an opinion about something."

She folded her arms across her chest and heaved a sigh. "How many mass shootings does it take for you to make an opinion?"

I stood and walked three feet away, giving myself space to breathe. When I turned back around, her face, usually so calm and serene, was now a force to be reckoned with. Still, I had to be frank with her.

"Gracie, I'm not going."

"It's the right thing to do."

"It won't change anything." I looked across town, noting how old-fashioned all the stores were, the owners too stubborn and proud to change anything. Remodeling came at a price, and no one wanted to pay it. Just like the gunmakers. Why would they support a law that damaged their revenue? I wasn't in support of them, by no means, but I had a decent understanding of economics and how things worked thanks to my dad.

"Well then." Gracie finally stood, dusting the back of her black dress. "I guess I'll have to ask someone else. But your presence would have made a big statement."

"Because I'm the only one left?"

Gracie sighed, a bit of her soft side returning. "Because people look up to you. Whether you admit it or not, you're a big deal in this town. And people count on you. You can't just run from this. It'll destroy you."

"I'm not running." Moving on wasn't the same as running, or was it? I shook my head and headed toward the door. "I need to get back to work."

"Of course," Gracie said, smiling politely, though I could tell she was still livid. "If you change your mind, you know where to find me."

****

I shouldn't have been so cold. Now would be the time to call and apologize, but I don't have the courage. What would I even say? How could I explain it? I've shut down emotionally, and I'm still not sure if it's something I did intentionally. I'm sure a therapist could give me an answer, after dissecting my brain apart. But do I want to be put through that?

I don't want to give anything to anyone right now.

I don't want to care.

I want to be free.

Maya

Dawn arrives at eight o'clock, and I'm more than ready to go out. I squeezed into my little black dress, braided my hair, and put on lots of dark eyeliner and mascara. Dawn's going-out style is the exact opposite. She wears a white blouse and a baby blue skirt. Boring. And her curly red hair is pulled back with a headband. Dorky. But she's been dressing that way since we were kids despite my attempts to sexify her.

"You look like you're going to an eighth-grade dance," I tell her when she enters the apartment.

"You look like you're out to get laid," she fires back, hanging her bulky blue purse on the coat rack.

"Not tonight." I wiggle my hips side to side. "Already took care of that earlier."

Dawn rolls her eyes but smiles. "Nicole?"

I nod. "But I probably won't be seeing her again."

"I figured. Did you read her Facebook post?"

"No. What'd she write this time?"

Dawn takes out her phone to show me.

Nicole: **You don't deserve me, you cunt.**

Ooh. Nicole has already gotten forty-three likes and sixteen comments.

I laugh. "What a drama queen!"

"She had it bad for you." Dawn slides her phone inside one of her oddly huge pockets. "What happened? Did she get too attached?"

"Don't they all?"

"Well, that often happens to girls. Not that I'm going from any kind of experience in that territory. But maybe you should go for a guy next time."

"I'm very picky when it comes to guys." And I

have very good reasons for that.

"Size is important." Dawn and I share a bit of the same humor, but she's tame around other people, whereas I have no filter. She walks into the kitchen and grabs a pitcher of water from the fridge.

"You're not pre-gaming?" I ask.

"With what? Your grandma doesn't have any wine." Dawn limits her alcohol intake to red wine and champagne, claiming her freckles spread when she drinks liquor or beer. What a load of crap. She won't admit she turns into the biggest flirt when she's drunk and makes a fool of herself.

"She doesn't buy it cause she knows I'll drink it," I say.

Dawn smirks as she pours herself a glass of water. "You'd drink cough syrup if she bought it."

"God no. That involves way too much puking."

I motion for Dawn to follow me back to my room. I don't have any red wine, but I do have an excellent assortment of recreational drugs. I open my Betty Boop jewelry box and pull out a few small bags. Nothing too extreme. Just leaves, gummies, and painkillers.

"What'll it be?" I ask.

"We're just going to Dave and Buster's. They have really good appetizers."

"Gummy?"

Dawn rolls her eyes. "No, thank you. I don't do that stuff." The worst she's done is smoke a teeny, tiny joint, and she freaked out the entire time.

"It'll be fun."

"Maya, no." She sighs and runs her fingers across her skirt as though to smooth out the non-existent wrinkles. "I'm driving, remember?"

"So nothing?"

"I'll have a couple of drinks when we get there.

But that's it."

Groaning, I put my lovelies back inside my jewelry box. "You know it's never a *couple* of drinks with me?"

Dawn smiles and takes my hand. "Yes, I know, little cousin. Now, let's go. Traffic is going to suck."

"When I collect my inheritance, we'll take Ubers everywhere. Maybe even a limo ride now and then."

"That's if you stay."

Her smile fades, and her big blue eyes suddenly seem gray.

I give her hand a little squeeze and pull her toward the door. "No plans yet," I say. "So for now, I'm here."

****

It's a forty-minute drive into the city. Grams lives in the suburbs because she's terrified of being mugged, raped, or murdered. I don't fear such things anymore. I still go into the city, whenever I want, with nothing in my wallet but a fake ID, some cash, and gift cards—all replaceable. You can't replace an unlived life. Unless we reincarnate, then we get a second chance. But I'd rather take all the opportunities I can with this life.

I never had a sister and neither did Dawn. Our fathers were brothers, and our mothers were polar opposites in terms of upbringing. Grams had my mother; my mother had me. My mom didn't have a lot of cash until my dad came along and turned her into a princess. Whereas my Aunt Meg and Uncle Lou were childhood sweethearts and went to elite private school together, destined to marry and be rich forever. Dawn has been their pride and joy for the most part. She's older by three years, majoring in nursing, and hoping to take care of NICU babies someday. Uncle Lou and Aunt Meg are surgeons and disappointed that Dawn "only" wants to be a nurse. Nothing's ever good enough for them. It must run in the family because nothing was ever good enough for my parents either.

"Did you eat yet?" Dawn asks, distracting me from my annoying thoughts.

"Chips." I rub my stomach.

"How about some protein? Burgers?"

"I'm good."

"You look thinner than the last time I saw you."

"Is that a hickey on your neck?"

"It's a birthmark, asshole."

"Whoops, I forgot."

She rolls her eyes and turns into the parking garage. It's almost full, so we have to park on the top floor, six stories up. As soon as I get out of the car, I light up a cigarette. I've been dying for one all day. Despite my lack of control with drinking, I have disciplined myself to only smoke at night. So instead of dying from lung cancer at forty, I might just make it to fifty. That's if my liver survives that long.

"Ew." Dawn immediately voices her disgust when she gets out of the car. She grabs her purse and swings it over one shoulder. "You're going to smell now."

"Good. Then no one will come near me tonight."

"Is that what you want?"

"I'm here to have fun. With you, dear cousin." I take two more puffs of my cig and toss it over the ledge. "Shall we?" I loop my arm around hers and pull her toward the elevator, which smells like piss.

When we reach the ground floor, we gasp for air, even though the city air is anything but fresh. It's a two-block walk to Dave & Buster's. The sidewalks are crowded and the streets filled with honking cars moving five miles an hour. I don't fear anyone, not even the so-called dangerous ones. I make eye contact with all the sketchy people. The weirdos. The dudes with face tattoos. The girls with possible man parts. The druggies. The drunks. Bring it on, world. Show me what you got. I'm not scared. Not anymore.

Dawn is my divergent, walking cautiously, not making eye contact with anyone, and leaning in close to me. Her red curls waft my face. She smells like summer. Must be her perfume. She would never come into the city alone. Not even for a job interview.

The line for D & B is only a million miles long. A group of college-aged girls stands ahead of us, all on their phones, and a middle-aged couple is behind us. Dawn relaxes somewhat, and I think about what it'll be like when I have lots of money. We'll be able to go to much better places than this. With VIP access. No more lines. No more waiting.

"Pinball or basketball first?" I ask.

Dawn doesn't answer. Two gunshots from across the street cause everyone around us to either panic, run, or drop to the ground. Dawn screams bloody murder and cowers behind a trashcan. I don't. Because it's just some guy robbing a convenience store. Maybe someone's been shot, maybe not, but the police will be here any minute. I doubt this is going to turn into a bloodbath.

An unsuppressed AR-15 will make your ears ring. What just fired sounds like your typical handgun, easy to conceal and typically used for robberies, not mass shootings. From my experience, in either case, the worst thing you can do is panic. Of course, everyone panics.

Dawn starts pulling me down the sidewalk. "Let's get out of here!"

"You don't want to play pinball anymore?"

She snatches her hand away and completely loses it. "Are you out of your mind? Someone just fired a gun. How is this not traumatizing you?"

Because the worst thing to happen already did, so there's not much left to fear. Death could be a never-ending pleasure zone, who knows?

Rather than explain all that to Dawn, I opt for a more generic answer. "We're in a city. It happens. No need to go spoiling the night."

Dawn shakes her head. Her red curls go flying. "You need help, Maya!"

I laugh and wiggle my leg. "I'm fine. Look, I don't even limp anymore."

"Not your leg. Your head. If you have zero fear right now, you're more messed up than I thought."

Now she's being a turd. "Lay off, Dawn. For real." Seriously, I already got this speech from Nicole today.

"Oh, now we're for real?" She hits the button for the elevator. Several people are behind us, all with the same idea to flee. I don't want to be stuck inside a car with her hysteria for forty-plus minutes.

"You know what?" I say, stepping back. "I'm not ready to go home yet. If you want to leave, that's fine. I'll take an Uber home."

"What? Where are you going?"

"Don't know. Don't care."

"You can't walk around the city by yourself. Don't be stupid, Maya."

I light up another cigarette and back away from her. The people behind me flood the elevator, trapping her inside. I blow my cousin a kiss and walk away. Because of the gunshots, the sidewalks are way less crowded. It means I'll be able to go anywhere I want without having to wait too long in line. I could return to Dave & Buster's to top my pinball score.

But first I need to pee.

The closest and cleanest place to pee is Starbucks.

But in the city, they're anal about letting you use their toilets unless you buy something first. So, I hop in line just for a bag of chips. Once I pee, I relax in a lounge chair to eat my overpriced food and check my phone.

I have several missed calls and texts from Dawn.

Dawn: **Where are you? Please get home safely. Don't do anything stupid.**

I have one giant text from Nicole.

Nicole: **I'm sorry I got so mad earlier. If you don't want a relationship, I get it. But I feel sorry for you. I think deep down you're still hurting because of what happened to you. If you would just let someone love you, you'd be able to heal.**

And lastly, I have a text from an unknown number reminding me I have an appointment with the bank next week to collect my inheritance.

I don't respond to anyone, and I delete the message from Nicole. As much as I enjoy having sex with women, it's getting harder for me to handle all the emotions and hysteria. And while I equally enjoy having sex with men, I don't like being forced into the submissive role or told what to do. I've also had guys who want to "save me", and I don't need that kind of chivalry. There has to be someone out there who is non-clingy and non-assertive but also great at sex. Maybe I just haven't met them yet. Does such a person exist?

Why am I suddenly logged in to my support group, anxiously awaiting Kicked123's return?

It's after 9:00 PM. He's probably out with friends. Then again, didn't he just go to a bunch of funerals? I doubt he's going anywhere tonight. He's probably crying or drinking or doing whatever he's gotta do to get on with his life.

Still, I type.

LookingForMyLostSock: **heres a story**

LookingForMyLostSock: **when i was 8 my parents took me to fantasy land but we got separated in the forest**

LookingForMyLostSock: **i didnt try to find them just started going on all the rides by myself had a way better time without them**

LookingForMyLostSock: **probably like the happiest moment of my life**

I send all the messages, even though he's not online. A small window pops up, asking if I want to send it as an email instead. I hit yes.

While I wait for something to happen, I finish the bag of chips and think about what I just shared. I've never even told Dawn about my rebellion in the forest. So why Daniel? In some ways, it's easier to spill your deepest and darkest secrets with strangers because you don't have an emotional connection with them. But should you lessen the boundaries, you risk them using the information against you. Do I anticipate getting close to Daniel?

I get a new message alert. He's back.

Kicked123: **What happened after that?**

Wow. That was fast.

LookingForMyLostSock: **they found me eventually and i pretended like i had been looking for them the whole time**

Kicked123: **You didn't tell them about all the rides?**

LookingForMyLostSock: **hell no they would have flipped**

Kicked123: **That's cool you went to Fantasy Land. That's that big amusement park down in Georgia, right?**

LookingForMyLostSock: **yup**

Kicked123: **I've always wanted to go. We were**

supposed to go when I was in middle school, but my mom ran out on us, so it never happened.

LookingForMyLostSock: **did she ever come back?**

Kicked123: **No.**

LookingForMyLostSock: **why she leave?**

Kicked123: **She stopped loving my dad.**

LookingForMyLostSock: **and u?**

Kicked123: **She tried to get custody, but my dad wouldn't let her take me. The court wouldn't either.**

LookingForMyLostSock: **where is she from?**

Kicked123: **Puerto Rico.**

LookingForMyLostSock: **have u ever been there?**

Kicked123: **Once. When I was three. I don't remember it. And I never had a desire to go back.**

It was the opposite for me. When our plane departed from the airport, I kept staring out the window, wishing one of the engines would catch fire, so I could parachute out and land right back in Fantasy Land. But nothing happened. My parents drank wine and champagne, while I sat behind them sipping on a Juicy Juice, wondering when our next "family" vacation would be.

That was the last big trip. Their work and social lives got too busy. When they needed a break, they took trips by themselves and left me with Aunt Meg and Uncle Lou. At least I had Dawn to keep me company. Without her, I probably would have started drinking way sooner.

LookingForMyLostSock: **fantasy land was the only place i ever wanted to go to as a kid if i could have any job in the world id be a fantasy land elf princess**

Kicked123: **What kind of elf? Lord of the Rings**

or Santa's helpers?

LookingForMyLostSock: **id be arwen from lotr**

Kicked123: **Do you look like her?**

LookingForMyLostSock: **i got the hair i could be her or princess jasmine**

Kicked123: **That's crazy.**

LookingForMyLostSock: **no its not**

Kicked123: **No. You having Princess Jasmine hair is crazy. Because I have Aladdin hair.**

LookingForMyLostSock: **really?**

Kicked123: **Yes.**

LookingForMyLostSock: **too bad u dont have a profile pic**

Kicked123: **It doesn't allow you to upload one on this site. We'd have to be Facebook or Instagram friends for that.**

LookingForMyLostSock: **i dont want u to see pictures of me**

Kicked123: **Why not? I bet you're pretty.**

I could send him a pic. Maybe even a dirty one for him to jack off to. But I'm not feeling that generous yet. Besides, the more I share, the more he could use it against me. He's still a stranger for now.

LookingForMyLostSock: **just want some privacy**

Kicked123: **You just shared a childhood memory.**

LookingForMyLostSock: **its not the story u want**

Kicked123: **Maybe you have several stories you want to share. It doesn't have to be about the serious stuff.**

LookingForMyLostSock: **thats all people want to talk about here**

Kicked123: **I don't.**

LookingForMyLostSock: **u want to laugh?**

Kicked123: **I just want to be happy. And find some pleasure in life again.**

For the first time in forever, I'm genuinely surprised (in a good way) by another human being. I didn't expect this. Everyone—and I mean *everyone*—I've chatted with on this site has never spoken about happiness or pleasure. It's always been about justice, regret, fear, or absolute sorrow. All subjects I loathe to discuss. My aunt and uncle say it's because I'm still in denial. I don't deny anything that happened. I choose not to let it torment me. If I did, I wouldn't be able to find pleasure in anything. And what's the point of life if you can't enjoy it?

Kicked123: **Have you heard of the Chinese Proverb about love, pleasure, sorrow, and happiness?**

No! He was doing so well. Now he's throwing in love and sorrow?

Still, I am curious about this proverb.

LookingForMyLostSock: **no**

Kicked123: **"You cannot love without knowing pleasure, have sorrow without knowing happiness. You need to know all of them to know one, and that balance came out."**

LookingForMyLostSock: **no one is that balanced**

Kicked123: **I know. I just wonder if it holds any truth. Can you omit one and still have three?**

LookingForMyLostSock: **which one would u pick?**

Kicked123: **Sorrow. What about you?**

LookingForMyLostSock: **love**

Kicked123: **You'd take sorrow over love?**

LookingForMyLostSock: **yes**

Kicked123: **Why?**

LookingForMyLostSock: **sorrow u deal with on your own but love u need somebody else**

Kicked123: **I disagree.**

LookingForMyLostSock: **explainnnn**

Kicked123: **Sorrow is something you can do on your own, but 9 times out of 10 it requires help from someone else.**

LookingForMyLostSock: **im the outlier**

Kicked123: **You've dealt with your sorrow all on your own?**

LookingForMyLostSock: **i guess so**

Kicked123: **How?**

Will this require a lengthy explanation, or can I get away with my usual charm and sarcasm?

I have nothing witty to say. And there's no way to explain what happened or why I chose to suppress most of it. It's a trainwreck in my memory and would require complete sobriety to dig up. But I remember the aftermath. One day I had a family. The next day I did not. One day I was a star athlete, the next I was in a wheelchair. It was chaotic for a while, but I moved on.

I also had painkillers and alcohol to keep me company and give me pleasure. And when that wasn't enough, I turned elsewhere.

LookingForMyLostSock: **i put all my attention elsewhere**

Kicked123: **Into what?**

Dare I tell him? About the first time I hooked up with someone, without being in a relationship. How much I enjoyed it, how high it got me. And when it was over, I didn't have to give a shit about that person. I didn't have to worry if they gave a shit about me. It was such an empowering experience. And a complete fuck you to the conservative parents who never taught me a thing about the world but expected me to always be a good girl.

LookingForMyLostSock: **pleasure**

Kicked123: **And that helped?**

LookingForMyLostSock: **yes**

Kicked123: **And did pleasure lead to happiness and love?**

LookingForMyLostSock: **not love**

Kicked123: **What about happiness?**

Am I happy? I'd say I'm content, most of the time. I'm chill. I laugh a lot. But does all that mean I'm happy? What the hell am I getting into with this guy?

LookingForMyLostSock: **pleasure is my only thing**

Kicked123: **So according to the Chinese proverb, you're only 25% complete.**

LookingForMyLostSock: **haha nice**

Kicked123: **I'm aiming for at least 75%.**

LookingForMyLostSock: **where are u now?**

Kicked123: **Zero.**

LookingForMyLostSock: **we need to fix that**

Kicked123: **We?**

I squirm in my seat. I don't know jack about this guy other than his name, age, and that he lives in Morville where some guy obliterated a football team at an end-of-the-year award ceremony. He knows even less about me, just my trip to Fantasy Land and my lost sock. I've gathered some other facts about him like his mom leaving, but nothing that truly paints a picture of what he's going through. Do I even care what he's going through? I never care about anybody's drama. But for some reason, this doesn't feel like drama. This actually might be fun.

LookingForMyLostSock: **u can get to 25**

Kicked123: **But I want 75%.**

LookingForMyLostSock: **u really need love?**

Kicked123: **And happiness.**

LookingForMyLostSock: **cant help with the love part but i can help with pleasure**

LookingForMyLostSock: **lets start with that**

Kicked123: **Shouldn't we start with my story?**

LookingForMyLostSock: **only if it has a happy ending**

Kicked123: **It doesn't. You should know.**

I bite my lip. I've heard every story out there. Shootings happen at concerts, churches, schools, and clubs to children, old folks, blacks, whites, gays, and straights. Bullets don't discriminate. But despite every situation, I've never been able to help anyone. I've never been able to connect. I didn't *actually* join this site because of my sarcasm. I joined because my counselor (who I was forced to see to avoid legal trouble due to my underage drinking) said it would be good for me to talk to others like myself. The problem is, not many people are like me. I've been waiting a long time for someone to even come close.

I thought this guy might be the one. But he wants to share his story. That could easily ruin things. He could get emotional and end up like everyone else.

Still worth a shot. What have I got to lose?

LookingForMyLostSock: **go for it**

Kicked123: **I can't do it like this. Too soon.**

LookingForMyLostSock: **then lets go back to pleasure**

Kicked123: **Sure. What do you suggest?**

LookingForMyLostSock: **do u drink?**

Kicked123: **Sometimes.**

LookingForMyLostSock: **girlfriend?**

Kicked123: **No.**

LookingForMyLostSock: **boyfriend?**

Kicked123: **I'm straight.**

LookingForMyLostSock: **smoke?**

Kicked123: **No.**

LookingForMyLostSock: **what gave u pleasure before?**

Kicked123: **Football and my friends.**

I'm late making the connection. He said earlier he was a *football* kicker. And he's from Morville where the varsity *football* team got massacred. Not the whole team though, according to the reports. One guy wasn't there.

The kicker.

The kicker stayed home.

LookingForMyLostSock: **must be hard to do now without a team**

Kicked123: **Did you just realize that? Or did you know before?**

LookingForMyLostSock: **just realized it**

Kicked123: **They were my life.**

Kicked123: **I got a scholarship to play football for Notre Dame. I'll have a whole new team to play for. But I don't want it anymore.**

I can relate to having your passion taken away. But in my case, I didn't have a choice. Gymnastics requires two strong legs, and I only have one. If I still had both sides working, would I still be a gymnast?

I haven't thought about that until now. I wouldn't be able to drink like I do and expect to win medals. I'd have to be sober. I'd have to be serious. So many of my life decisions would have gone in the opposite direction had I just been able to return to my sport. But no. That asshole had to put a bullet through my femur of all places. I know the head is one of the hardest targets to hit. But only 5% of people survive it. Knowing my luck, I'd be in that 5% group, suffering from brain damage.

Is that what I wish had happened? That I had died too?

I shake my head. Counselors throw those kinds of

questions at you, to make you feel like you're suffering from survivor's guilt, to make you feel like you're messed up so they can prescribe medications more addicting than alcohol and recommend additional therapy sessions. Why is it their jobs to find out as many wrong things about you as they can? Do they even care what you want?

LookingForMyLostSock: **what do u want?**

Kicked123: **I just want to feel good again. I don't feel anything right now. But I'm told that's normal. You can feel numb for a while.**

LookingForMyLostSock: **just aim for pleasure and forget the balance part**

Kicked123: **Are you suggesting I drink, get a girlfriend, and smoke something?**

LookingForMyLostSock: **no girlfriend just someone for sex**

LookingForMyLostSock: **alcohol for sure**

LookingForMyLostSock: **gummies or joints**

Kicked123: **I don't have anyone to do those things with. And I'm not down for doing them by myself.**

LookingForMyLostSock: **masturbation is overrated**

Kicked123: **Ha!**

LookingForMyLostSock: **just trying to keep it real u dont live too far from me**

Kicked123: **Really? Are you in PA?**

LookingForMyLostSock: **close**

Kicked123: **You're not going to tell me? Even though you know where I live.**

LookingForMyLostSock: **im not suggesting we meet up**

Kicked123: **I'm not either.**

But we could meet up. Eventually. I squirm in my

chair just thinking about it, but I shouldn't let those kinds of thoughts become verbal. I don't want Daniel to presume I'm into him.

LookingForMyLostSock: **but seriously get laid drink smoke eat a pizza**

Kicked123: **Just ate a whole large pizza.**

LookingForMyLostSock: **now go find a hot girl and get with her**

Kicked123: **Not tonight. I'm too full from the pizza. And tired.**

LookingForMyLostSock: **do it soon and tell me about it**

Kicked123: **Ha! Every little detail?**

LookingForMyLostSock: **YES!**

I doubt he will succeed. He seems way too vanilla when it comes to pleasure, but maybe he'll change when he realizes the flavors are endless.

Kicked123: **I'll see what I can do. But hey I need to sign off now. Talk soon? Tomorrow?**

LookingForMyLostSock: **sure**

Kicked123: **Okay. Bye Maya. Thanks for listening.**

LookingForMyLostSock: **same bye**

When I finally look away from my phone, I realize there's hardly anyone around, and the baristas are getting ready to close. How long have I been sitting here?

The desire to play pinball and get wasted has passed. I want nothing more than to get back on my phone and research everything I can find on the Morville Massacre.

But mainly, I want to know more about Kicked123.

Daniel.

Daniel

"Sorry, it took so long to get home."

Dad stands in my doorway, still in his work clothes. I'm in bed with my laptop. Jojo is asleep by my head, slobbering up the pillow. It's almost 11:00 PM.

"Sorry, I ate all the pizza." I nod my head at the empty box.

"It's fine. Hallie made banana bread."

"She's been bringing in a lot of food lately."

"Well, she knows I don't cook. And no one expects you to right now, given everything you've been through. But you can't keep eating take-out. We need to figure out something else in the meantime."

"It's fine, Dad."

"No, it's not fine." His voice takes an edgy tone, something I haven't heard since before Mom left. He rarely yelled when they fought (even though she did and never in English). He spoke sternly and paused between sentences to formulate the most logical responses. And that pissed Mom off even more. That he wouldn't stoop to her level of hysteria. He stayed calm even when she packed her suitcases, broke dishes, and threatened to never come back.

I take a deep breath, not sure if I'm ready for this conversation.

Neither is he. But he's never been one to back down from being a father. No matter how uncomfortable it makes him. That's the one thing I will always admire and respect about my dad. He's always there for me, even when he has no idea what to do.

"May I?" He points at my desk chair.

I nod. "Sure."

He sits rigid, like he's in a courtroom, about to be

sworn in. His hands clasp together, he breathes in through his nose and out through his mouth, yet his words sail out as though written prior. "I know it's late, and we've both had long days. Several long days. But it's important we talk about things."

"I don't want to talk about what happened."

"I know." He nods several times. "But you can't keep quiet forever. It'll be summer soon, and with the football season only a few months away, you need to be ready to play again." He shakes his head at the pizza box. "You need to be healthy, both mentally and physically."

I look at the ceiling rather than his serious face. "You think it's that easy?"

"Of course not. But you have to try."

"Why though? Why do I have to try?"

"Don't you want to go to college?"

"I'm not sure what I want right now. I'd like to be able to feel something for starters."

"That's why I suggested you talk to someone."

"I have."

"Who?"

"I joined one of those online support groups. Like you suggested."

"Oh?" He loses the serious tone. "Well, good!" He smiles and almost chuckles. "That's very good to hear."

"Yeah, so maybe that'll help."

"It's a start. A good start." Dad nods several times, seemingly okay with everything. Then he looks around my room. "Where are all your trophies?"

"In my closet."

He walks around, noting the missing headlines, jerseys, and anything else that would remind me of football. Then he pauses in front of the only picture of me and my mom. Halloween, several years ago, I dressed as

Batman, and my mom was Catwoman. She was the only mother on the block who dressed up every year until middle school came and I was too embarrassed to go trick-or-treating with her. Despite her temper and glass-breaking skills, she was a fun person to be around. She loved to host parties, make exotic meals, and sing at the top of her lungs in or out of the shower.

"Gracie came by the hospital earlier," Dad says, not lingering on the photo for long. "How is she doing?"

"She's upset. Just like everyone else." I don't mention the D.C. protest.

"And what about you?" Dad asks. "You said you wanted to feel something again. Have you really not felt anything this whole time?"

I sigh and rub my forehead. "I just feel ... emptiness."

"But no sadness? No sorrow?"

I swallow hard, thinking of my convo with Maya. How I would omit sorrow if I could. But the problem with sorrow is it can linger inside, and you have no idea it's even there. Sorrow has a way of numbing you, so you don't feel anything at all. And then once you release it, there's no going back. It's a never-ending ride of pain and torment.

I learned that from my mother. After she left, I went numb for a while, and then my emotions exploded. I could barely get through the day without crying. I was only thirteen, and I never thought in a million years she could be that upset with my father she would abandon me as well. What kind of mother does that?

Football took the place of having a mother. Now I've lost football and all my friends. What will take the place of that? Pizza? Dog walking? There has to be something to fill the hole.

"It's okay," I finally say, trying to break the

awkward silence. "It's better if I just move on. Like you did when Mom left."

Dad's eyes widen. "I didn't just move on."

"Yes, you did. You didn't cry once. You didn't even get upset."

"I did cry. And I was very upset. But I never showed any of that in front of you."

"Why not?"

"I had to be strong for you. If I fell apart, it would have taken you longer to heal. I didn't want you to give up on life. Just like I don't want you to give up now."

"I always thought…" I shake my head. "I guess I misunderstood."

"I should have been more open with you. I should have at least told you how I felt." He coughs to clear his throat. "But I will now. And right now, I'm worried about you. I'm worried you're holding all this in. You're not letting anything out."

"Do you need me to cry or something?"

"It's not what I need. It's what you need."

"I want to move on. In my own way."

"All right," he says, finally moving toward the door. "I know you'll figure it out. I just want you to know I'm here for you. Always."

"Thanks, Dad."

"Let me know how that online group goes. I hope it helps."

"I will."

"And I'll look into hiring someone to cook for us."

"Sounds like a plan."

I'm glad he has an idea of what to do to make things better. But I'm still out of whack on my part. Other than talk to Maya, I've done nothing to "deal" with my situation. Once Dad leaves, I return to my laptop, but

Maya is offline. It's almost midnight. Maybe she's asleep.

Still, I read through all our conversations. I make a mental note of anything that might hint at where she lives. But all I gather is she's somewhere close to Pennsylvania. Maybe Maryland or New York.

I want to know more.

I want to know everything.

What does she want?

My phone buzzes with a text from my ex. What the hell could she possibly want?

Anna: **Party tonight at the barn to pay our respects to the team. R u coming?**

The Barn belongs to Kurt Howard's family. Kurt was the quarterback of our team. He was cocky and short-tempered on the field but off the field a pretty great guy. We partied frequently with the junior varsity team, the cheerleaders, even the marching band. There was no division. We supported one another. We mourned every loss together and celebrated every win.

I received the invite days ago from Kurt's little brother, Alfie, a quiet freshman who plays the trumpet. I never responded.

Still, I think about what Maya suggested earlier.

I need to get laid.

Anna and I broke up two days before the massacre. And before that, it had been over two weeks since we last had sex. I should have known something was off when our frequency went from once a week to once a month. She claimed she had a yeast infection then a long period. And every other excuse. In actuality, she was hooking up with some college guy.

So, it's been almost a month.

Not that long. But still.

I need to get laid.

Wesley: The Told Story

Wesley Dover made the decision months in advance. It was carefully planned out. In his head, that is. He never wrote anything down. Never spoke to anyone about it. Initially, the police had little understanding of his motive other than he used to play for the Morville Eagles. But only as a freshman. He quit mid-season, no reason given, and became an outcast.

Then *some* of the facts came out.

He was bullied for quitting football. For the rest of the year, his former teammates would harass him in the hallways, calling him a loser, a pussy, a nark. Some would even go to the extreme of physically assaulting him. In the bathrooms, they'd dunk his head in unflushed toilets and shove wads of wet toilet paper down his pants. But Wesley never reported any of the assaults to the principal or police. He just took it. Day after day. Week after week. Then one day he snapped. While cornered, he pulled out a knife and threatened to kill the next person who touched him.

That earned him his first and only suspension. After that, the team left him alone. The whole school left him alone. He went to his classes. He graduated with decent grades. He didn't go to college or trade school. Instead, he lived at home with his mother, playing video games most of the day and working evening shifts at the grocery store. Though he had zero friends in Morville, he was well known in the first-person shooter world, winning many online games with the potential to go pro. If only he could control his temper.

Whenever he lost, he blamed everyone on his team. He was constantly getting banned from games and having to create new accounts to play. All because he couldn't keep his mouth shut.

When it was revealed how much time he spent playing the game, people ignored the whole "he was bullied" story and blamed the video game instead. Then they criticized his mother for being "neglectful". Though it wasn't her fault she had to work nonstop after her husband walked out on them when Wesley was a baby. The dad disappeared, paid no child support or alimony, and Wesley's mom was a high school dropout. She earned her money cleaning houses and waiting tables. She made sure Wesley had food and clothes, the necessities for life, but she had no idea he played video games all day. She had no idea how angry he was.

She had no idea he had driven to Texas one day to buy a gun with the sole purpose of annihilating an entire football team. Nor did she know about all his trips to the shooting range. He spent every penny earned on ammo.

Every May, right before graduation, the high school held an award ceremony just for Morville athletes. The biggest highlight of 2018 had been the football team's state victory. They hadn't won since the year Wesley quit football. It took seven years to regain the title, and it was Daniel Nowak's 42-yard kick that brought the team to victory once again.

Daniel hadn't missed a single field goal all season. Because of his consistency, he was to be honored with the *Player of the Year* award, but he caught strep throat and was advised to stay home.

He and his teammates were to be honored with *Team of the Year*, which often went to the varsity football team even if they didn't win states.

There were over five hundred people in the auditorium. At 7:56 PM, Principal Canter called the head varsity coach, Hank Colebrook, to present the awards. It took nearly five minutes to announce all the athletes because of the overwhelming applause. Every boy received a plaque and certificate. Coach Colebrook held on to Daniel's plaque for all the pictures, making sure to announce Daniel's achievements, including his scholarship to Notre Dame.

Wesley shot from backstage. He didn't make any grand entrance. He went through the back door, which had been propped open due to the AC malfunctioning, and waited until all the athletes reached the stage.

Coach Colebrook said, "Let's give them one final big round of applause."

During the clapping, Wesley made his move. Without hesitation, he marched forward with his assault rifle and opened fire.

It was an instant blood bath. The team was angled in a way that gave Wesley a clear shot of each and every one of them. Wesley tried aiming for torsos but dialed in—he went right for heads. Twelve of the nineteen boys died instantly. Four died on the way to the hospital. Three on the operating table. Coach Colebrook was the only survivor, as he dove or "fell" into the orchestra pit the second Wesley fired his gun. Colebrook suffered one shot to the shoulder.

When it was clear that he had gotten the entire team, Wesley turned to face the auditorium of screaming people. But rather than fire on anyone else, he turned the gun toward himself and blew his face right off.

But why the varsity team? Even if his motive had something to do with football, the boys he murdered were in elementary school when he played for Morville. They weren't the boys that bullied him in 2011. So, what really set him off?

Maya

"We're here," the Uber driver calls from the front seat.

I look up from my phone, surprised at how fast the trip took. I've been nonstop reading articles, blogs, and police reports. It's after midnight now.

"Thanks," I say, quickly slipping out of the car. I've already paid and tipped. Still glued to my phone, I walk through the apartment building door and down the long, wall-papered hallway. A couple of dogs bark as I pass their doors. A lot of old people live on the first floor, and they all have poodles or pugs.

Once I'm back in my room, I get on my laptop to see if Daniel is online. He's not. Probably asleep. Now that I've read almost every story about the Morville Massacre, I want to talk to him about it. Not because I'm having sudden "feelings" for him. It's an interesting story without a full conclusion. Plus, Daniel is on a mission to regain some pleasure in life, and I'm all for helping with that.

So rather than sleep, which I should, I Google more about the massacre, specifically Wesley Dover. I pull up a couple of photos of him. Seven years ago, he was a smiling young freshman with short red hair and freckles. In the junior varsity team photo, he seemed happy alongside his teammates. Like he belonged.

Fast forward seven years, he's a caveman with a big red beard, bloodshot eyes, and scruffy, neck-length hair. The dude looks like he hasn't seen the sun in months. Definitely hasn't been laid. Did he die a virgin?

I shouldn't joke about that, even if no one else is around. Eventually, it's going to stab me in the back. You know what they say about karma. But I've already experienced the ultimate horror, so what else could happen to me? The chances of being in two mass shootings during one lifetime are pretty rare.

I stop thinking about myself and take a closer look at the 2011 junior varsity photo. I study every athlete, wondering which ones bullied Wesley after he quit the team. They wouldn't say in the articles who did what to him, but someone must've come forward to admit the truth.

Too tired to keep reading, I close my laptop and rummage through my phone. Dawn is content now that I'm home safe and sound; I did text her back. Nicole has been added to my blocklist because she wouldn't stop texting me the whole ride home.

I send Daniel one last message.

LookingForMyLostSock: **u r probably asleep but if u wanna chat im still here**

Daniel

Why did I come here?

It's a sob fest. A bunch of teenagers, mostly athletes, crowded around a big bonfire, drinking and crying. I'm not even outside my car and my comfort level is at a negative ten. If feeling something means I have to get wasted and weep until snot pours out of my nose, then I don't want to feel anything, ever again.

But Anna texts me before I can retreat.

Anna: R u in your car? Come out.

Damn. She spotted me. I shrink into my seat.

Before I can put the car in reverse, she opens the passenger side and slides right in, smelling like clinker and vodka. Her bleach-blonde hair is long and wild, and she's not wearing any shoes. Her feet are coated in dirt, and her legs are bruised. She has that kind of sensitivity that if you poke her too hard or even look at her too hard, she bruises. I could never tickle her or hold her too tight. She'd whack my hands and scream, "Stop! You're giving me bruises!"

By all standards, she is attractive. Thin, but not skeletal. Tall, but not too tall. Does her makeup every day. Shaves regularly. Nice nails. Which always makes me wonder how long we would have lasted had she not cheated. I did love her at one point. But did she ever love me back?

"Where's the douche?" I have no problem calling him by his real name.

Anna doesn't seem to have a problem with it either. "He's not here. We kind of broke up today."

Good riddance. "Is that why you weren't at Charlie's funeral?"

"That and I'm kind of tired of funerals."

"There have been a lot…"

"How was Charlie's?"

"Uh, normal, I guess. Gracie sang."

"She's here."

"She is?" I squint my eyes at the bonfire, hoping she'll stand out.

"Yeah." Anna folds her hands behind her head to stretch or show off; her yellow tank top is see-through. "She's pretty wasted too."

I don't let my eyes linger for more than a second. "I didn't know she drank. She's only fifteen."

"She just lost her brother. I'm surprised you're not drinking. Do you want me to get you something? There's a keg."

I shake my head. "Alcohol won't give me any pleasure."

"Pleasure?" She laughs like I made a joke, but I'm dead serious. Alcohol is the last thing I need right now.

"Alcohol won't make me *feel* good," I correct myself, so she better understands. "That's what I meant by pleasure."

"Oh, I see." Biting the bottom of her finely glossed lip, she reaches a hand toward my leg.

Every inch of my body clenches just thinking of how awful she is but also how talented she is with her mouth. "What are you doing?" I ask.

She pulls her hand back slightly. "Look. I never got the chance to tell you how sorry I am for what I did."

"Well, you have been kind of busy with your boyfriend. But now that you two broke up, you'll have all the time in the world to think about it."

"I've been thinking about it for a while."

I roll my eyes. "Rather than give me some lame-ass apology, could you tell me why you did it?"

"I fell for another guy."

"Why didn't you break up with me first?"

"Because I was selfish. I wanted to get through the school year. We had senior banquet and prom. And I wanted to do all that with you. Not him."

How could I forget those *precious* moments? Seemingly outraged we weren't crowned king and queen, she refused to go to the after-prom with me. In reality, it was all just an act so she could go hook up with someone else.

"You used me. Great." I throw my hands up. She never loved me. "At least you can admit to your shallowness."

She laughs, thinking I made another joke. "You're still a great guy."

Seriously?

"Let me make it up to you." She tip-toes her fingers toward my leg again. "I'll do anything you ask."

"Would you?" I gesture at my crotch.

Her cheeks flush red, but she smiles. "If that'll give you some *pleasure*."

"Let me think." It doesn't take too long to consider what would really give me pleasure. "Get out of my car. And don't come near me ever again."

"What?"

I reach over and open her door. Then without any warning, I shove her as hard as I can. She lands on the ground, cursing through the dictionary. I hope she bruises everything. I hope she caught an STD from that zit-faced douchebag. Hopefully one curable, just in case she passed it on to me. Then again, we always used protection, and we haven't done oral since January. Damn. How could I go for five months without knowing something was wrong? Am I that naive?

She stumbles to her feet. "I saved your life!" Here

it comes. "If it wasn't for me, you'd be dead!"

I knew she'd say that at some point. She thinks she's some kind of hero because she gave me strep, which kept me from the award ceremony, thus preventing my death. But what if it hadn't? What if instead I had been there and spotted Wesley creeping around backstage? What if I had been able to warn everyone? Any extra seconds would have given some of the guys a chance to run or "fall" into the orchestra pit as the coach did.

The chances of me being able to do something beneficial would surely have been minimal. Then again, I was to receive a special award, which could have changed how the guys were lined up, the timing, everything. It's the little details that matter most in any death scenario.

But why am I even considering this with someone like her?

"You didn't save me," I tell her. "You just delayed my death. Now please close the door and move, unless you want your feet run over."

"You're ... *awful!*" She slams the door and scampers back to the bonfire, probably to tell everyone just how awful I am. But I don't care what anyone thinks of me, not anymore. I only cared about my teammates. And they're gone now.

Just as I'm about to back up, Gracie approaches my car. She's in a blue tube top and shorts that expose 90% of her legs. She squints her eyes at my headlights and runs to my side of the car. Now I'm trapped. Will I ever get the chance to leave this horrible place?

She taps the window.

I roll it down halfway.

"You're here!" she exclaims, leaning forward. I didn't know she owned such revealing clothing. She always dresses so pristine at school.

"I'm leaving," I say. "I don't feel well."

"What? No! Stay!" She reeks of Bud Light. "We need you here. We need you to say something."

"Say something? No, sorry, I can't do that."

"You didn't speak at any of the funerals. This is your chance."

"I can't."

Her eyes water and fume, a plethora of emotions ready to burst. "What do you mean you can't? You can't or you won't?"

"Both."

I'm letting her down, yet again, and it's destroying her. I think of Charlie, how he looked whenever we lost a game, which was rare this last year. Gracie's dark eyebrows press together, her bottom lip sticks out, and she breathes heavily through her nose. Fighting back those tears. Always fighting. Charlie would punch me in the face if he knew how insensitive I was being right now. Would it kill me to say a few words?

"Do you wanna go for a ride?" I ask, instead. "We could talk, just you and me?"

Her eyes brighten. "Sure."

****

I'm not sure which situation puts me in a more vulnerable position. At a bonfire, surrounded by sobbing drunk people. Or face-to-face with a not-so-sober Gracie, parked near a dark building on the outskirts of town. It's kind of creepy, unless you look straight up. You can see the stars for miles.

"So, who drove you to the party?" I ask.

Gracie enjoys the McDonald's French fries I just bought her. "Some of the squad."

"And your parents are okay with you being out this late?"

"They know where I went. They know why I needed to be there."

"Right."

"What about you?"

"I'm eighteen, so…"

"No, I meant do *you* know where you need to be?" She puts the greasy bag on the floor and turns toward me. Her legs are so long, her knees hit the dashboard. "What's going on? Why are you being so quiet? You went to all the funerals, but you barely spoke to anyone. And you didn't go to any of the house gatherings."

"I'm still processing everything."

"Processing? You weren't even there! You didn't see them die. You didn't see Charlie…" Her voice quivers, but she doesn't cry. Not yet.

"I should have been there."

"No." She shakes her head. "Don't say that. No one wanted that. No one." She cradles her hands against her chest and takes a deep breath. "The fact that you're alive means something. I just wish you would see that. You were meant to survive."

"I don't know what I see. I just … need space right now. From everyone."

"But everyone is suffering. The whole junior varsity team is scared. They don't know what they're going to do next year. Like seriously, it's going to be a mess trying to put together a new varsity team. It may not even happen. And that'll be such a letdown. After everything that happened, we won't have Friday night football anymore."

"I know. That really sucks."

"Not for you. You're going to college. You're going to play for Notre Dame."

"Yeah … maybe."

"What do you mean *maybe*?" She's back to yelling and throwing her hands up like she means to hit something or someone. "You have to play. If you give up football, then they win!"

"Who?"

She smacks her hands against the dashboard. "The NRA! The shooter! All those horrible politicians! If we stay silent, they win. We have to keep protesting. We have to demand more change. That's why I asked you to go with me. You have the strongest voice right now. You need to be there."

"I don't have any voice right now."

"Daniel, yes you—"

"No. I'm going to stop you right there." I turn toward her, my voice raised but nowhere near hysterical. "You need to listen to me. I'm not the same Daniel I was two weeks ago. I am a different person, a changed person. I'm empty. I have no feelings or emotions right now. And I want to have that again. But I'm not going to get there by faking tears. I have to start with something that actually makes me feel good. I have to remember what happiness feels like. What pleasure feels like."

"Pleasure?" She nearly spits. "You want pleasure at a time like this? You have got to be kidding me."

I rub my forehead. "I just want to go home."

"And do what? What is there to do at home?"

I look down at my phone, resting inside the cup holder. I know exactly what I can do at home. But I don't want Gracie to know about Maya.

"Do you want me to drive you back to The Barn?" I ask.

"Just take me to my house." She folds her arms across her chest and glares out the window. Big salty tears run down her face. A part of me wants to wipe them away, to show some of me still cares, just deep down and out of reach. But I can't allow myself to go that route.

Am I being selfish?

Maya would say no.

And maybe that's why I like Maya. Because she gets me. She understands what I'm going through. She doesn't try to force anything out of me. She talks to me. She makes me laugh. She keeps it real without being too real.

If I could pick one person on the planet to be with tonight, it would be her. And that's without even knowing what she looks like, minus the Jasmine hair.

"Just so you know," Gracie says when I pull into her driveway. "I always liked you."

It takes me a few seconds to tear my mind away from Maya, so my next words come out a tad forced. "I always ... liked you too."

Gracie smirks and smashes her empty McDonald's bag. "But I don't anymore." She throws the trash at me. "So good night." She gets out of the car and slams the door.

I went out tonight with the intent of getting laid, and I pissed off two girls. Will Maya be disappointed or amused by my failure?

As soon as I get home, I check my email. I have one missed message from Maya, about twenty minutes ago. I wonder if she's still awake.

Kicked123: **Hey. I'm here.**

Maya

I'm looking at vacation options for Fantasy Land when I get the notification that Daniel has messaged me. I am so excited that I nearly spill my chips.

LookingForMyLostSock: **u r awake????**

Kicked123: **I went out for a bit.**

LookingForMyLostSock: **u get laid?**

Kicked123: **No. I just pissed people off.**

LookingForMyLostSock: **how?**

Kicked123: **I refused to be like them.**

LookingForMyLostSock: **nice!**

Kicked123: **I don't feel guilty about it. I don't feel anything, that's the problem.**

LookingForMyLostSock: **just leave town**

Kicked123: **Nowhere to go.**

LookingForMyLostSock: **plenty of places to go if u know the right person**

Kicked123: **Are you suggesting something?**

I just started talking to this guy today, and now I'm considering letting him in on my sudden plan? Does that mean I no longer think of him as a stranger? Are we online friends now? Either way, if I hadn't opened up to him, I never would have thought of going back to Fantasy Land to fulfill my childhood dream. It would only make sense to include him, right?

I click on the Fantasy Land tab. For the ultimate vacation, I'll need a week or two to complete the best parts. I want to hit up the main park, the forest, waterfalls, plus resort stuff like sunbathing, drinking, watching fireworks, and having lots of sex with...

Maybe I'll omit the last part. Nicole has been my sex buddy for months. I don't have anyone suitable to take her place right now, and it only takes a couple of days for the cravings to return. Dawn once accused me of being a nymphomaniac. I jokingly took it as a compliment. But sometimes it feels like a curse to want pleasure so much that if I don't have enough of it, life sucks and nothing makes sense. And if I have to fill the hole, I drink more, and that's when life can go dark. Literally and figuratively.

I wasn't always a sex addict/alcoholic. I drank before the incident. I had a glass of wine now and then, just like my mother, though she kept her extra servings a secret. For a lady to drink whiskey, especially straight-up, was vulgar. I had sex but only with my boyfriend. Those were the standards my mother preached. The few times she conversed with me, it was never about what I wanted or enjoyed but what was expected of me. Those standards must've died with her. Cause God knows I didn't want to end up all bitchy and uptight like my mom. Every rule she created, I broke with pleasure.

There's no sense in trying to "behave" myself. I won't survive Fantasy Land without sex. With all that moisture in the air and bodies scarcely dressed in the heat, I'll end up doing something stupid like sex with a stranger. I can't be *that* kind of nympho. I have standards, qualifications, and safety measures to consider.

But if Daniel came with me, could he take Nicole's place?

I don't know him well enough. Nicole and I were friends for several weeks before we had sex. She seemed to have her act together and understand the no-strings-attached policy, and yet she *still* fell for me. If Daniel followed the same path, I'd have to do the same thing to him that I did to Nicole. Inviting him would be a huge risk. I could destroy his obliterated life even more.

But the ungodly images in my head overpower the

"what-if" thoughts.

How can I be having sexual fantasies about a guy I haven't even met? Is it because I already presume he looks like Aladdin? He could have the hair and be ugly as sin.

LookingForMyLostSock: **brb**

For all the research I did on Wesley Dover, I hardly did any on the people he murdered. In just a few short clicks, I'm guided to the Morville High School website, which has a memorial page for all the victims. A short blurb follows each individual picture. I scroll to the end of the page, searching for Daniel. He's highlighted as the only surviving teammate.

And he isn't ugly.

Not at all. His eyes alone would make me turn around more than once should we pass each other on the sidewalk. By his timid smile, he seems like the type of guy not to see himself the way others do. His light brown skin probably glows in the sun. His midnight-black eyebrows and dark eyes don't reveal much joy, but I guess he's not one for candescent senior pictures. I'm glad I was never in high school long enough to endure all the stupid traditions of senior year. Two years was enough. And since I was sixteen by the time I officially dropped out, I opted to earn a GED. I can thank Dawn for pushing me through that stupid exam.

Even though his skin is dark, he has a white-boy face. I see it in his eyes, how they narrow slightly, and the slender shape of his nose. I don't know why I'm focusing on such detail, but it's the only physical representation I have of him and so far, it's pushing me to invite him to Fantasy Land.

But he doesn't have Aladdin hair. Unless he's grown it out since the picture was taken. Should I ask?

It doesn't matter. He wouldn't want long hair in

Georgia. I can endure any kind of heat. I don't sweat like normal people.

LookingForMyLostSock: **sooooo im going to fantasy land**

Kicked123: **Nice. When?**

LookingForMyLostSock: **next week when i turn 18**

Kicked123: **Congrats. Who are you going with?**

LookingForMyLostSock: **no one yet**

Kicked123: **Isn't Fantasy Land super expensive?**

LookingForMyLostSock: **im getting money for my birthday**

Kicked123: **Enough for your whole vacation?**

LookingForMyLostSock: **more than enough**

Kicked123: **Sounds like a plan then. What made you decide to do this?**

LookingForMyLostSock: **i want to live there**

Kicked123: **Ha!**

LookingForMyLostSock: **i do!**

Kicked123: **I'm sure it would be a dream come true.**

LookingForMyLostSock: **u should come with me**

I bite the inside of my mouth and pinch my eyes shut, convinced he's going to freak out and never talk to me ever again. Will I regret this?

Kicked123: **Really? You don't even know me.**

LookingForMyLostSock: **i know enough**

Kicked123: **You'd really be okay with meeting me for the first time in Fantasy Land?**

LookingForMyLostSock: **yes**

Kicked123: **I don't know if I am. I don't know you well enough. We just started talking.**

He's hesitant, of course. That's a normal reaction,

I guess. He needs to know more about me, a fair concern. But how much am I willing to tell him to gain his trust? I already shared a pretty private childhood memory. What if he asks about my family?

LookingForMyLostSock: **i dont turn 18 for 3 more days**

Kicked123: **So we have three days to get to know each other?**

LookingForMyLostSock: **yes but with rules**

Kicked123: **What kind of rules?**

I want the freedom to cut ties easily and immediately if this guy turns out to be another Nicole.

LookingForMyLostSock: **no phone calls or social media**

LookingForMyLostSock: **no questions about my story**

LookingForMyLostSock: **if u want to know ill give u a hint and u can google the rest**

Kicked123: **I'd like to talk on the phone. Is that really a no?**

LookingForMyLostSock: **no for now**

Kicked123: **I've been told I have a sexy voice.**

I snort, laughing.

LookingForMyLostSock: **still a no**

Kicked123: **Alright. I agree.**

LookingForMyLostSock: **for real??**

Kicked123: **As soon as you give me the hint. What should I Google?**

I don't respond. A minute passes by.

Kicked123: **We have to establish some sort of trust if you expect us to go on vacation together.**

LookingForMyLostSock: **rightttt**

I do a quick Google search to make sure I give him the right hint. The first thing that pops up when I type "country concert mass shooting" is the 2017 Las

Vegas shooting. That's not what I survived. Wrong state. Wrong crowd. Wrong everything.

Country music was playing at my shooting. But it was a country *Christian* band. When I add the Christian part to the search, two main articles pop up, both with excessive details, pictures, and videos. There's also a Wikipedia page about the killer. And a memorial site for all the victims. I've never viewed any of these pages.

But here I go, sharing them with someone I haven't even met. Whose rules am I breaking now?

LookingForMyLostSock: **country christian concert mass shooting**

Kicked123: **That's it?**

LookingForMyLostSock: **yes going to bed now ttyl**

Kicked123: **Alright. Sweet dreams.**

LookingForMyLostSock: **same**

I'm not going to bed, not yet, even though my eyes are ready to explode. I just don't want to think about sharing any more personal details with Daniel. I know he'll want to pick my brain. All people do once they discover the truth about you. And as much as people hate pain, they are drawn to it, like a moth to a flame.

No one goes through life scratch-free. But you can control how much pain you take in, how much you show, and how much you share. And people will judge you based on what you choose.

Take in too much = can't function.
Take in too little = can't move on.
Show too much = emotionally unstable.
Show too little = disconnected, unemotional.
Share too much = asking for attention.
Share too little = asking to be left alone.

But there's good news, so I've discovered. You can get past having to worry about any of that by constantly being in a state of bliss. Do things that make you feel good. It's science. You do pleasurable things, your body releases hormones and chemicals that make you happy. Oxytocin is a natural pain reliever, releasing endorphins throughout the body. You get that from sex. Noradrenaline gives you pleasure and peace. You get that from riding roller coasters and visiting places like Fantasy Land.

But instead, people think the key to pain management is talking out their feelings, crying, and bonding with others on an emotional level. To me, that sounds like suffering. It sounds like the opposite of pain management.

With Grams gone for the weekend, I have no issues with being able to smoke a joint in my room. I strip down to my underwear and lie across my bed, musing about my trip to Fantasy Land with Daniel, and the possibility of moving there, permanently.

One or two weeks in Fantasy Land will cost me a few grand at least. But moving there? Is it even possible?

Google tells me I'd have to be a multi-millionaire to afford a house near Fantasy Land. So much of The Forest is protected wildlife, so getting permission to build or buy is near impossible.

The amount I'll be receiving on my birthday: $1,895,323.

Maybe I'll live a few miles away from the park.

All by myself?

Princess Jasmine was alone for years before she met Aladdin. If she can do it, so can I. Then again, she was never happy in her palace.

I guess that means I'll have to buy a tiger too.

Allen: Wikipedia

Allen Timberlee was an American mass murderer responsible for the Coors shooting in which he opened fire into a Music Hall, where roughly 500 people were in attendance for a Country Christian Music Festival, held annually in the town.

Born: Allen Martin Timberlee, May 1st, 1960, Baltimore, Maryland, U.S.

Died: April 23, 2016 (Age 55) Coors, West Virginia, U.S.

Cause of death: Gunshot

Occupation: Retired real estate agent, truck driver

Known for: Perpetrator of the 2016 Coors shooting

DETAILS:

Date: April 23, 2016 = 8:01-8:04 PM

Location: Coors Music Hall, Coors, West Virginia, U.S.

Target: Country Christian Music Festival audience

Killed: 19

Injured: 52

Allen Timberlee was born in and lived in Baltimore, Maryland at the time of the shooting. He was a retired real estate agent, avid golfer, and deer hunter.

Early Years and Education: Timberlee was born to Martha and Dylan Timberlee in 1960, but his mother died shortly after his birth due to complications from labor. He was raised by his father until the age of ten when his father unexpectedly died of a heart attack. He lived with his uncle in Coors, West Virginia for five years where he was repeatedly abused and neglected. His uncle was highly religious, believing in physical punishment for any sin committed. Timberlee was forced into self-flagellation and suffered horrendous scars on his back as a result. In 1975, Children Protective Services, newly created at the time, stepped in and removed Timberlee from the home, but no charges were brought against the uncle. Timberlee lived in foster homes until he graduated from high school.

Career: Despite his tragic childhood, Timberlee went to college and earned a degree in Business from the University of Maryland. He planned to start his own real estate company but lacked management skills. Instead, he worked under a local branch, earning a decent income for most of his life. In 2009, he lost his license after a physical altercation with a client. He retired from real estate and worked as a truck driver on and off until his death.

Personal Life: Timberlee met his wife, Alison Toran, in 1985. They married the next year and had twin boys. One of the boys died of leukemia in 1989. Timberlee and Toran divorced the following year. She received full custody of their son Jeffrey and moved to Boston. During this time, Timberlee suffered frequent alcohol and drug abuse and was arrested for a DUI in 1992. When his son came out as being gay, Timberlee was mortified, having been brainwashed by his uncle to despise homosexuals. When the government legalized gay marriage, Timberlee joined the protest group, at one point making a statement: "If my son marries another man, they both should be crucified."

Shooting: Using a semiautomatic modified to fire like an automatic, Timberlee entered the town music hall at 8:01 PM and immediately opened fire. Nineteen people were killed, including all four members of the band Purple Cross. Fifty-eight people were injured. Timberlee was fatally shot four times in the chest by a police officer in attendance.

Investigation: It is still unclear why Timberlee chose to target the Country Christian Music Festival. While it was a family-friendly event, the lead singer of the band, Purple Cross, was openly gay. Investigators believe the abuse Timberlee suffered under his uncle caused him to be highly homophobic and hateful toward anyone who sympathized with or accepted homosexuality.

The location of the festival was held in Coors, West Virginia, where he lived with his uncle. After his uncle died in 2001, Timberlee inherited the house and would often stay in it whenever he visited Coors, which became more frequent leading up to the night of the shooting. It was discovered that Timberlee had gathered many weapons over the years, including whips, chains, and branding sticks. He had twenty-six guns altogether. He only used one for hunting.

Daniel

As I watch the bread turn crisp inside the toaster oven, I think about how long it will take for Wesley Dover to have his own Wikipedia page. It's all I thought about last night. It's all I dreamt about too.

Do all mass murderers have their own Wikipedia page?

How many victims have their own Wikipedia page?

Not even the police officer who took down Allen Timberlee got his own Wikipedia page, and he was a hero.

I understand Gracie's anger now. The perpetrators are glorified on the web, while the victims get #thoughtsandprayers then silence. But the silence doesn't just come from the White House or the NRA. It's everywhere and everyone.

How many people, besides the people of Coors, care about the Coors shooting anymore? It happened a little over two years ago. I vaguely remember hearing about it on the news, but it was also during a time when Morville had been struck by a tornado and two people died, so we were dealing with our own tragedy. Have we become that numb to mass shootings?

Until it happens to you…

Yet I'm still numb. Maybe if I had been there and survived, then I would feel something.

I add butter and raspberry jam to my toast. Jojo slobbers and pants as I sit by myself at the kitchen table. Dad is still in bed. He's always so exhausted by the weekend that he sleeps through most of it.

After breakfast, I return to my room to see if Maya has signed on. It's only eight o'clock. Even though

I stayed up until two in the morning reading articles, I'm wired to constantly wake early. I have nothing planned for the day. There aren't any more funerals to attend, and graduation has been postponed to the end of June to give people more time to mourn.

I need to stop by the Animal Hospital at some point to walk Samantha. Another doctor comes in for the weekend, but he doesn't give Samantha much attention other than her food and water. I don't understand why Dad doesn't bring Samantha home for the weekends. Jojo wouldn't mind, too much.

I shower, shave, and comb my hair, which is getting thicker and longer every day. I imagine what I'd look like dressed as Aladdin. Would Maya find me attractive?

Would I find *Maya* attractive?

There were several articles about the Coors shooting, but I'm sure Maya didn't want me to read through the memorial pages. Coincidentally, both our shootings had nineteen victims. Twenty if you include the killer.

Of the nineteen killed at the concert, most were adults. I skim through the profiles of each, trying to see if any of them could be related to Maya.

Anthony and Marilyn Floros. Husband and wife. Died protecting their daughter, Maya, who was injured during the concert.

Her name is Maya Floros.

I ignore the individual photos of Anthony and Marilyn and zoom in on Maya. She *is* Princess Jasmine. Everything about her radiates babe from the length of her neck to her smoldering brown eyes. Her hair is down to her waist, thick, wavy, and black, just like mine. She may be paler than a vampire in quarantine, but so what? Those eyes could melt/destroy/fuck diamonds. Her arms are muscular and those shoulders, damn. Gymnast? Weightlifter? Will she answer if I ask?

I look down.

I have a boner.

Then she messages me.

LookingForMyLostSock: **did u sleep?**

Kicked123: **Eventually. You?**

LookingForMyLostSock: **like a baby**

Kicked123: **Nice.**

LookingForMyLostSock: **what r u doing today?**

Kicked123: **I need to go walk a dog. And figure out questions to ask that you'll actually answer.**

LookingForMyLostSock: **u can ask whatever u want**

LookingForMyLostSock: **if i dont want to answer i wont and then we move on**

I can't move anything at the moment. Now that I'm talking to her, it's getting even worse. I haven't gotten hard in forever. Not after what Anna put me through. And then the massacre. There's no room for arousal in any of those situations.

Kicked123: **I saw a picture of you.**

LookingForMyLostSock: **u found the memorial site?**

Kicked123: **Yes.**

LookingForMyLostSock: **its an old pic so dont get too excited**

Too late for that.

Kicked123: **What's your sport? Do you have one?**

LookingForMyLostSock: **i used to be a gymnast**

Kicked123: **Did you quit?**

LookingForMyLostSock: **i had no choice**

Kicked123: **How come?**

LookingForMyLostSock: **not answering that**

Kicked123: **Okay. Are you an only child?**

LookingForMyLostSock: **technically no**

Kicked123: **Technically?**

LookingForMyLostSock: **brother died a few hours after birth**

Kicked123: **I'm sorry.**

LookingForMyLostSock: **he had kidney problems and parents wouldnt abort him**

Kicked123: **They knew he would die?**

LookingForMyLostSock: **basically**

Kicked123: **Were your parents really religious?**

LookingForMyLostSock: **methodists**

Kicked123: **What about you?**

LookingForMyLostSock: **atheist**

Kicked123: **Always or just recently?**

LookingForMyLostSock: **always**

Kicked123: **Same.**

I'm pretty sure my mom was raised Catholic, but the second she came to the states, she forgot about God.

LookingForMyLostSock: **what about your dad?**

Kicked123: **Same. We never talk about religion.**

LookingForMyLostSock: **pretty boring topic**

Kicked123: **I don't find it boring. I just don't get anything from it. It doesn't make sense to me. I was raised to believe in science.**

LookingForMyLostSock: **science makes sense!**

Kicked123: **But evolution and things exploding in space sound weird to me. I think there's a much simpler explanation for everything.**

LookingForMyLostSock: **life is better when I dont have to explain and just do it**

Kicked123: **I hate having to explain. Especially right now. Everyone keeps pressuring me to do things I don't want to do. And then when I say no, they ask why and get angry as if I owe them something.**

LookingForMyLostSock: **u dont owe them shit just do what u want to do**

I take a deep breath and stretch my fingers against the keyboard. If there's any emotion to be felt right now, it's guilt for wanting to escape.

But I feel no shame in telling Maya.

Kicked123: **I'd like to get out of here.**

LookingForMyLostSock: **and go to fantasy land?**

Kicked123: **I haven't made my decision yet. I have to talk to my dad first.**

LookingForMyLostSock: **u r 18**

Kicked123: **It doesn't matter. I live with him so he needs to know where I'm going.**

LookingForMyLostSock: **will he be cool with this?**

Kicked123: **I might have to lie a bit.**

LookingForMyLostSock: **about?**

Kicked123: **I would have to make it seem like I know you. That we've met before.**

LookingForMyLostSock: **why does that matter?**

Kicked123: **I don't know if it will matter. But it might matter.**

LookingForMyLostSock: **tell him this instead**

LookingForMyLostSock: **the founder of the online support group invited u to fantasy land to vacation with other victims**

LookingForMyLostSock: **to share love and support**

LookingForMyLostSock: **cost is covered because u won a raffle**

Kicked123: **That's not a bad idea. He is the one that encouraged me to join this site.**

LookingForMyLostSock: **perfect!**

Kicked123: **Let me talk to him first before I**

give you my answer. How long will we be gone?

LookingForMyLostSock: **wednesday til ????**

Kicked123: **So I have to let you know by Tuesday?**

LookingForMyLostSock: **or sooner so i can book**

Kicked123: **When's your birthday again?**

LookingForMyLostSock: **monday i get my inheritance**

LookingForMyLostSock: **its huge so dont worry about paying for anything**

Kicked123: **That's good. Because I don't have much money in the bank right now.**

I idiotically bought Anna a super expensive necklace for Valentine's Day, which she didn't offer to return to me after we broke up.

LookingForMyLostSock: **u can have whatever u want if u promise me a few things**

Kicked123: **Which are?**

LookingForMyLostSock: **remember that chinese proverb?**

Kicked123: **Yeah?**

LookingForMyLostSock: **no love and no sorrow**

Kicked123: **Are you worried I'm going to fall in love with you?**

LookingForMyLostSock: **not in fantasy land**

Kicked123: **So I can fall in love with you afterward?**

LookingForMyLostSock: **no!**

I'm joking, but a part of me wishes it could be real. That I could find something or someone to love again. But Maya is not a candidate for that. So I best forget about love and sorrow. Just as she said. My goal is to be happy, right?

Kicked123: **I promise I won't fall in love with**

you. EVER.

LookingForMyLostSock: **i dont do drama no tears no nothing**

Kicked123: **I haven't cried since my mom left.**

LookingForMyLostSock: **good!**

Kicked123: **I guess so.**

LookingForMyLostSock: **it will be fun just let me know how the convo with dad goes! gotta run bye!!!**

I check my phone. I have a couple of nasty messages from Anna and one from Luka, the kicker of the junior varsity team.

Luka: **Look what this guy wrote!**

I click the link. Someone on Twitter posted a picture of our varsity team with Xs across all the players, except for me. I'm circled with the caption, "Missed one!" The guy who posted doesn't have a profile pic or any followers, which means he created the account simply to be cruel. Likely, his account will be suspended in the next hour. But the comments have already gotten out of control. Most people are giving him heat, but some agree with him, adding in stuff about our team being stuck up and a bunch of rednecks. So we live in a cow town and some of the players were cocky, but does that warrant their death? Hell no.

And what about me? Why would they target the lone survivor? To make me feel guilty? To make me depressed? To make me want to end myself?

I don't want to be known as the survivor. I don't want to be known as the one who got away—the one who lucked out. I didn't ask for those titles. I would have gladly accepted Player of the Year, but now too much baggage goes with it.

I stop reading before my head spins loose and send Luka a quick text.

Me: **Just ignore it. People are assholes.**

Luka immediately writes back.

Luka: **Can't. People are dying because of assholes.**

And there goes my boner. Well, at least one problem has been solved this morning.

****

Around ten o'clock, I head to the hospital to walk Samantha. After which, I take her home. She is overjoyed to be in a car again, wagging her giant tail in my face as she sticks her head out the window. I wish things such as car rides excited me as much as they excite a dog. Dogs are forever young.

Jojo barks nonstop when I bring Samantha inside. And Samantha whines and cowers behind me, scared of little Jojo. All the racket causes my dad to finally wake up. He grumbles into the kitchen wearing his blue bathrobe and Where's Waldo? glasses.

"Why is Samantha here?" he asks.

Always *why*.

"She shouldn't be in a crate all the time," I say. "She needs more exercise."

"Daniel, we can't have two dogs here."

"We can until she's adopted. Look, she and Jojo are already starting to get along." To the point of not making any noise. Jojo gives us the googly-eyed "am I being replaced?" look.

"Fine. Then perhaps we should work on getting her adopted." Dad turns on the coffee maker. "Did you eat yet?"

"Yes."

He opens the refrigerator. I used to make biscuits with gravy every Saturday morning. I bet he misses that. He opts for toast.

"I'd like to talk to you about something," I say,

sitting at the table. Jojo rubs her nose against my leg, her cue to be picked up. As I hold her in my lap, she growls at Samantha who lingers nearby. Samantha hides behind my chair.

"What is it?" Dad asks, sniffing all the jars of jam to figure out which one to pick, though he typically goes for raspberry.

"You know how I joined that online support group?"

"Yes?"

"Well, they had this uh, raffle thing for a vacation to Fantasy Land, and I kind of won."

Dad's eyebrows shoot so high they look like black arrows. "Really?"

"Yeah. But the trip is soon."

"How soon?"

"Like next week soon."

"For how long?"

"I can't remember the exact timeline. A week or so." A week sounds about right.

"And is it just you that won?"

"I won the free trip. But other people are going from the support group. It's kind of like a bonding experience, for us to connect and share our stories. I'm hoping it'll help me."

Dad nods his head. "Well, you don't need to ask for permission. If you want to go, you should go. Just be safe."

Really? It's that easy for him to be okay with me leaving? Only two weeks after the massacre? Is he that static from everything?

"You're not worried?" I ask.

"Why would I be worried? People go on vacation all the time."

"After what happened here, you're not concerned

about something bad happening to me?"

"Have I ever been one to overly fret about bad things happening to you?"

"No, you've been pretty chill." Calmest parent on the block.

He removes the slightly burnt toast from the oven and loads it with raspberry jam. Both dogs sniff their noses in the air. Dad nods while pouring coffee, likely formulating another perfect round of dialogue.

With a deep breath in and out, he sits at the table and begins. "I don't fret about bad things happening because I know they're bound to happen. Even when all precautions are taken. The only thing I can control is how I handle each situation. In this case, I will encourage you to do whatever is necessary to ensure you have a successful future. I know you don't want to think about college or football right now, but you do have a full ride waiting for you. It's yours for the taking. You may think it doesn't matter right now, but it will someday, especially if you decide later on in life to go to school. College debt is no joke. I just finished paying mine off, and I'm forty-five years old." He finally bites into his toast, jelly falling off the edges.

"I understand." But I don't want to talk about it. "I just wanted to make sure it was all right. Me leaving for a while."

"It's more than all right. I hope it helps you." He sips his coffee. "But Samantha can't stay here while you're gone. She'll have to go back to the hospital. And I'll have to arrange for someone else to walk her while you're gone."

"Okay," I say, petting Samantha's furry head. Jojo growls. I pet Jojo too and notice she is wheezing. "Hey, is this normal?"

Dad glances once at Jojo before getting up for

more coffee creamer. "For a fourteen-year-old dog, yes that's normal."

He could have given me another perfect round of dialogue, possibly explaining what was going on with Jojo, but he opted for the safe route. I know Jojo is old and slowing down. She's not going to be around much longer. But just how long?

I give Jojo a little extra squeeze, remembering when I got her. I was four years old. Christmas Day, Mom surprised *everyone* with a puppy. Dad said nothing of it, which meant he wasn't okay with her going behind his back. But Dad grew to appreciate and love Jojo.

Do I love Jojo? Am I capable of love anymore?

Maya

I'm high when Dawn surprises me with an afternoon visit. She's wearing yoga pants, and her hair is in a messy bun, which means she probably came straight from the gym. Her nostrils flare when she steps inside. "Have you been getting high?" She immediately turns on one of the ceiling fans.

"Grams won't be home until tomorrow."

"You need to air this out now. Gross. How can you even breathe?"

"Pretty well actually."

Dawn opens one of the windows then proceeds to Febreze the entire apartment. I eat chips and lounge on one of the armchairs, watching her enter "big cousin" mode. She washes the dishes in the sink and throws out the garbage. She can't have a conversation until everything is perfect, which means she has something big to say. Or she just wants the place cleaned up before Grams returns, which is equally lame. It's not even her grandmother.

"There," she says, finally sitting down. By the amount of sweat coating her forehead, she looks like she did an additional workout.

"So?" I lean back into my chair, stretching my arms overhead.

"I came over to first of all say, don't ever do that again."

"Do what?"

"What you did to me last night. You scared the shit out of me."

"I was fine. I just went to Starbucks. And then I took an Uber home."

"You went to Starbucks? For what? They don't

put whiskey in their coffee."

"Chips. But whiskey would be an excellent addition to their menu."

Dawn smirks and folds her arms across her chest. "Secondly, I'm here to talk about next week."

"What about next week?"

"Your birthday."

"You wanna make me a cake?"

Dawn rolls her eyes. She means business today. "You haven't told anyone your plans yet. We all know you're finally cashing in on your inheritance. And it's well over a million dollars. Plus, you'll have control over your parents' estate, which is worth a shit ton as well. Just exactly what do you plan to do with all that money?"

"Why is it anyone's business?"

"Because if you plan on moving away, we need to know."

"Why?"

"So we can keep track of you."

"Keep track of me?" I laugh and toss my empty bag of chips toward the coffee table, but it slips off the edge.

Frustrated, Dawn carries it to the kitchen trash can. "My mom and dad are really worried about you. You've been under your grandmother's care for two years, but after Monday, you're an adult."

"I know. Isn't it great?"

"They're worried you're going to be reckless with the money."

"Well, it's a good thing Grams got assigned to be my guardian. I would have run away even sooner if I had to live with your folks."

"See, that's just it. You're going to run away, aren't you?" Dawn rubs her forehead. Her face pinches up like she's going to cry or scream. I know I'm her favorite little cousin, but it's not like she's lacking in the friend department. She and her nursing school friends go out all the time. But I'm sure they're not nearly as fun as I am.

Distance should not be that big of a deal. "It's not running away," I explain. "It's called *moving* away."

"Where?"

"I don't know yet. I'm going to start with Fantasy Land."

"Fantasy Land?"

"Yeah, I'm going there for a little while. I need a vacation."

"By yourself?"

"No. Not by myself."

Dawn's face softens just a bit. She finally sits back down. "Then who with?" If she expects me to say her name, she's dead wrong. But she'll never accept me going with someone I met online.

"New boyfriend," I say instead.

"Boyfriend? An actual boyfriend?"

"Yes."

She blinks several times. "When did this happen? Didn't you just break it off with Nicole?"

"Nicole was not my girlfriend, so nothing got broken off. I just put a stop to all the sex."

"And what about this new guy? Is he from around here, or did you meet him in the city last night?"

I lean my head back and stare at the ceiling fan. Sometimes I envision myself as a teeny tiny person getting caught in the blades and spun around endlessly. I don't imagine it would hurt, but instead, be highly pleasurable like a never-ending Merry-Go-Round. I shake the thought away as a yawn overcomes my entire face. "I'm tired, Dawn. We'll talk later."

"You aren't going to tell me about this guy? Not

even his name?"

I fold my arms behind my head, prepared to pass out in Grams' chair.

Dawn leans forward, her face all pinched and pissy again. "Come on," she says. "Tell me something."

"His name is Kicked123."

"What?"

I close my eyes and fake snore, which makes Dawn livid. She stands and kicks the front of my chair; my eyes jolt open. Is she going to kick me next?

"You're a shitty cousin! I've looked out for you. I've lied for you. I helped you to earn your GED. I've been there for *everything*. And now you're just going to leave and act like it's no big deal?"

"It isn't a big deal. Nothing is. Why can't you people get that?"

"You people? Don't categorize me like that. I'm your cousin."

"You're annoying."

"You're ill! Very, very ill. Please get some help because obviously nothing I do for you makes a difference."

I give her the silent treatment. I give it to anyone who tells me to get help. Because I don't have to explain why my life choices are better antidotes than whatever Dr. Hump-a-lot has to suggest.

Dawn shakes her head and calms herself, somewhat. "If I don't see you before your big adventure, then I don't see you. Just remember, you still have a family here. And we love you. Even if you are a little shit."

She waits a few seconds for my response, but I don't say a word. Rather than yell or kick something again, she quietly leaves. I take a deep breath through my nose. Despite her attempts to eradicate the smell of marijuana, it's still here. It'll leave when it's ready.

In my case, I've been ready to leave since the day I tasted freedom in Fantasy Land.

It's go-time.

Daniel

I spend the rest of the morning in my room with both dogs, while Dad attempts to clean the house and finish paperwork. I offer to help, but he insists I rest. There are no more funerals to attend, so there's no need to put on a collared shirt and tie. In another life, I'd go to graduation parties, sign yearbooks, and get psyched for college.

But in this life, I lounge in my boxers, play video games, eat Nutella straight from the jar, and research Fantasy Land. I always thought Fantasy Land was a place for Lord of the Rings fanatics and Dungeons and Dragons geeks. But it's much more than that. Not only does it have some of the most intense roller coasters in the country, but some of the sickest live shows based on classic fantasy books and medieval legends. There's even a nightclub where bouncers dress as centaurs and exotic fairy dancers hang from the ceilings. The website says: *Fantasy Land will take you through the wardrobe to Narnia, across the sea alongside Captain Nemo, and up Mount Doom with Frodo Baggins.* You don't even have to be a human while you're there. Elf ears or fairy wings (your choice) are included with any 4-night stay or longer.

It sounds like a blast. And since school hasn't let out yet for most states, the crowds won't be too unbearable. But I can't say the same about the heat. I don't do well in humid environments unless I have a fan tied to me. Or maybe on-demand buckets of ice.

Will I have a good time with Maya? She seems like a fun girl, and she's hot based on her two-year-old picture, but what if in person, she's nothing but trouble?

She could be one of those crazy girls, like legit kill-you-in-your-sleep psycho.

I take a risk going with her. But if I stay here, I'll be numb and unmotivated to do anything for who knows how long. This trip could be my chance to start over. Maybe I'll discover something new about myself. Maybe I'll find happiness again. Even some pleasure.

****

In the evening, Maya finally signs online.

LookingForMyLostSock: **u talk to yr dad?**

Kicked123: **Yes.**

LookingForMyLostSock: **and?**

Kicked123: **The lie worked.**

LookingForMyLostSock: **just gotta pack yr suitcase**

Kicked123: **If I decide to go.**

LookingForMyLostSock: **u still dont know? dont you know enough about me?**

Kicked123: **I know that you used to be a gymnast. I know about the shooting.**

LookingForMyLostSock: **what else is there to know?**

Kicked123: **I just want to know if you were different before the shooting.**

LookingForMyLostSock: **what do u mean?**

Kicked123: **You told me you live for pleasure. But were you always like that? Or did you feel other things?**

LookingForMyLostSock: **like when i was a kid?**

Kicked123: **Yes.**

LookingForMyLostSock: **i dont think about childhood**

Kicked123: **But you remember that trip to Fantasy Land.**

LookingForMyLostSock: **that was different**

Kicked123: **What about when you left Fantasy Land? Do you remember feeling sad at all?**

LookingForMyLostSock: **maybe but lets not dive into feelings**

LookingForMyLostSock: **stick to the rules**

Kicked123: **I know. But one of my uncertainties is having such a good time that when I return home I'll be miserable.**

LookingForMyLostSock: **maybe u wont return**

Kicked123: **What's that supposed to mean?**

Is she planning to abduct me?

LookingForMyLostSock: **keep an open mind**

LookingForMyLostSock: **when i was alone in fantasy land i didnt worry**

LookingForMyLostSock: **i just had a good time thats what u should do always**

Always? How can you always have a good time when there are negative things you cannot control? Like other people? The weather? They say happiness is a choice, so it might be possible. Just not something I expect myself to figure out anytime soon.

****

Maya and I talk on and off throughout the weekend. It helps to pass the time, and her sarcasm and jokes amuse me. I disable all my social media accounts, so I'm not plagued by posts and pictures about the massacre. I don't read any more articles about Maya's shooting or my own. If I'm not online with Maya, I'm with Jojo and Samantha in the backyard. Jojo is too old to play fetch anymore, so she sits on my lap while I throw the frisbee across the yard a thousand times for Samantha. This hermit life isn't so bad. But it isn't something I want long-term. I suppose I've already made my decision about Fantasy Land, but I have yet to tell Maya. I hope my answer will make us both happy.

Maya

"So that's it?" Grams cries, bawling her eyes out in my doorway as I pack up my room. "You have your money, and now I'll never see you again?"

It's Monday, at last. All my belongings are either in boxes or bags. Most of the luggage is coming with me to Fantasy Land; the rest goes into storage. I've taken down all my posters, folded up my comforter, and stacked my pillows, that stuff can stay, along with the furniture. I'll buy way better stuff whenever I get a place of my own. A king-size bed, lots of mirrors, and a jacuzzi tub for sure. That's the kind of bedroom I want—comfortable, big, and fun.

"You don't need to cry," I say, trying to be nice. "I'm not leaving forever. I'll come back to visit." Maybe. "You knew I wouldn't stay here after I turned eighteen."

"I didn't think it would be this soon! Oh, dear!" Grams covers her face and sobs into the wall. She's your typical Italian grandmother, overdramatic and loud with black fuzz above her upper lip. She uses her hands to convey every emotion. If she isn't sobbing into them, she's throwing them up left and right like she's trying to make pizza out of the air.

"I was planning to make you a cake, but I don't think I can now!" she wails.

"Hey, no worries. I don't need cake." I just need to get the hell out of here. And Grams needs to calm down and leave me alone, so I can talk to Daniel. I want to book the trip, but I'm still waiting for his answer.

Grams dries her eyes with the bottom of her ankle-length skirt. "Will you call me whenever you get there? When are you leaving?"

"Hopefully tomorrow or Wednesday at the latest."

"Couldn't you wait another week? Just so I have time to process all this? And so we can say some proper goodbyes to everyone else?"

"I already said my goodbyes."

"A Facebook post is not proper."

"It is for me." I'm starting to lose my patience. I'll leave tonight and stay in a hotel if she doesn't back off.

"Fine." Grams throws her hands up. "But I am making you a cake! A great big chocolate one! And you're going to eat it! And like it!" She storms out, slamming the door behind her.

I immediately open my laptop, the only thing I haven't packed.

LookingForMyLostSock: **got the money so i can book now**

LookingForMyLostSock: **i can get a flight from charleston at noon tomorrow and theres a flight for u from pittsburgh at 3 pm does that work?**

Kicked123: **Which hotel are we staying at?**

LookingForMyLostSock: **its a surprise**

Kicked123: **Will we share a room? Or what?**

LookingForMyLostSock: **ill get a suite**

Kicked123: **Okay.**

LookingForMyLostSock: **as in yes?**

Kicked123: **As in yes.**

LookingForMyLostSock:
YAYYYYYYYYYYYYYYYYY!!!!!!

I'm ecstatic. This is the best I've felt since the night I got invited to dance on stage with the lead singer of Blood Bath Drama Kings.

For the next half hour, I collect Daniel's info so I can book his flight. Then I secure the hotel and purchase park tickets. I also arrange for a personal driver to pick Daniel up from the airport, so he doesn't have to take an Uber or bus. Once that is taken care of, I reorganize my luggage, making sure my drugs are thoroughly hidden. I stuff my marijuana gummies inside my vitamin container. The leaves will have to stay behind due to their obnoxious smell. I put all my pills inside a tampon box, though is that necessary considering they're mostly prescriptions? My Jack is more problematic, so I opt to get more when I'm in Georgia. The only problem is I have to use a real ID when I check into the hotel, and my real ID says I'm eighteen. My fake says I'm twenty-two. What am I going to do? Risk using the fake or come up with a better plan?

Don't procrastinate. It's a minuscule problem to deal with. I'm sure I'll be able to get booze if I ask someone to buy it for me.

Two hours later, I'm ready to go, and Grams is frosting a three-layer chocolate cake. I'm not much for sweets, but I'll eat a small piece to appease her.

I sit at the kitchen table while Grams sings happy birthday, then showers me with forehead kisses, takes my picture, and claps as I blow out all eighteen candles. She tries not to cry again, but birthdays always upset her. Any holiday makes her upset because she thinks about my mother.

Grams grew up poor and married poor. So poor that my mother had to sleep on a sleep sofa until she was twelve years old. Grams encouraged her daughter to marry for love and happiness, but my mother sought the wealthiest, most successful man she could find. Grams' greatest joy from that marriage ended up being me. And if she wasn't so scared of the slim chance of me breaking my neck while competing in gymnastics, she would have attended my meets. But she did come to school events. She was a part of my life. And thank the holy stars the judge listened to me when I asked to live with her instead of my aunt and uncle after my parents' death.

"I have something for you, now that you're eighteen," Grams says, as she cuts us each a slice of cake.

"Lottery tickets?"

"No. You don't need any more money." She reaches into her purse nearby and pulls out a black jewelry box. "Your mother was supposed to inherit this after my passing, but now it goes to you. I want you to have it now. Before I go."

"Thanks, Grams." I open it. It's Grams' teardrop ruby necklace. "Wow, Grams, didn't Grandpa give this to you like a million years ago?"

"*Forty* years ago. Right before his passing." She smiles through her pain. I am the only family she has left. Maybe I should be more sympathetic.

"You don't want it anymore?" I ask. "You want me to have it?"

She stands and takes the necklace from me. She pushes all my hair to one side and loops the jewel around my neck. "It's worth a lot now, so don't go selling it. Please."

"I won't. I'll cherish it forever." I trace my fingers around the edges. "It feels kind of heavy though."

"The ruby is four karats, and there's about two karats worth of diamonds around it."

"Wow. How did Grandpa afford this?" The dude could barely put food on the table.

"I have no idea." Her lips veer to one side, which might suggest Grandpa did something scandalous to get that necklace. "Just keep it in a safe place when you're not wearing it."

"Sure." Tampon box or vitamin container.

Daniel

I only pack a carry-on.

If Maya turns out to be a psychopath, it'll be easier to gather my things and leave.

Also, I have no idea what to bring other than toiletries, clothes, and a phone charger. Maya said I'll sweat so much I won't want to wear *anything*. I hope she doesn't plan to lounge around the hotel without her clothes on. If I get hard just looking at a picture of her, I can only imagine what would happen if I saw her naked.

Monday evening, I make chicken parmesan for dinner. I'm not in the mood to cook, but I'm leaving Dad for a while, and it's the least I can do. As I pull the garlic bread out of the oven, Dad calls from the hospital, saying he'll be home late. I put aside a plate for him, eat my own, and Tupperware the rest. Samantha licks clean my dish, while Jojo lies on the couch, snoring away. Usually, she stalks me whenever I eat. Maybe Jojo is still upset Samantha is here. Or she knows I'm going somewhere. Dogs can sense those things.

While I'm rinsing my dish, the doorbell rings. It better not be anyone other than Amazon dropping off a package. Samantha barks and scratches at the door, chipping paint. Now I'm forced to answer it or risk demolition.

I grab Samantha by the collar and swing open the door. Samantha sniffs the intruder and immediately stops barking. It's only Gracie, back to her usual, sober self with cleavage-covering clothing. I'm surprised, nonetheless. Our last two encounters ended on a bad note. The third time's the charm?

"Hi, Gracie. What's up?"

"Your dad says you're leaving tomorrow."

"What? When did he tell you that?"

"I came to the hospital today, but you weren't there. He said you were home, packing for some trip."

This is not good. If Dad told Gracie, Gracie will tell everyone from school. I don't want people to know my business. That's one of the reasons I went off social media. So I can leave town discreetly.

"Yeah, I'm leaving for a while," I confess.

She frowns. "Where are you going?"

"Well, I'm, uh…" I notice the silver Cross around her neck. "I'm going on a spiritual journey."

"A spiritual journey?" Her lips twist to one side, suggesting a smile. "For what purpose?"

"To find God."

"Oh." Now she's full-on smiling, and it's making me sweat. "That's great, Daniel. That'll be good for you. Maybe you'll start to feel something again."

"Yes, that's the idea." I'll be feeling the heat of Georgia. "So, what did you need to see me for? Did you want to come in or—?"

"I wanted to apologize."

This is surprising. "For what?"

"For what I said to you. And for all the pressure I put on you. I wasn't being sympathetic. What you're going through is different from every other person in this town. And with all the crap people are saying online, it's just not fair."

"Gracie, it's okay. It doesn't bother me what they say."

"Then why'd you disable all your social media accounts?"

"Well, I…" I better think of something fast. "I need to be off social media for the spiritual journey. No electronics."

"Oh, right. That makes sense. What exactly are

you doing for this spiritual journey?"

"I'm going to connect with other victims of mass shootings. It's really hard to talk about right now. It's very…" I lower my head, hoping she'll back off if I show some hesitation and fear.

"No, I understand. I'm just so glad you're doing something. I'd love to have you with us next week in D.C., but finding God is way more important."

"Thanks, Gracie."

She smiles again and nervously scratches the back of her neck. "Yes, well ... I should be going. But I just…"

Oh, no. She's biting her bottom lip and squeezing her knees together. Girls do that when they want to be hugged or worse, kissed. Girls also do that when they're debating whether or not to kiss you first. Do I want to be in either situation? I'm still very much attracted to Gracie, but she's three years younger than me, way too political for my comfort, and the sister of my dead teammate. I also just lied to her face about the spiritual journey.

Something dropping to the kitchen floor startles us both. "Oh, no," I say, backing up. "I gotta go. It's the dog."

"Of course." Gracie immediately steps away. "Good luck on your journey! Tell me all about it when you get back."

I don't care that Samantha jumped on the counter and knocked over the tray I used to cook the chicken parmesan in. She licks it clean, and I thank her a million times for saving me from an unwanted situation.

Then the doorbell rings again. Gracie is back?

Samantha barks hysterically, growling like an armed robber is at the door. I look through the peephole, surprised to see Coach Colebrook holding a brown paper bag. Did we somehow travel back in time to when people knocked on your door whenever? Or could it be that I haven't returned anyone's calls in two weeks, so what choice have they but to come directly to my house?

I hold Samantha by the collar to open the door, but she doesn't stop barking even after she sniffs the coach. So I drag her away and step outside to talk to him.

"Sorry," I say. "We're fostering."

"That's okay, Daniel. I just came by to give you your plaques." He hands me the bag, but I don't look inside.

"Thanks."

"We had to have them professionally cleaned. That's why it took so long for me to get them to you."

I wish he hadn't told me that. That the blood of my teammates had splattered on all the awards. Now I'll have less of a reason to do much with the plaques other than dump them inside my closet. Or a trash can.

By my silence, maybe he realizes what he said was a mistake. He scratches the back of his shaved head and looks across the driveway. "Is your dad around?"

"He's working late."

"Oh." He nods his head and awkwardly shifts from right foot to left. "Well, I just wanted to give you your plaques. And to tell you again how sorry I am. But grateful you're still with us. It's going to be hard next year, working with a brand-new team, if we can even put one together. I'm hoping you'll be an inspiration to all the boys when you kick ass at Notre Dame."

"I, uh ... hope so too." Maybe if I continue to lie, he'll just leave. It worked on Gracie.

He starts to back away but pauses. "You know, I haven't spoken to anyone about this, but Wesley showed a lot of potential."

"What?" Why the hell would he say something like that?

"Nothing, forget I said anything!" he almost shouts. With a forced smile, he puts a hand on my shoulder and gives it a tight squeeze. He did that at every funeral, but this time it feels wrong. Like he shouldn't be touching me or anyone, ever.

"I have to get back inside," I say. "The dog…"

"Right. Take care now, Daniel." He finally removes his hand from my shoulder, but I'm pretty sure he would have kept it there as long as possible had I stayed outside with him.

I don't get upset with Samantha for scratching the hell out of the front door. We have paint in the garage. I'll fix it up before I leave tomorrow. It almost seems like Samantha tried her damndest to get outside, to protect me from Coach Colebrook. Dogs can sense a good person from a bad. But Colebrook has never been anything but kind and supportive for as long as I've known him. Why did the shoulder squeezing suddenly become creepy? Does he do that to everyone or just specific people?

Maybe it was the fact that he did it after mentioning Wesley.

What did Colebrook mean by Wesley's potential? Potential on the football field? Potential to *kill*? If the latter, why wouldn't Colebrook mention that to the investigators?

Probably because it would put him in a bad light. He's already been labeled #coward for falling into the pit rather than protecting his athletes. Though many say he "fell" because of the gunshot. Either way, the survivor's guilt must be eating him alive. Plus PTSD. If physical therapy doesn't work, his shoulder may give him problems the rest of his life.

I take a deep breath, feeling less weirded out by Colebrook's behavior. He gets a pass this time.

Samantha follows me into my bedroom and

lounges on top of my bed. She's acting like she already lives here. I sit down at my desk and Google Wesley Dover's name again. He still doesn't have a Wikipedia yet, but I scroll through all the pictures people and newspapers have posted of him. Some are sad and sympathetic, saying if he hadn't been bullied, he never would have snapped. Many still blame video games. Others just label him as mentally ill. *Should have been medicated. Should have been put into a special school. Should have been taken away from his neglectful mother.*

Should have.

But what about potential? There's nothing about Wesley being a good athlete, let alone an outstanding one. From what people have posted, he was a decent receiver but lacked the upper body mass to survive varsity. Wesley looked more like a soccer player, lean and long-legged. What could Colebrook see in that?

Maya messages me, interrupting my thoughts.

LookingForMyLostSock: **all packed?**

Kicked123: **Yeah.**

LookingForMyLostSock: **excited?**

Kicked123: **Getting there. Just had a couple of weird visits from people.**

LookingForMyLostSock: **did u tell them where u were going?**

Kicked123: **I'm on a spiritual journey.**

LookingForMyLostSock: **u r getting good at this**

Kicked123: **Deceiving people?**

LookingForMyLostSock: **its for yr happiness**

Kicked123: **I'm never going to be happy if I stay here.**

LookingForMyLostSock: **im in the same boat**

Kicked123: **Boats make me seasick.**

LookingForMyLostSock: **good thing we r not going on a cruise**

Kicked123: **I wouldn't survive that.**

I stare at the brown paper bag. No one got to hold their plaques for more than a few minutes. Why should I hold on to mine any longer? I toss the bag into my closet, alongside all my other awards just in case Dad wants to keep anything for sentimental value.

I chat for a few more hours with Maya, mainly talking about Fantasy Land and all the things we're going to do. Maya doesn't have a set schedule for anything other than needing to hit up the nightclub, something she wasn't allowed to do as a child. Since she's paying for everything, I don't care if she makes all the decisions so long as there are cool-down options like a pool or waterpark when it gets too hot.

Around ten o'clock, I fall asleep with Samantha lying by my feet and Jojo wheezing by my head. I dream about Coach Colebrook and Wesley Dover. Colebrook screams at Wesley to run faster, but Wesley can't keep up with the other guys. With every step, he grows smaller and smaller, until he passes out on the field with all his teammates around him, yelling at him to get up. Then they kick him.

If I wasn't going to Fantasy Land, I might be inclined to investigate Wesley Dover on my own. To uncover this so-called potential only Coach Colebrook seems to know about.

But more importantly, did his potential have anything to do with his downfall and decision to annihilate my team? Did he always have killer instincts?

I can't linger on what-if ideas. Maya would tell me to move on and let the police handle it. But what if after months and months of investigating, they still have no real answers?

The simplest explanation is usually the right one. A bullied, shooter-obsessed young man just lost it one day.

That doesn't sound simple at all.
There is no simple answer for anything.

Wesley: The Untold Story

Though Wesley had difficulty playing football in middle school, he improved tremendously by October of his freshman year. He put on mass and lifted weights to strengthen his upper body. Things were starting to look up for him. He had a place where he could fit in, a team to keep him motivated, and the support of his classmates. Though his mother was unable to attend the games due to her never-ending work schedule, he would regularly tell her about them and how much he enjoyed being on the team.

"Maybe if I work hard enough, I can get a scholarship," Wesley would say. Because there was no chance she'd have any money to pay for his education, let alone be willing or able to cosign on loans.

The last game Wesley played earned him his first highlight in the school newspaper. He caught the winning touchdown, and for the first time, he felt like he might have a chance to go somewhere with his life. Girls started paying attention to him, even though he was just average in looks. His Facebook blew up with friend requests. Teachers he didn't have suddenly knew his name and would regularly say hello to him.

The following Wednesday, Wesley was invited to meet with the varsity coach after practice. Wesley was stoked, thinking of all the possibilities ahead of him should he continue to improve. After showering and changing into fresh clothes, he waited patiently outside Coach Colebrook's office while the rest of his teammates went home.

It was 5:30 PM.

Wesley waited and waited, fiddling his fingers, wondering why it was taking so long for the coach to invite him in. He didn't know how much longer he could wait, considering it would be dark soon, and he had to walk home.

Finally, at six o'clock, Coach Colebrook opened his office door and invited Wesley in. At this point, the locker room was empty. No other adults were there, not even a custodian.

Coach Colebrook was just as intimidating up close as he was from far away. At 6'3", he weighed at least two hundred and thirty pounds, the majority of it in his chest. No player could out-bench him. He had a round, pudgy face, was completely shaven—including his head—and had cauliflower ears from boxing in the Navy. He spoke loudly, even indoors, indicating he may have lost some of his hearing but would never admit to it.

Wesley stood awkwardly in the doorway, unsure whether to stand or sit.

Colebrook relaxed in his revolving chair and gestured to the green cushioned chair across from his desk. He immediately stood once Wesley sat. "I've been watching your progress this year. I'm very impressed. You started just average, but you're improving every week. Do you enjoy your position?"

"My position?"

"As a receiver?"

"Oh, yes, very much so."

"Any aspirations to change positions?"

"Oh, no, sir. I'm fine where I'm at."

"Hmmm." Colebrook scratched his chin and sat on the corner of his desk. "Tell me more about yourself, Wesley. I never see your parents at any of the games."

"It's just my mom, and she works a lot."

"Oh, so she's not around much?"

"No. I'm usually on my own."

"And how about friends?"

"I'm friends with everyone on the team."

"What about girls? Do you have a girlfriend?"

"No." Wesley nervously rubbed the back of his neck.

"Why are you blushing, Wesley? There's nothing to be ashamed of."

"I'm, uh…" Wesley was visibly sweating now. "I've never had a girlfriend."

"What about a boyfriend?"

Wesley cleared his throat and sat up a little straighter. "No, sir. I'm not gay if that's what you're asking."

"Well, that's good, son. Because this is a small town, and most folks around here are God-fearing people. I would hate for it to get out that we have a future star player who's a homosexual. That just wouldn't settle right with people. And it would certainly harm the reputation of this school's football program."

Stunned, Wesley nearly choked on his following words. "I'm not gay."

"Are you sure? If you've never been with a girl, how can you know?"

Wesley wasn't book smart, but he knew when someone was trying to mess with him. What purpose did this interrogation serve other than to make Wesley second guess himself?

Wesley smiled politely and said, "If most folks around here are God-fearing people, then me being a virgin would not be seen as any fault to them."

"Touché," Colebrook said, lifting an invisible glass.

"Anyway." Wesley stood up, ready to leave.

"Yes?" Colebrook stood as well. He had a good six inches on Wesley and made no effort to give him space.

Wesley swallowed hard. "If there isn't anything else you wanted to talk about, I should be getting home. It'll be dark soon."

"Oh, I'm sure it already is. Why don't I give you a ride home?"

"I only live around the corner. It's not a big deal if I walk."

Colebrook placed his hand on Wesley's shoulder, giving it a good squeeze. "I insist."

****

Later that night, Wesley laid sideways in the bathtub, waiting for it to fill with enough water for him to drown.

It wasn't the physical pain that tormented him. He barely noticed the blood seeping between his legs, turning the water a pinkish red. It was his soul. Should he have one, it was taken from him that night, after he'd been humiliated and destroyed.

When the water covered his nose, causing him to gag, he sat up and grabbed a bar of soap. Violently, he washed himself, pushing hard against the fingerprint red marks on his arms. But no matter how hard Wesley scrubbed, he couldn't get the scent of Colebrook off his body. He kept smelling the man's awful aftershave and hearing his heavy breathing in his ear.

Wesley stayed in that bathtub all night, trying to rid himself of the smell, the pain, the shame, and the guilt.

Why?

Why didn't I fight back?

Wesley blamed himself. He never should have accepted a ride home with Coach Colebrook. He'd listened to the coach lament about how horrible high school was for him and how fighting in the Navy helped him to overcome many of his problems. Yet the coach never declared precisely what those problems were.

Wesley should have gotten out of the car immediately rather than allow the coach to put his arm around his shoulder, squeeze it repeatedly, and then let him fondle his ears and neck.

Why?

Why didn't I fight back?

By morning, Wesley decided the only way to survive the trauma was to shut down. To keep everything hidden away. If he opened his mouth, if he told anyone, would they believe him? Would his teammates take his side or the coach's?

Wesley didn't go to school for the rest of the week. The junior varsity coach called several times, asking if he would be well enough to play in Friday's game, but Wesley never responded. Instead, he spent most of his time in his room, trying to make himself feel as little as possible. The less space he took up, the less he would feel. He barely ate, barely moved. When his mother came to check up on him, he pretended to be ill. After a while, she knew he was faking it and threatened to tell the school. If a counselor or any of the coaches knew, they'd wonder why, which would lead to questioning. Wesley couldn't handle any of that. He wanted to be left alone.

When Wesley returned to school the following week, he was a completely different person. He didn't speak to anyone, avoided eye contact, and kept a low profile in the hallway. At first, a few of his teammates were genuinely concerned about him, thinking someone had died or Wesley had some incurable disease. Rumors quickly spread, but not one person speculated that the head varsity coach had raped him.

Wesley left his jersey outside the locker room with a note to all the coaches that he was quitting football and for no one to contact him about it. Immediately, the guys who were "concerned" then cornered Wesley in the hallway, demanding his reason for quitting. No one leaves Morville football unless they're seriously injured or sick.

That's when the bullying began. Everyone knows this part of the story. Several people witnessed the harassment, but no one spoke up about it until after the Morville Massacre. Even though the school had a "strict" no-bullying policy, they were lenient if the perpetrators were athletes. It was more important that the school won state titles than care about the loners and outcasts. Those are the unfortunate truths of many high schools in America.

The knife incident happened just before Winter Break. Wesley had been punched, pushed, and his head dunked into a toilet, but when three of his teammates cornered him in the bathroom, telling him to drop his pants so they could take a picture of his penis, Wesley finally snapped. He opened a switchblade and slashed at the air, screaming, "If you ever touch me again, any of you, I will kill you!"

Wesley was suspended for bringing a weapon to school. The other boys claimed they hadn't touched him and were merely trying to get an answer for his betrayal to the football team. Their "harassment" earned them lunch detention.

The years went by. Eventually, no one bothered Wesley, and he was forgotten about. Though whenever someone new inquired about him, the responses were harsh. "Don't mess with him. He's crazy and might blow up the school one day." He met regularly with the school psychologist and was prescribed Lithium, which numbed him to a point where he wouldn't notice the rain on his back. Nothing brought him joy or happiness anymore, but that was okay. He would rather spend the rest of his life desensitized than feel any ounce of his past.

He played video games to pass the time. At first, it was just a hobby, but Wesley showed skill in the first-person shooter world. Because his medicine fatigued him, he ditched Lithium to spend more time online. He became highly competitive to the point that he would express rage toward his teammates whenever they lost a match. The things he screamed matched many of the hurtful things thrown by his former teammates.

And then one day, something changed in Wesley. After being banned from another match, he got ready for his evening shift at the grocery store. As he walked through the parking lot, a truckload of loud high school kids zoomed by, nearly hitting him. Wesley waved a fist and yelled at them to slow down but halted when he realized it was the varsity football team, celebrating their state victory.

Suddenly, Wesley was taken back seven years prior when the varsity team won, and the town went wild for them. While Colebrook celebrated his victory, Wesley chowed down on Lithium and curled up in his room all alone. Would Wesley take that route again? Not this time. Drugs no longer pumped through his veins anymore—only rage.

After that, it just became planning. Target practice. Buying a gun. Planning it out. Figuring out when the team would be together, close enough for one flawless attack. Since football season was over, the team would only come together for the end of the year award ceremony. At first, Wesley considered wiping out the entire auditorium with a homemade bomb. Because it wasn't just Coach Colebrook who failed Wesley—it was his teachers, his classmates, his teammates, the whole town of Morville. But Wesley knew destroying the football team alone would damage the town beyond repair. So he made his decision. And he carried it out to near perfection except for two targets. Colebrook escaped with a shoulder shot, and Daniel Nowak wasn't even there.

Part Two: Pleasure
Daniel

When I exit the terminal, the first thing I notice is a tall James Bond-looking fellow holding an enormous pickup sign: KICKED123. It must have been Maya's idea. I shake my head and laugh. What am I getting myself into?

"Are you Daniel Nowak?" the man asks when I approach him.

"Yes."

"I'm Maddox DeVario." He hands me his business card to show he's legit, though the black suit, sunglasses, and squeaky-clean shoes are enough. "I'll be driving you to the resort."

"Is, uh, Maya here?" I wonder if she'll pop out of a bush or drop from the ceiling.

"No, sir. She arrived earlier today." He takes my carry-on. "Is this all your luggage?"

"Yes."

"Follow me, please."

When I step outside, the heat hits me like a smack in the face, and I immediately start sweating. I expect DeVario to lead me to a fancy car, maybe even a Tesla, but it's a black stretched limo. Just how much money did Maya inherit?

DeVario opens the door for me before putting my luggage in the trunk. The interior is something out of a movie. There are plush leather seats, a flat-screen TV, and an open bar with glass bottles of soda, ice, and an enormous bottle of Jack Daniels. Is that some kind of a joke because of my name? Or does Maya expect me to drink hard liquor before my arrival?

"Sir, do you need any assistance?" DeVario asks

from the front seat. "Is the temperature all right?"

"Uh, yeah, everything's great." The AC blasts, cooling the sweat underneath my mop of black hair.

"Miss Floros has instructed me to tell you to relax and to have a drink."

"Oh, right." I opt for a bottle of Evian. It's too early to drink whiskey. Plus, I haven't had any alcohol in weeks. If I am going to drink, I'll start with something less intense.

Once we vacate the airport, I message Maya.

Kicked123: **Fancy ride.**

LookingForMyLostSock: **did u have a drink yet?**

Kicked123: **Evian.**

LookingForMyLostSock: **a real drink?**

Kicked123: **It's too early for liquor.**

LookingForMyLostSock: **its never too early for liquor**

LookingForMyLostSock: **take a shot for me pleaseeee**

Kicked123: **I'll take a shot with you later.**

LookingForMyLostSock: **bring the bottle with u im having issues getting alcohol here**

Kicked123: **I imagine so.**

LookingForMyLostSock: **its soooo annoying!**

Kicked123: **Any other surprises?**

LookingForMyLostSock: **wait and see**

Kicked123: **Will one of those surprises include me getting your phone number? You know it'd be a lot easier to communicate via text or an actual phone call.**

LookingForMyLostSock: **patience my young padawan**

Kicked123: **Padawan?**

LookingForMyLostSocks: **star wars**

Kicked123: **I haven't seen any of those movies.**

LookingForMyLostSock: **u have to watch them!**

Kicked123: **Aren't there like a thousand Star Wars movies?**

LookingForMyLostSock: **u only need to watch the original 3**

Kicked123: **As long as there are pizza and chips.**

LookingForMyLostSock: **def chips**

Maya and I chat back and forth the rest of the car ride. I eat chips per her suggestion and drink a can of ginger ale. It's almost dinnertime. Hopefully, Maya will surprise me with real food when I meet her at the hotel.

It takes twenty minutes to reach the entrance of Fantasy Land, which is surrounded by trees tall enough to be mountains. The ride through the forest lasts about ten minutes before we come upon the various hotels and cabins. Based on the fancy limo ride, I wouldn't be surprised if Maya booked a castle for us.

"What hotel are we staying at?" I finally ask.

"Miss Floros instructed me not to tell you until we arrive," DeVario says.

"Another surprise?"

"I believe so."

Kicked123: **Are we staying at a 5-star hotel?**

LookingForMyLostSock: **4 stars**

LookingForMyLostSock: **dont wanna be around rich stuck up people**

Kicked123: **4 is still nice. Even when I traveled for football, the nicest we stayed at was a 3.**

LookingForMyLostSock: **looking forward to spoiling u**

Kicked123: **Will that give you pleasure?**

LookingForMyLostSock: **for sure**

Kicked123: **Then spoil me all you want.**

Our messaging has gone from harmless to flirting to possibly something more. Likely, I'm just reading into things. Maya has made it clear she's sarcastic, so suggestive comments can only be taken with a grain of salt. Does she have a serious side at all? Or is everything just fun and games? Should I be worried about that?

DeVario heads toward one of the hotels partially hidden by gigantic trees. I strain my eyes, trying to take in everything all at once. If this is a 4-star hotel, the 5-star hotels *must* be castles. This near-castle is surrounded by waterfalls, boulders, trees, bushes, and trails. Everything looks handcrafted, from the ledges to the doors, yet it feels part of nature.

"Welcome to The Fairy Fountain Lodge," DeVario says, pulling up to the front entrance.

"A fitting name," I say, noticing all the fairy figurines and statues.

Once he parks, DeVario immediately runs out to open my door. A group of teenagers gathers around, probably expecting to see a celebrity. DeVario shoos them away before retrieving my carry-on from the trunk.

"Shall I escort you in, Mr. Nowak?" DeVario asks.

"I'll be fine, thanks." I take my carry-on from him. "I, should, uh, probably tip you?"

"No, sir. Miss Floros has already taken care of that."

"Right. Well, thanks again."

"Mr. Nowak, please don't forget the whiskey." He reaches inside the limo and grabs the bottle. Then from his jacket pocket, he pulls out a brown paper bag for me to carry it more discreetly. Maya thought of everything, and I mean everything.

I hurry inside, not wanting to linger in the heat any longer. Even though several people are ahead of me to check in, the wait is nothing as I'm distracted by all the views. The lobby is the size of a ballroom with fairy totem poles, rainbow headdresses, and sparkly furniture. Of the people, it's mostly parents with young kids.

It surprises me that Maya would pick a family-oriented hotel when her favorite pastimes are mostly 21+. But the view from one of the windows points me straight at the main amusement park. Of course, she would want to stay at the hotel closest to all the rides. I just wish there wasn't a giant body of water separating us from the entrance. The thought of being on a boat makes my stomach curl.

After I check in, a bellhop takes my carry-on even though I can do it myself. He takes me to the top floor. I'm certain Maya has tipped in advance, but I ask anyway, and sure enough, she has. I thank the bellhop, and he leaves.

"Maya?" I squeak.

There's a wooden table with chairs directly to my right as I walk in. I leave my luggage beside the table and wander across the living room. There's a bright purple couch and two armchairs, a flatscreen TV, and a mini-bar without any alcohol. Sliding doors lead to a balcony with an epic water view. I can see all the rollercoasters and the descending sun. Turning around, I notice a welcome basket on the coffee table with two sets of fairy wings. Maya is out of her mind if she thinks I will dress up like a fairy at any point during this vacation.

Through an arched doorway, I find the bedroom. The *only* bedroom, but at least there are two beds. Both are queen-sized with wooden frames. There is a painting of King Oberon over one bed and Queen Titania over the other. Even Shakespeare found his way into the resort. I find another TV, but no Maya.

Her stuff is everywhere. There are three big

luggage bags, all opened. Clothes are thrown left and right like she had a meltdown trying to find something to wear. Both bathroom sinks are covered with girl stuff, from tweezers to purple toenail polish to an unopened bag of potato chips. The most interesting item is a vintage-looking Betty Boop jewelry box.

I feel awkward being here all by myself, surrounded by bras and potato chips, so I adjourn to the living room to send her a message.

Kicked123: **Hey, where are you? I'm here.**

LookingForMyLostSock: **nearby**

Kicked123: **What should I do?**

LookingForMyLostSock: **take a shower eat and meet me at the dock in a half hour**

Kicked123: **Okay...**

LookingForMyLostSock: **also take a dramamine**

LookingForMyLostSock: **non-drowsy kind next to tv in bedroom**

Why would I need a Dramamine? Does she think I'm going to get motion sickness from the rides? Or...?

Kicked123: **No boats.**

LookingForMyLostSock: **u will be fine!**

Kicked123: **But what should I eat besides potato chips?**

Knocking at the door startles me off the couch. It's room service with a pepperoni pizza. This is getting almost too weird, how everything just magically happens. Maya said she wouldn't plan anything, but so far, she's done nothing but plan.

I do as she instructs, but I don't finish the entire pizza. I'm too nervous to eat that much food. I take a longer-than-usual shower, scrubbing where I don't often scrub because subconsciously, I'm still thinking about Maya naked. I change into shorts and a T-shirt, all light colors, comb out my hair that feels longer by the second, and stuff my pockets with my wallet, phone, and gum. I chew three pieces as I walk through the hotel, down the elevator, and to the dock.

My heart thumps like I'm about to kick a 50-yard field goal in front of Tom Brady. Worst scenario, Maya is a 50-year-old man. In which case, I would sprint to the nearest airport and fly directly home.

But Maya is easy to find amidst the crowd, even with her back toward me. She stands with one hand on her hip and the other holding a brown slushie-like drink. Jet black hair falls to her waist, slightly curling at the ends. She has on fake elf ears, and I wonder how comfortable they are. Her bottom is covered by a glittery blue T-shirt about two sizes too big, hanging so low that her black shorts only peek out by a millimeter. Her legs are long and athletic, but one looks slightly thinner. It could be how she's standing or the light reflecting from the sun.

How do I announce my presence? Call out her name? Tap her on the shoulder?

I send her a message instead.

Kicked123: **Boo.**

Maya checks her phone and then immediately turns around. I'm about thirty feet away, but I doubt I stand out as she does, with the way her hair moves with the wind, landing perfectly across her pale-white shoulders and back. Her midnight eyes scan for my presence as her red lips wrap around her drink straw.

Suddenly, her mouth is open, and she's flapping her arms like a deranged fairy, spilling her drink everywhere. She tosses it into the nearby trash can, shoves her phone in her pocket, and charges at me.

As a football kicker, I've never had to worry too much about being tackled, but it happens occasionally. But by a girl? Never in my life have I been more intimidated.

Maya

"You have Aladdin hair!" I exclaim, halting in front of him. He looks terrified, so I immediately step back, even though every bit of me wants to grab him.

He chuckles nervously. "And you have Jasmine hair."

"I know, right? I should totally dress up like her. You can dress up and be whoever you want here."

"Great." He puts his hand out. "It's nice to finally meet you."

I shake his hand. It's relatively huge for an average-height guy. Which instantly makes me wonder what else might be relatively huge. "Likewise," I say. "Do you like the hotel?"

"It's nice and, uh, glittery." He's short for words, which means he's still nervous. I need to tone it down, so I don't scare him off.

"Sweet." I take another step back. "So, are you ready to go to the main park?"

"Is that where we're going tonight?"

"Unless you want to do something else? You want to hit up the nightclub instead?"

"No, no." He steps forward this time and smiles. "We can do whatever you want."

My lips twist to one side. "Oh, don't tell me that. I'll take total advantage if you give me that kind of freedom." I grab him by the elbow but check to make sure he's not freaked out by the sudden contact. He continues to smile, so I lead him to the fairy boat. He hesitates slightly, but I give his arm a teeny squeeze, and he makes the final step.

"Will this be a long ride?" he asks, veering away from the other passengers.

"Ten minutes. The Dramamine should work. Trust me. I know plenty of people who have motion sickness."

"I don't have motion sickness." He looks down at the little blue waves. "It's just something about water. It makes me queasy."

"Don't look at the water then. Look at this lit view! Breathe it in." Seriously, how is he not mesmerized? The sky is picture-perfect blue. Hot, sticky air surrounds us. The sweat from his arm penetrates my skin. Though warm, it sends shivers down my spine.

With the slight stubble on his face, Daniel could pass for twenty-one, but he'd have to nix the Aladdin hair. His athletic body shows dedication, hours of gym time, and healthy eating, or maybe just good genes and a bit of luck. I used to have that "athletic" look. The six-pack abs. The shoulders. Now I'm just skin, bones, blood, and alcohol.

"Yeah, this view is pretty lit," he says, looking right at me.

I smile and detach my arm from his. "So, did you remember the Jack?" I ask, leaning my arms across the white railing of the boat. Daniel is sweating so much, he could probably fall into the water and continue sweating.

"It's in the hotel room," he answers.

"Did you drink any?"

"I'm not a big drinker."

"Are you a super clean eater because of football?"

"Sort of. But I've been pretty bad about my eating lately. Lots of takeout food. So much pizza." He rubs his stomach like he's fat or something. Seriously, I don't have to see him naked to know he's ripped. However, I would like to see him naked for other reasons.

"Well, you're on vacation now, and you're going to walk eight miles a day while you're here, so eat and drink whatever you want."

"How are you getting alcohol if the fake doesn't work here?"

"Oh, it's so easy to bribe people with a little bit of flirting or cash."

"So you bribed your way to get that slushie?"

"Of course."

"I don't have the talent or necessities to do that."

"Don't worry. I got you covered." I touch his arm again, but he doesn't coil or seem alarmed. He just smiles, and I melt a little more.

When I see something I want, I don't hesitate to claim it. That's something I want to teach Daniel. If he falls down the path of "oh, woe is me, I don't deserve anything!" he's doomed to a life without pleasure.

"What is it?" he asks when he notices me staring into his brain.

"Just taking you in," I say.

"Am I different from what you expected?"

"Yes and no."

"Is that a good thing?"

"Depends." I bite my bottom lip, still tasting the slushie.

"On?" He looks down at my fingers, now drawing little circles around the dark hairs on his arm.

"Do you consider yourself a leader or a follower?" I ask.

"Neither."

"Introvert or extrovert?"

"Do I have to be labeled?"

I finally let him go. "Of course not. Labels don't mean anything unless they mean something to you."

"They don't," he says, looking at the water again. "Not anymore."

"And they never should again."

As though taken aback by my last comment, he stands tall, opening those shoulders to their full girth. I don't have to strain my neck to meet his gaze, but I feel the red rush to my cheeks. I think about everything I want—his hands grabbing my waist, his mouth down on mine, and his body pressed against mine.

"When are you going to touch me back?" I ask, ready to skip the rollercoasters and go straight to the hotel. My fingers trickle around his elbow to the end of his T-shirt dampened with sweat.

His eyes widen, only for a second, then relax. "I'm being respectful. I just met you, and I'd like to spend at least an hour with you before I go tickling your arm."

Hot and admirable. With a smile stretching my face apart, I release his arm, returning some of his space. "What happens after two hours?" I ask.

"Maybe I hold your hand."

"And after three?"

"Will we make it to three? I might fall asleep."

"Ooh, burn." But we both laugh.

The boat docks. Daniel steps off the boat like a champ, which is already an improvement. Once we're both on land, we walk to the jam-packed entrance. Security guards check bags left and right, but visitors get in and out pretty quickly. It's not like Fantasy Land has any staffing shortages.

Then I notice the metal detectors, and my heart launches into my throat. Even though it's rare for an alarm to sound over an IM rod, I still don't like the idea of something or someone scanning my body for metal I know is there and always will be.

Daniel goes first, passing without question. Then it's my turn.

"I have a rod in my leg," I tell the male security

guard before moving. I point to the vertical scar.

He motions for me to step through, but nothing happens. At the airport, they scanned my whole body. Thankfully, this dude doesn't ask any questions and just lets me into the park.

"Are you Wolverine?" Daniel asks.

"I wish. It's titanium, not adamantium."

"Does it hurt?"

"Does what hurt?" I ask, moving ahead of him so he'll stop staring at my leg.

He catches up with a single step. "So this is Fantasy Land!" He takes in the view, the crowds, but mostly the giant stone castle guarded by a fifty-foot red dragon. "Looks like every kid's dreamland."

"It felt that way the first time I came here."

"What does it feel like now?"

I'm not as awe-struck as I thought I'd be. Then again, the mind of an eight-year-old is vastly different from an eighteen-year-old. As a kid, all I saw was a world outside my own, a place where problems could be forgotten, where life was simply one fantasy after the other. And it got even better when I separated from my parents and felt the added gratification of freedom. I could be a pirate, a princess, and a dreamer all at once. I could run from place to place, ride every ride multiple times, and eat sugar, all without being told to slow down or watch out, or that's not ladylike! I could be the person I needed to be. The person I wanted to be.

Now all I see are screaming kids, couples arguing, and overpriced merchandise. Everyone looks sweaty, even the children. It baffles me why all the old people wear long pants and why six-year-olds still need to be in strollers. And why does that fat husband think wearing plastic armor will impress his wife? Maybe I need to be high to enjoy this. Too bad I left all my goodies in the hotel room. I thought the slushie would be enough.

Before I can answer Daniel's question, he grabs my hand and pulls me through the marketplace, away from all the vendors, straight toward the castle. We pause in front of the dragon, who looks way less intimidating than I remember. Daniel surveys the castle, his grin stretching by the second.

My eyes fall to our conjoined hands.

"It hasn't been two hours," I tell him.

He gives my hand a tiny squeeze. "I said maybe I'd hold your hand after two hours. Which also means maybe I'd hold your hand sooner."

"Charming."

"I thought I was Aladdin."

"You can be both."

He smiles to one side. "So, where do you want to go first?"

"Let's go on The Dwarf Demon."

"Which is…?"

"An underground roller coaster. All in darkness."

"Sounds terrifying. Lead the way, my lady."

Daniel

I decide to treat this evening as a date, minus the fact that Maya is paying for everything.

I let her choose what rides we go on, and she chooses everything, even the "Gypsy's Carrousel" full of screaming kids. Some of the rides are lame, but Maya finds pleasure in everything. She takes pictures with anyone dressed as an elf or fairy. On our way up "Mount Doom", she pretends to be scared but then on the way down, releases the most epic scream of the year followed by insane laughter. Inside the costume shop, she tries on one of the most scandalous elf outfits that barely covers her bottom, but rather than buy it for herself, she hands it over to a fifteen-year-old who hasn't enough cash and wants to wow her boyfriend. Maya finds pleasure everywhere, even in generosity.

Nearing eleven o'clock, fireworks explode across the water. Maya looks happy, but her hand tremors against mine. I wonder if the loud noise triggers flashbacks of the concert shooting. Does she think about her parents' deaths? Does she remember being shot? Is it something she still fears? I want so much to ask about her experience. How she's managed to survive all this time on her own. And to be so nonchalant about it. Like it wasn't even that big of a deal.

"Are you okay?" I ask once the show is over.

She laughs. "I need a drink." Her eyes scan the area for a vendor, but only beer is sold outside the restaurants.

"Do you want to go back to the hotel?" I ask.

"But we haven't gone on all the rides yet."

"Yeah, but the park closes in like an hour anyway. We can come back tomorrow and spend the whole day here if you want."

"True. Let's go then."

My legs are cramping by the time we make it back to the boat. I haven't exercised in weeks, and my body isn't used to this humidity.

Maya is noticeably limping, favoring her left side over her right, but she doesn't voice any complaints. Even if she was in pain, I don't think she'd be keen to express it. Instead, she looks out across the dark water and smiles nostalgically. I wonder what she's thinking about.

When we dock, she lets out a weird little yelp. "Are you okay? Are you in pain?" I ask, deeply concerned she's trying way too hard to hide her discomfort.

"Just sore," she says with a wide grin. "A couple of drinks should numb it out."

"What about some Tylenol?"

"Tylenol? I have much stronger stuff."

Of course, she would have prescription pain medication. The one time I hurt myself playing football, my eighth-grade broken ankle, I was prescribed Vicodin, but my dad only let me take it for two days before switching me to Tylenol. He even joked, saying I only earn Vicodin if I take a bullet someday. I'll never dare remind him of that.

"Do you have to take pain medication often?" I ask. "For your leg?"

She laughs like I made a joke. "Vicodin doesn't mix well with alcohol, so unless I want to get blackout drunk, I don't take it unless it's absolutely necessary."

Couldn't that kill a person?

"Besides," she continues, "I only get refills if I visit my doctor. So my supplies are limited."

"Aren't you supposed to see a doctor? For follow-ups and stuff?"

"Hey, do you want to check out the nightclub before we go to our room?" she asks, obviously not interested in answering my question.

"I'm not sure I have the stamina for a club right now." I've never actually been inside a club. Barn parties are more my style.

"Maybe another night," she says after a yawn.

She seems tired enough to crash, but the minute we get back to the hotel room, she kicks off her shoes and goes straight for the bottle of Jack. I've seen people do shots of whiskey at parties, but never have I seen a girl drink straight from the bottle.

"Much better," she says after a long swig. "Your turn."

I stand under the AC vent. "I said I'd take a shot with you. That was like three."

"Then just take one, and you can catch up later."

"Why do you like whiskey so much? Is it the taste?"

"Hell no." She laughs. "It's the burn. It was also my father's favorite…" She cuts herself off and shakes the bottle in front of my face. "Come on, just one shot. Pretty please?"

How can I say no to that face? My face warps in every direction after I take my swig. Maya giggles as I search the fridge for a chase. Thankfully, there is coke.

"I can go down to the bar and get you a slushie if you want," she says. "They're really good."

"No thanks," I say after downing half a bottle of sugary soda. "I'm good."

"You're not going to party with me? This is our first night at Fantasy Land!"

"Maya, it's kind of late."

"It's not even midnight."

"And I need to shower again."

"You don't smell."

"And I haven't drank in a while."

"One more shot. Please?"

"I'd rather have the slushie."

"I'll go get you one!" She leaps for the door.

At least that gives me a chance to shower in peace. Maya must not have a working nose. Guys always smell bad when they sweat. Unless they're vegans, then they smell like gold.

I wash with cold water to keep cool and prevent a boner. I could just drink a ton, and then I wouldn't have to worry about anything rising. But getting shit-faced would cause a horrible hangover and ruin tomorrow.

I want to relax. I want to feel good without losing control. Can I strike a balance with Maya? She seems to go straight for the highest setting on the remote.

As I slip into boxers, the main door opens. I hobble for a corner to secure privacy, but Maya barges straight into the bedroom with two slushies.

"What are you doing?" she asks suspiciously.

"Putting on clothes."

"Oh." She sets down our drinks and enters the bathroom, shutting the door behind her. I panic for a second, thinking she's up to no good, but then I hear the water turn on. She's just taking a shower.

I finish dressing, grab my drink, and head for the living room. Feeling stressed at this point, drinking helps to mellow me out. I turn on the TV and lean back into the sofa.

I'm on vacation. I shouldn't stress about anything.

About fifteen minutes later, Maya moseys in with her melting drink and wet hair. The sleeves to her extra-large purple t-shirt are cut off, and she's not wearing a bra underneath, so anytime she raises her arms, it's a clear shot of porcelain white side-boob. I don't think I've ever been with a girl so unreserved. Then again, have I ever been alone with a girl in a hotel room? How many first-time moments will I have during this trip?

"Feel better?" she asks, tapping her finger against the side of my glass.

"I feel pretty good."

She smiles and wraps those perfect lips around her straw. For the next hour, we watch TV and drink. Eventually, hunger strikes. Maya eats potato chips like it's the only food on Earth while I finish the last of the pizza.

"So, Daniel, tell me something real?" Maya asks, rubbing her bare foot against mine.

I take the bottle of whiskey from her. "My mom wanted to call me Jack."

"Really?"

"Yes. But Daniel is a family name on my dad's side. Every other generation names their son Daniel."

"I have no idea why my parents picked Maya." She laughs, trying to take the bottle back. "They probably just went with whatever was trendy at the time."

"How about I hold onto this for a while?" I ask, cradling the bottle as if I need it more, even though I'm at the point where I've had enough to feel good but not enough to get sick or crazy.

"Are you going to drink more?" she asks.

"Maybe we should save some for tomorrow night." I tuck the bottle underneath the couch. When Maya tries to retrieve it, I grab both her hands. She throws her head back and laughs.

"You're really strong," she says.

"Am I hurting you?" I ease my grip, but that gives her another chance to grab the Jack. I move faster, grasping her forearms this time. She laughs once more, and then it happens. She kisses me.

It's near-instant how she goes from lying next to me to being on top of me, her fingers in my hair and her tongue down my throat. This is exactly what I feared would happen. She'd want to have sex with me almost immediately, and I wouldn't know what to do. But I don't panic. How can I? Everything feels amazing. Now the only fear that comes to mind is she'll jump off me and shout, "Just kidding!" Which wouldn't be the end of the world but would make this moment confusing.

I push those thoughts aside and allow my body to lead. My reactions are as near-instant as hers.

My hands wrap around her waist and up her shirt. I touch every part of her upper body, caressing the lines of her back, finding the muscle definition that still exists despite her lack of mass. When my hands reach the back of her neck, she lifts her arms, taking her shirt right off.

In all my life, I've never had it happen like this. Most girls in Morville want committed relationships before taking off their clothes, which I respect, until they do things like cheat on me.

I shouldn't think of Anna. She's nothing compared to Maya, with her long black hair now tangled in my own. Maya, with her pulsing hips and frisky hands and an uncontrollable mouth that just can't seem to separate from mine.

I'm going nuts with her on top. I feel trapped on the couch, so with little effort, I stand, hoisting her up with me.

"What are you doing?" she asks, finally pulling her mouth free.

"Bedroom?" I suggest.

"I can walk." She tries to wiggle loose.

"I want to carry you."

"I'm not a baby."

Her eyebrows narrow, so I ease her down. She immediately grabs my hand and pulls me toward the Titania bed. She wants me to lie down, so she can be on top. Now I'm tempted to ask questions like are you sure this is what you want? She might be too drunk to think clearly, making me feel like I'm taking advantage of her.

But she shows no signs of being too impaired. Her tolerance is likely way higher than the average girl's if she can chug whiskey. What about me? Am I drunk? Am I thinking straight?

And then she takes off her shorts and underwear. How the hell am I supposed to think *clearly* about anything now?

But strangely, I notice the scar first. A single line, about a foot long, running vertically down her thigh. I wonder how much damage was done. How much of her femur is left, and how much is metal? What was her recovery like? Is she still in recovery?

Maya opens one of her suitcases and pulls out a condom. I don't say anything, even though a part of me wants to ask what kind, what size. She yanks off my shorts and boxers and slides the condom on with ease. It doesn't feel restricting, so it must be right. I'm sweating again, so I take the liberty of removing my shirt myself.

As soon as all my clothes are off, she's on top of me with her mouth covering mine and her hair everywhere. There's no turning back now. I just hope I don't disappoint. If she's an experienced drinker, does that make her experienced in other ways?

Shut up, brain. You will disappoint her if you don't stop thinking.

When we finally connect, it's like I'm in another world. Maya doesn't care about anything other than total satisfaction, and I join her in the pursuit. She feels tight, but not virgin tight, more like she hasn't had sex in a while tight. Maybe that's why she's so anxious to do this.

Or maybe she's actually into me. Which ups my confidence and my performance.

Fifteen minutes later, I fall backward, exhausted, taking her with me. Her forehead lands on my shoulder, and her arms dangle lifelessly across the bed. I close my eyes and listen to her breathe. Thoughts melt like candle wax, and I finally find a moment of quiet inside my head.

Maya

I wake up sore.

It's a big change going from girl to guy. And, in this case, a good one.

Daniel is lying beside me, gently snoring as the morning light sneaks through the curtains. His lower half is covered by white sheets, leaving the rest of him on display. He has curly black chest hair, dark nipples, and a perfect six-pack. I'd have to ditch alcohol and potato chips if I ever wanted to look that good again. But the whole working out part would probably do me in. How long has it been since I've done a pull-up? Or even hung from a bar?

I roll out of bed and stumble over clothes to the bathroom. I need to pee, hydrate, and put my head under cold water. Some people need meds, sleep, and quiet time to battle a hangover. I just need a temperature change, chips, and another drink. Then everything returns to normal. I'm back on the horse, ready to ride.

After chugging sink water, I throw on clothes and head out the door, leaving Daniel to snooze. I buy one bottle of water and two bottles of OJ from the nearby vending machine. That'll mix nicely with Jack.

When I return to the room, Daniel is awake but still in bed, rubbing his forehead and looking at me like he has amnesia.

"Morning, sunshine," I say, handing him the cocktail.

"This is terrible," he says after one sip. "Did you mix this with whiskey?"

"Yes."

He sets the bottle on the nightstand. "I'm good. Thanks though. How are you?"

I sit beside him with my chips and offer him the water instead. "Can't complain. Do you want to go into the forest today? We could do zip-lining. There's also this sick mermaid lagoon. And a waterfall."

He drinks nearly half the bottle before answering. "Uh, sure. What about the park? You wanted to finish doing all the rides."

"We can do that in the evening." I offer him some of the chips.

He turns them down. "How about breakfast?"

"This is breakfast for me."

"Are you on a chip diet?"

"Ha." I fill my mouth with two chips, then crumble the empty bag. "You can call for room service. Or we can grab something on the way out."

"I should probably put on some clothes first."

He seems embarrassed, walking naked to the bathroom. I want to tell him to relax, get over it, and let's act normal, but from what I'm sensing, he's not used to such excitement after one night with someone like me. This may require some sensitivity on my part but not too much.

While he showers and whatnot, I brush and braid my hair. I consider ordering us breakfast, but I'm not sure what he wants, and the only thing that sounds appealing is the hash browns. Maybe I have a potato addiction.

After a half-hour, I knock on the bathroom door. He's procrastinating. Or worse, texting somebody for girl advice. I can give him whatever advice he needs. I won't hold back or make him guess what I'm thinking.

"I'm shaving," he says after I knock again.

"Can I come in?"

He unlocks the door. I stroll in and take a seat on the toilet. Daniel is in front of the mirror with a towel wrapped around his waist. Half his face is covered with shaving cream.

"Do you have to shave a lot?" I ask.

"Every other day. Or I start to look like a bear."

"Not me," I say, rubbing the stubble on my leg. "I'm not on a schedule."

"It doesn't bother me," he says, "in case you're wondering."

"I'm not." However, I have showered more in the last week than in the last month. And I spent way too much time yesterday choosing an outfit to meet him in. Am I self-conscious about the way I look and smell around this guy? Does that equate to *caring*?

He whooshes his razor through the soapy sink water. "Are you wondering about anything else?" he asks. "Are you okay?"

"Okay with what?"

He takes a deep breath. Oh no, here it comes. "With what happened last night?"

I bite my lip to avoid laughing. "Why wouldn't I be?"

"I just don't want you to feel, you know ... weird or bad."

"Bad?" I take the razor from him. If he's too distressed or emotional to shave, I'll do it for him. "Daniel, listen. I only do things that make me feel good. It's my life motto, you could say. So if you're at all concerned about last night, don't be. What we did was fun. And it's something we'll likely do again, many times, while we're here together. Because it only makes sense that two people who are obviously attracted to one another have sex with each other. It shouldn't make either of us feel weird or bad."

"Who said I was attracted to you?"

I pause for a second, but then I notice his slight grin. "You wouldn't have come on this trip with me if you weren't."

"It's one of the reasons I came." But he looks down when he says it.

"Don't be ashamed of that. No one falls for your personality or brain right away. It's the physical part that sets the ride in motion."

"But it's the emotional part that keeps the ride going."

"Or ends the ride." It just so happens I'm shaving around his Adam's Apple, so I pause, but Daniel mistakes my stoppage as something else.

"Do you ever think about that part?" he asks.

I shave the last section around his neck, holding his face still with my left hand. Once I finish, I hand him a towel to wipe his face.

"Me on top of you," I say. "That's what I want to think about."

Fire rushes to his cinnamon cheeks. "That's on my mind too," he says, looking right at me. "But it was very unexpected."

"As I recall, you didn't hesitate."

"It was tough not to."

"Good. That's how I want it to be every time. Now let's get some breakfast, ride some rides, and have some drinks."

"More drinks?"

"We're on vacation, Daniel. But if you don't want to drink, I have alternatives."

"We can't smoke weed in Fantasy Land."

"Hell no. That's what gummies are for."

His eyes bulge. Then he laughs. "Let me guess. You have some?"

"Of course. I'm always prepared. You want one?"

His lips twist to one side. "Would that make you happy?"

"I'm already happy. Aren't you?"

"I'm getting there."

"Getting there?" I roll my eyes and scooch past him. "Man, oh man." I dig through my Betty Boop jewelry box for my vitamin container. "Here we go." I pop a green gummy into my mouth and place his gummy on the bathroom sink.

He gapes as if I offered him a suicide weapon. "I'll be honest." He picks it up and sniffs it. "I haven't done anything more hardcore than alcohol since Homecoming, which was over seven months ago. And I only took maybe a couple of hits of a joint."

"You'll be fine."

"I also haven't been with somebody, you know, like just for sex. I've always been a relationship-type person."

"Why?"

"Why what?"

"Why do you have to be in a relationship to have sex?"

"It's how I've always been. It's what's expected of me."

"By who?"

"Everyone. My town is super conservative."

"Ugh, vomit much."

"Super liberals aren't much fun to be around either."

"I agree with you on that. The middle ground is more forgiving. But let's not get politics in the mix. How has it been for you? The whole relationship thing?"

"It's been…" He laughs again and nervously rubs the back of his neck. "It's been terrible. I've had two serious girlfriends. Monica and I dated in ninth grade for about six months. After we lost our virginities to one another, she completely freaked out and broke up with me. And now she's a lesbian."

I laugh. "Dang, you must have been a horrible first lay."

"Everyone's first is bad."

"Not always, but mostly."

He smirks. "And then I got together with this girl named Anna at the start of junior year, and we had a solid relationship for a good chunk of time. But senior year, she started acting weird. And then she stopped having sex with me. And then I found out she cheated on me."

"Let me give you some advice, if I may." I take the gummy from him and try squeezing it inside his mouth, but his lips remain sealed. Now he looks even more attractive, freshly shaven, smelling like alpine mint. A part of me just wants to pull off his towel and end this conversation, but he wants to listen. How can I deny him my knowledge?

"Go ahead," he says, gently pushing my hand away.

I set the gummy down. "First off, screw expectations. If you want to have sex with someone, hell, let's say you want to have sex with an old woman, who gives a fuck what other people think? Though I wouldn't go around bragging about such a conquest. Maybe keep that one to yourself."

"Maya, I would never—"

"And secondly, if you're with someone, relationship or not, and they stop having sex with you, they're going to, if not already, start sleeping with someone else."

"Lots of relationships go through slow spots, but that doesn't mean someone will cheat."

"Oh, but it happens. Trust me."

"And you know this because of all the serious relationships you've been in?"

I twist away from him and grab my bottle of suntan lotion. "I've been in relationships. Just no recent ones. Are you going to get high with me?"

"Tell me about your relationships." He puts the gummy inside his mouth but doesn't bite down. Instead, he swallows it like a pill. Now I feel obligated to share. But is it such a big deal to tell him about that part of my past? It's not like I was ever madly in love with someone and had my heart broken.

I remove my tank top, so it's easier to distribute the lotion. "Do my shoulders and back, and I'll tell you about a few." I hand him the bottle and move my braid out of the way. "I had my first boyfriend in seventh grade. He had bad breath and acne and used way too much tongue to kiss. I dumped him after a month. Then there were a few more guys. Nothing serious. They lasted maybe one or two months at most. Then there was Connor." I pause, not liking how it sounds to say his name, but I can't let Daniel know, so I smile as though I'm having good thoughts. "We dated in ninth grade and some of tenth. He was nice but way too romantic. Flowers, poems, cards, stuffed animals."

"What's wrong with that?" He gives me a massage while he rubs the lotion in, digging deep around my shoulders.

"I'm not a flower and card kind of girl. I want to have fun. He wouldn't even go on rollercoasters with me. And when we started having sex, he never wanted to try anything new. Just the same old routine, over and over again. No oral. And we could only do missionary or positions that put him on top."

But is that really why I lost interest in him? Or was it more so that my mom 100% approved of our relationship and constantly referred to him as such a good influence on me? Like I was that corrupt of a kid? I hated how during family dinners, she talked more to him in one hour than she would talk to me in an entire week. It's like my whole existence was an afterthought. Don't even get me started on how much attention my dad gave Connor. He was always inviting him to play golf at the country club, yet he wouldn't even come to my goddamn gymnastic meets. He always had an excuse.

"Please tell me you didn't cheat on him," Daniel says, pulling me from my negative thoughts.

I force another smile. "I thought about it, but it never happened. Even when we went on a break."

"Why not?"

Air catches in my throat. With all my strength, I swallow it down, crushing any bit of emotion from barfing its way out.

"Why not?" Daniel asks again, digging his thumb into a tight spot on my back.

"Cause he died."

"Oh." Daniel's hands halt against my lower back. "Was he at the concert too?"

"With his folks." Damn, why am I talking about this? This is not like me, but Daniel starts massaging me again, and the words slip out. "It was a family event."

"Did he—?"

"After that, I wasn't with anyone for a while because I was in the hospital. But after I got out, I decided to nix the whole relationship thing and be with whoever I wanted."

"Multiple partners?"

"One at a time. I'm not a slut."

"I didn't say that."

I'm getting defensive. This means some bit of emotion has wiggled loose. I take a deep breath, hoping the gummy kicks in soon.

"Are you okay?" Daniel asks.

Shit, he knows I'm getting upset. So I continue explaining myself. "I'm with one person as long as we're having fun and enjoying each other's company. No labels. No long-term commitments."

"And have you been safe?"

"I always use protection, and I get tested every few months." Dawn thinks it's ridiculous I'll go to the gyno, but I won't go to the regular doctor, AA, or any other form of therapy.

"I've never been tested, in case you're wondering," Daniel says, removing his hands from my back. He wipes off the excess lotion. "I've never had a reason to because I've only been with two girls."

"But didn't the last one cheat on you?"

"Yeah, but we barely had sex while she was cheating. And we used protection. So…"

"You're fine, Daniel. Don't worry." Seriously, everything is curable except for the serious shit. And the serious shit you can avoid if you're not a dumbass.

"I'm not worried. I mean, I am worried. But it's fine. I'm just wondering about the last person you were with."

"Nicole."

His eyes grow wide. "You've been with girls too?"

"Yes."

"So you're bisexual?"

"I am what I am. Right now, I'm with you. I like you."

"I like you too."

"Good. Now, is that enough sharing? Can we please just be high and go zip-lining?" Seriously, get me out of this bathroom!

Daniel nods and trickles his fingers under my shorts. "Just one more thing." He kisses my neck. "If this is all about pleasure, then it would give me immense pleasure if you could let me be somewhat romantic with you."

"I just told you, I'm not into that."

"Please?"

"*Daniel.*"

"Can you meet me halfway? I took a gummy for you."

And I shared way too much of my past. Drugs will cycle through your body like a load of laundry. Some leave stains. Some need another wash. But words are forever.

Still, I meet him halfway.

"You can hold my hand. As hard and as long as you want."

Daniel

List of things I've done since meeting Maya:
1) Had sex on the first "date"
2) Ate a marijuana gummy
3) Agreed to be "with" Maya, but I'm not her boyfriend.

It's not a bad deal. Most guys would consider it a dream. A girl who willingly throws herself at you, offers you drinks and drugs, and takes you to Fantasy Land. A girl who doesn't expect flowers or cards, loathes romance altogether, and only wants to have fun and live in the moment, forever without labels. A girl who thrives on pleasure.

But what happens if you take the pleasure away? What if we remove the alcohol, the drugs, the sex, and the fun? What would Maya be underneath it all? Would she be able to survive? Is she mentally strong enough? Would she break down, or would she go numb?

For the past couple of weeks, I have felt nothing. No pleasure. No happiness. No love. No sorrow. I've lied to people. I've abandoned all my dreams. I haven't "dealt" with anything happening back home. But was that ever the goal?

The goal was to move on and find something new to bring me joy again. So far, Maya has done a lit job of making me feel good. Even though this is a no-strings-attached kind of relationship, she still talks to me. She listens without judging. If this were my daily life, I don't see why I'd have to search for anything or anyone else.

But this isn't everyday life. This is a fantasy, exactly as advertised. A temporary bliss. A wrinkle in time. And even though Maya has clarified that we're not to talk about the future, I can't stop thinking about it because I don't know what I'll do when all this ends. Do I go back to my mundane life in Morville? Do I investigate Wesley's motive? Do I go to college? What is my purpose in life anymore?

I'm high from the gummy, which makes my brain think even more. But when I focus on the now, like Maya said, everything is clear. Right now, I belong with Maya here in Fantasy Land.

We stop downstairs for breakfast. I order a bagel with cream cheese and coffee. Maya eats a hash brown and drinks the rest of my bottled cocktail. After some coaxing, she drinks water as well.

"Aren't you going to eat anything else?" I ask.

"No. Why? Are you still hungry?"

"Yes."

She giggles and gathers our trash. "I'll buy you something to suck on when we get to the forest."

"Can that be you?"

"Later." She tosses our trash and then immediately grabs my hand.

****

The official entrance to "The Forest" is three miles away, so we take the bus like normal people. However, I wouldn't mind a private ride, considering how paranoid I feel. It's not in my nature to make eye contact with every person around me, but I'm convinced everyone knows I'm high, and they're going to tell on me. And then I'll be kicked out forever and ruin the whole trip.

Maya squeezes my hand and warns me that if I don't relax, she will pull down my pants in front of everyone. That would get both of us kicked out.

So I close my eyes and pretend to sleep until we get there.

The Forest surprises me. Though mostly

"natural", mini-rides, attractions, bars, and restaurants are built into the trees and ground. You can walk or zip-line your way to different areas. To keep people from getting lost, fairy drones guide you where you want to go. Hiding in the trees, wizards call out random facts about the forest creatures. *Beware of the goblins lurking under the bridge! If you're quiet enough, you might catch a pixie!* The geek level is extreme, so I understand why Maya would want to be high here.

High Maya is more chill and quieter. She holds my hand and takes me from tree to tree, rolling her eyes whenever a wizard shouts at us and asking the fairy drones bizarre questions like where's the orgy pool?

Around noon, I'm starving again, so Maya suggests we eat at the Werewolf Buffet and Bar. Like a wolf, I eat everything in sight while she bribes whatever guy she can to buy her a drink. It works the first time. She asks a college guy, and he gets her a mixed drink, no questions asked. But the second guy doesn't let her slip away so easily.

When he snatches her arm, demanding she talk to him, I bolt from my hiding spot and interfere like I'm ready to get my knuckles bloody.

I grab her hand. "Is everything okay?" I ask.

The guy, who has a good four inches and forty pounds on me, scorns and huffs. "Why can't your boyfriend buy you a drink?"

"He's not old enough, and he's not my boyfriend," Maya answers.

"In that case, why can't we hang out?"

"We're good," I say, trying to pull Maya away, but she seems intrigued by this guy, which pisses me off.

"Maybe later," Maya says with a smile so sly one would think she wanted to invite the dude back to our room. "When my drink is empty."

Oh, burn. I didn't see that one coming.

The guy is livid now. "Bitch."

"Hey, don't call her that!" I get up in his face, which is probably not a good idea with nachos and "granny wolf" sausage in my stomach and THC running through my veins.

The dude raises his fist like he's going to punch my face, but Maya throws her drink at the guy's face, giving us just the second we need to escape and catch the next zip-line.

Maya laughs nonstop until we're clear on the other side of the forest.

Once I'm certain we're safe, literally by scanning every face around us, I start laughing as well. "Don't you need another drink?" I ask.

"Ah, screw it. I'm having way more fun without one." She grabs my shirt and pulls me in for a kiss.

A woman with three small children gasps and tells us to knock it off, but we tune her out. Nothing will spoil this day.

****

Around three o'clock, we're so exhausted from The Forest, we return to the hotel to take a nap. It's after six when we wake, both sober, hungry, and ready for more fun. We drink what's left of the Jack, about two shots for Maya and one for me.

"Damn, we're out," Maya says, sulking at the bottle. "I'll call DeVario to get us. There has to be a liquor store somewhere."

"He's okay with providing alcohol to us? Won't he get in trouble with his company?"

"DeVario has me in the system under my fake license, so he thinks I'm twenty-two. And he knows I tip well, so he's fast to respond."

"Nice."

"Do you want him to take us anywhere else?"

"I thought we were going back to the park?"

"I know. But we could go for a ride first. Just you and me."

"How about we go out to dinner?"

"Ooh ... like a date?" She laughs and rolls her eyes.

"I mean like whatever. No labels."

"In that case, let me put on my little black dress."

She's only hung up three things out of thirty, one of which is a slinky black dress. It falls past her knees, hiding her scar, but shows off her long white back. While I eat chips to manage my hunger, she twists her hair into a messy bun and shoves a bunch of pins in to keep it from falling loose. Then she puts on a gigantic ruby necklace.

"What's that?" I ask.

"Part of my inheritance. I haven't worn it yet. What do you think?"

"It's, uh, huge."

She hits my shoulder playfully. "What are you wearing? Shorts and a tee again?"

"I didn't bring much."

"No, you didn't. So we need to go shopping first."

"But I'm starving." I crumble the empty bag of chips.

"Then it looks like we'll have to get you another bagel before we go."

Maya

After a stop at the liquor store, DeVario takes us to the nearest strip mall. I Google the best place for men's clothing which leads us to a store called Martin's Way.

Daniel immediately backs away, convinced I'll dress him in layers. "I don't want to sweat."

"You can still wear shorts." I drag him into the store by the elbow. "You just need to wear something a little more…" I grab a pair of black textured shorts off the first rack I see. "These. And…" I grab a black and white striped dress shirt. "Put this on and roll up the sleeves."

"I'm gonna sweat."

"You'll sweat regardless."

"Why this?"

"So we look sexy together! You can take it off later."

"All right." With a reluctant grin, he takes the clothes into the dressing room. While he changes, I gather socks, a pair of solid black sneakers, and two pairs of sunglasses (one for me). As though overcome by sudden confidence, he walks out like he owns the place, puckering his lips and nodding his head at all the mannequins.

"Here," I say, handing him the accessories. "Just add this and you'll be complete."

Daniel laughs. "New socks too?"

"Socks are important."

"Like the one still stuck between the washer and dryer?"

I roll my eyes. "Yep, still stuck."

He sits down to finish dressing. I notice a few girls checking us out from across the store. One has straight blonde hair, reminding me of Nicole. I'm tempted to talk to her, but when Daniel stands, and she immediately blushes and whispers something to her friend, I get that she's only interested in Daniel. Not me.

For some reason, that doesn't disappoint me as much as it makes me jealous. Is he better looking than me? Sexier? Through one of the mirrors, I notice the youth still in his face, the definition of his muscles, and his overall well-being. He'll probably look good for the rest of his life, reaching the ultimate level of sexiness around thirty. I wonder what I'll look like at that age. Will I even be alive?

While I usually laugh off such an idea, it radiates a strange sadness. Luckily, Daniel throws me a quick smile, and the negative thoughts depart.

After we pay and leave, I light up a cigarette, my first in two days.

Daniel immediately steps away. "I didn't know you smoked," he says, disgusted.

"Once in a while."

"Why the sudden urge right now?"

"Just had a craving." And I don't want any more bad thoughts to creep in.

"Can I substitute that for something else?" Without waiting for me to answer, he takes the cigarette from my hands and presses his lips against mine.

My knees go weak, and the urge to be with him takes over. I wrap my arms around his waist and push our hips together. Screw this so-called date. I want him now.

But I'll settle for the limo.

We sprint to the parking lot.

DeVario meets us out front, not questioning our short stay.

Once inside, Daniel turns the music up; I unzip his new shorts.

"Really? In here?" he asks with his hands in my hair, destroying the bun I made.

"Why not?"

"We'll be back to the hotel in like fifteen minutes."

"I can't wait that long."

He takes my hands and puts them around his neck. "Yes, you can. Let's just take it nice and slow this time."

Nice and slow is not my tempo. Nice and slow reminds me of Nicole. Even memories of Connor slip in. That boy loved to kiss my face and *only* my face.

"I promise you it'll be worth it," he says.

In that case, sure, why not?

So for the next fifteen freaking minutes, Daniel kisses me. He starts with my neck and face, then my shoulders, arms, and every finger. I don't think I've ever kissed anyone for so long without some article of clothing coming off.

"You're killing me, Daniel," I say. The anticipation is murderous.

The limo finally stops, so I know we're back at the hotel. I adjust my dress. Daniel grabs the two bags of liquor, and we leave as casually as possible. As soon as we're back in the lobby, I pick up the pace, determined to get upstairs, while Daniel takes his good, sweet time, holding my hand and kissing my shoulders.

"You better be enjoying this," I say.

"Oh, I am."

Three other people enter the elevator with us, so forget anything naughty. But Daniel surprises me. He sneaks his hand down the back of my dress and beneath my underwear. I nearly collapse from the pressure. I'm shocked by his bold move but worried I might not be able to keep my mouth shut for much longer. Thankfully, the elevator dings, and the people in front of us get out.

I release a much-needed gasp. Then his lips come down on mine, and we don't separate until we reach our room.

"I can't believe you did that," I say, kicking off my shoes.

He shuts the door behind us and drops our bags on the table. "I told you it would be worth it."

I run my teeth across my bottom lip, nervous about what might come next.

Daniel wastes no time now that we're alone. He takes off my dress and slides my underwear down to my ankles. Then his face disappears.

I'm shivering.

But I'm in heaven.

I close my eyes and run my hands through his hair. He's not only talented with his fingers but his mouth as well. So much I might not be able to hold out for much longer, and I actually want this to last. I don't want it to be quick. I want build-up. I want everything and more.

But then his lips go somewhere forbidden.

I jerk away from him.

"What is it?" he asks.

Both hands cover my scar, the only place on my body that makes me feel weak and exposed. "Don't kiss me there. You can go anywhere else, just not there."

"Does it hurt?"

"No. I just don't want you to kiss me there."

"Okay," he says, coming toward me again. "I'm sorry. Do you want me to stop?"

"No, don't stop. Keep going."

I let it slide because, God damn, he knows how to go down on a girl better than a girl does. His tempo choice and his way of leading might be superior to mine. All because of the anticipation. The not-knowing part.

Since Connor, I've always been in charge of sex. I'm the dominating one. The one who decides the tempo and the direction. Probably because I've never been able to trust someone to do it better.

Or maybe because I don't trust people in general.

And that's when I let go. I give up control and allow myself to come. So hard I nearly fall into the coffee table.

Daniel cushions my landing with his hands and guides me to the couch instead. My lips find his almost instantly. And the song plays on.

Seconds later, we're in the bedroom, both naked. Daniel has a condom on, but this time he's on top. And while typically I would fight like hell to reverse positions, I don't care anymore. When we connect, my head arches back, and I gasp at the ceiling. Daniel has me pinned, and I savor the suffocation. The consumption. But the thoughts in my head spiral out of control as the pleasure below reaches a new high. I beg for the strange flashbacks of my mother's dead body to go away and for Connor's scream to vanquish. I want to push out all the darkness and return to the light. Let the past be buried, and let my present be everything.

It gives me immense satisfaction when Daniel collapses next to me, panting and shaking, all of him soaked in sweat. We lay like that for several minutes. Once I regain my strength, I roll on top of him and kiss him.

"Are you alive?" I ask.

"Very."

"Good."

"Was it good?" he asks.

"Very."

He stretches his arms over his head and then wraps them around my shoulders. "I didn't think that was possible," he says.

"What do you mean?"

"I've never ... done it like that."

"Like what?"

"Just so ... aggressively."

"For real? If what we did is considered *aggressive* to you, then you have a lot to learn about sex."

"I'm sure I do. I just get afraid sometimes. Of hurting people. Of hurting you."

I roll my eyes, not liking how his confidence has shifted. "Oh, Daniel." I run my hands through his sweaty black hair, pinching the ends until drips of water wring out. "Don't get all emotional on me."

"I'm not emotional," he says, squeezing my lower back. "I just want you."

"You have me."

"I want all of you."

I scoot away from him. I can sense it coming. He's getting like Nicole. Too touchy-feely. Too attached. Too emotional. And this is only our *second* time hooking up. What will he be like the third time? In tears?

"Where are you going?" he asks, sitting up.

"I have to pee."

A girl should always pee after sex, but I also need a few minutes alone. I need to remember why I'm here and what I want. I didn't expect Daniel to take so much control so quickly. Maybe he was a little aggressive, leading as he did. That's never happened before. If things continue as is, will I eventually submit to him emotionally? Can I keep this strictly physical?

I value pleasure more than anything. I have to focus on that, which means more sex and less talk. More fun, less downtime. More alcohol and drugs. I'm pretty sure I was almost sober having sex this last time. And while it felt incredible, is it worth it to be fully coherent or a little buzzed? With alcohol, my brain shuts off—no worries of strange thoughts coming to the table.

The only drug I have to wipe my brain completely is also the most dangerous. But I'm tempted. I open my tampon box and stare at the tiny bottle. Only four pills left. No refills. I probably couldn't get more even if I tried. For now, I have to be content with what I have.

Daniel seems to have read my mind because when I come out of the bathroom, he's pouring us each a shot of Jack.

We drink and watch TV. Order room service. Shower and sleep. I'm glad the day is ending non-dramatically. Let's see how long we can keep this up.

Is forever an option?

Daniel

I'm in paradise.

In just a week, I've had more sex with Maya than I ever had during my near two-year relationship with Anna. More alcohol than at high school parties. More laughs. More thrills. More of everything. The rapture rises every day.

From start to finish, our days are packed with pleasure. If we're not in our room having sex, we're at the park, forest, or lagoon. By now, we've been on every ride, seen almost every show, and taken pictures with over a hundred elves. Things that bothered me before don't matter, especially the heat. I sweat until my clothes are drenched, and I eat and drink to my heart's content. I feel healthier and active, and I am constantly having fun.

Amidst all the entertainment, I've convinced Maya not to smoke cigarettes this week and to include more than chips and alcohol into her daily intake of calories. She's opened up to sandwiches and French fries.

Maya has persuaded me to do some pretty extreme things as well. Saturday, I agree to go shirtless and drench myself in "fairy dust" for the ultimate nightclub experience. She does the same but covers her nipples with starfish pads. Dancing straight in the center of the club, the lights fall on us, and the fairies hanging from above try to pull us off the ground. Then a fight breaks out between two elf lords, and the whole club is cleared out, except for Maya and I, lounging in the trees with the fairy world. One of them offers me a strange pill with a smile on it. Maya whacks the fairy's hand away. "No one cranks my man except for me." We leave right away, Maya somewhat livid. The pill was Ecstasy.

As I hold her hand in the elevator, I have the

biggest smile.

"What are you so happy for?" she asks.

"I had a good time tonight," I say. "You'd never see me shirtless and covered in fairy goo back in Morville."

"I think you sweat most of it off," she says, wiping a finger across my glistening chest.

Little does she know, I'm smiling because she called me *her* man.

Behind those brown eyes, there's a part of her that cares. Or wants to care. Maybe in time, she'll let go.

****

One afternoon, while taking a break from everything, Maya takes a phone call out on the balcony. Her phone has been buzzing nonstop for the last couple of days, so whoever's calling now must be important.

While Maya has her conversation, I check through my phone, noting all the missed calls and texts from Gracie.

Gracie: **Hope you're having success on your journey. How's it going? Have you found God?**

Before I left, I made it clear that I wouldn't answer any calls or texts, nor be on social media anytime soon. My dad hasn't even tried to reach out, but he respects my wishes. He'll only contact me if there's an emergency.

For a few seconds, I think about the Morville Massacre and how everyone is doing back home. But then the balcony door opens, startling me, and Maya comes in, her cheeks somewhat flushed and not from the sun.

"What is it?" I ask. "Is everything okay?"

"Nothing. Just the realtor."

"Realtor?"

"My parents' house is finally getting sold."

"Oh."

"It could've been sold before I turned eighteen, but my grandmother didn't want to deal with all the paperwork. She's not too keen I sell it now. But it's more money in the bank for me."

"It doesn't have any sentimental value to you?"

"No." She huffs and tosses her phone on top of the bed. "Why would it?"

"I don't know. I don't know much about your parents."

"It's best you don't know anything." She peels off her tank top. In one week, she's gotten maybe a shade tanner with patches of sunburn around her shoulders. "What?" she asks when she notices me staring.

"Nothing. You're just beautiful."

"Aw." She pecks my lips and then slips into the bathroom for a shower. I follow her, removing my clothes. "What are you doing?" she asks suspiciously.

"Showering with you."

"I prefer to shower alone."

"I'll make it worth it."

"Fine." She seems annoyed but allows me in. She turns the water on and immediately starts washing her upper body while I take care of her legs. I don't realize where I'm touching when she practically knees me.

"Stop!" she yells, backing into the corner of the stall.

"I'm sorry. I forgot. I won't wash you there."

"Just get out. Please."

I can't tell if she's going to cry, if she's even capable of crying, or if she's on the verge of screaming at me. But she needs her space, so I get out, grab a towel, and retreat to the bedroom. Now I can't put the past out of my head. I need to know what happened to Maya. Why won't she talk about her parents? *Anthony and*

Marilyn Floros. They died trying to protect her. Why does she seem to hate them so much?

Through Google, I discover that Anthony was the CEO of a pharmaceutical company, and Marilyn was the principal of an elite private school. Both were highly well-educated, career-driven people. And their daughter, Maya, was a gold medalist gymnast, ranking first in West Virginia and 14th overall in the country. That means she could have tried out for the Olympian team. I find tons of pictures of Maya competing and also of her on the podiums. Maya is stunning in every photo. She's happy and healthy. But there is not a single picture of Maya with her parents at any of the events. That must explain some of the resentment. My dad always kept his work schedule open for Friday night football. Only emergencies kept him from attending.

I don't even hear the water turn off. Maya comes out wrapped in a towel, smelling like rosebuds. "Sorry for snapping," she says.

"It's fine," I say, nearly dropping my phone. "I was just looking up stuff to do."

"Have we extinguished all options around here?"

"Just about. But I don't mind repeats."

She allows her towel to fall loose. "Do you want to have sex without a condom?" She sits on my lap.

Is she for real? I was expecting her to suggest something like another Mount Doom binge.

"Why?" I ask.

"Because it'll feel amazing, or so I hear."

At least I know she's never done anything so reckless. But why take the chance now? Especially since we're not boyfriend-girlfriend. And I wouldn't exactly call ourselves mature enough, either.

"Are you on birth control?" I ask.

"No."

"Then it's a stupid idea."

"It's not stupid."

"*Maya.*"

"I never get my period. It's fine. Nothing's going to happen."

"You don't get your period? Why not?"

"I was a gymnast for most of my life. It delayed a lot of things. And my diet doesn't support a period right now."

"Maybe you should work on that."

"Maybe you should work on getting hard." Her hands try to help, but nothing happens. Between her outburst in the shower and now asking for unprotected sex, it's almost like she's trying to keep something from spilling out. She was acting weird after the phone call too. Was she really talking to a realtor?

"Why can't you just talk to me?" I ask.

"I talk to you all the time."

"I'm concerned about your health. Am I not allowed to be concerned?"

"You can be concerned all you want. But don't expect anything to change." She scoots off my lap, disappointed by my lack of enthusiasm, and searches for the next pleasure.

Drugs and alcohol.

I could say so much right now. She's reckless. Her lifestyle will kill her someday or at least cause her a lot of pain. She bypasses problems with temporary highs, and one day, those problems will grow so big she won't have any highs to help her. She won't accept the lows of life no matter what. But the low will happen someday, and I wonder if she'll have anyone around to help her when it does.

Too many people in my life have died or abandoned me. I'm not ready to add another to the count.

But for now, my worries would only push Maya away, and she needs me, even if she won't admit it. She needs me, and I need her.

"Just stay," I say, reaching for her hand. I ease her back into my lap, this time cradling her.

"You have to stop pushing," she says in a near whisper. "Don't ruin this."

"I don't want to ruin anything. I just want you..." How do I word this without revealing my concerns? "I want you to have pleasure for the rest of your life." Aka, I want you to stay alive for as long as possible.

"That sounds perfect." Her mouth reaches for mine. "I want the same for you." She loosens my towel, and before I know it, she's made her request come true, and I'm not doing anything to stop it.

I can't deny that it feels incredible. But I know the risks. It's not just an unwanted pregnancy I'm worried about. It's what I'll feel afterward. It's what she might feel.

"Is this what you want?" I ask, just to be sure.

"Yes. This is how I want it. This is how I want it every time."

There's no way to take this slow, especially with her on top. But it doesn't matter because we don't care about the tempo anymore. Our lips conjoin, but we don't kiss. We exchange air. Every movement below takes us one step higher to our eventual peak. She lets out this weird cry, almost like she's in pain. And then she goes still, with all her hair in her face. I try to kiss her, but she turns her head away. Either everything was so intense, she's dizzy and needs a second to regain herself, or she's unable to handle the reality of what we just did.

It's no longer casual sex when you remove barriers like that. It's something more. She has to know that. She has to know what she's doing.

Is she in that much denial?

****

Later we go to The Forest, even though Maya is anxious to hit the nightclub again. There's one show I've been wanting to see, but Maya has avoided it, always coming up with an excuse like she needs another drink or wants to take a break and return to the hotel.

Based on reviews, "Festival of the Fairies" is one of the most popular live shows in Fantasy Land. When we finally sit to watch, I can see why it's so popular. But also why Maya tried twice to avoid it.

The show is all acrobatics, dance, and gymnastics—fairies flipping through the air, exotic dancers, and drummers. The most physically fit employees of Fantasy Land are all right here, putting on a spectacular show, showing off talent that can only be achieved by years of training and hard work. And while it's enjoyable, I see no joy on Maya's face.

I have happiness and pleasure when I am with Maya. But it isn't enough. Unlike her, I can't survive on those two elements alone. I need more. If I've learned anything from this spiritual journey, it's that I need to allow myself to feel again, even if it hurts.

Does that mean I'm falling in love with Maya? Or have I already?

She doesn't say anything when the show ends. She just gets up and exits along with everyone else. Once outside, she walks ahead of me and grabs hold of one of the trees. Her eyes closed, she pushes her forehead against the bark and takes several deep breaths. I have no idea what to do other than give her space until she decides to speak.

She stays pressed against that tree for almost a minute before she lets go with a red mark across her forehead. "I could do that," Maya says, her eyes on the ground.

"Do what?"

"I could flip like that. I was good. I was really good. I could have gone to the Olympics. I could have been like Simone Biles. I had that kind of talent. I had passion."

"Maya, you could still—"

"No, I can't." Her eyes shoot daggers. "I lost my chance. Even if I started all over again, I'd never get back to where I was. I'd reinjure myself trying."

"I'm sorry, Maya."

"It's fine." She laughs and rolls her eyes. "I'm not mad or anything. The life of a gymnast is all work, no play. My life now is way better." She starts walking away.

I remain where I am. "Is it? What happens when the money runs out?"

She spins around, her eyes narrowing. "What are you talking about?"

"How much did you inherit?"

"Why is that any of your business?"

"I'm just asking."

"A couple million. Probably more after I go through all the shares and investments."

"You could blow through that in just a few years."

"Then I'll become a Fantasy Land Princess!"

We're both shouting now, which means it's happening. We're having our first fight in the middle of Fantasy Land. I've been close to pushing Maya's button many times in the last few days, but I've always backed off. While a fight might be helpful to get some things out in the open, I would prefer no audience.

"Let's not fight here," I say, trying to grab her hand. "I shouldn't have pried like that. But you started to open up to me, and I would like you to do that more often."

"Isn't opening my legs for you enough?" She pulls away from me and heads toward the exit, but my stride is almost double hers. She tries running to escape me, but eventually, her weaker leg gives, and she resorts to a hobble-skip.

"You're going to hurt yourself," I say. "Slow down."

"Just back off, Daniel. Give me some space."

I ease off by a couple of feet to ensure she doesn't try to run again. I follow her to the bus, but she sits next to someone else while I am forced to stand. There's so much I want to tell her, but every time I look at her, I think of one more thing to say. And because of how emotional I'm feeling, how can I filter what comes out of my mouth?

She gets off the bus before me. My gentleman side takes over, and I allow the older woman to my right to walk ahead of me. By the time I reach the lobby, Maya is nowhere in sight. She's probably already on the elevator, planning to chug whiskey the second she gets to her room.

I fly up the stairs and nearly leap across the room to grab the bottle of Jack before she can.

"What are you doing?" she yells in a high-pitched voice that echoes to the world's end.

I shut the door before she screams again. "Getting drunk..." I can barely breathe after that sprint. "...and having sex is not going to solve anything."

"I don't have any problems to solve other than you being in my way."

I take a few seconds to steady my breathing before I unleash a series of questions that may lead to World War III.

"Why don't you ever talk about your parents?

Why don't you seem to care that they're gone? That they died. That Connor died. That you almost died. Why do you not feel anything anymore?"

"It's their fault that they died!" Hands clenched, every muscle tensed, she lands on the couch like she wants to break it.

"How is it their fault?" I ask.

She growls. "Connor hated country music. He only went because he knew I'd be there, and he used it as another opportunity to get me back. I didn't want to be there either. My parents dragged me to that stupid concert all for appearance. To show the town what a great wonderful family we were. And look at what happened! They all died and left me unable to do the one thing I loved."

"Gymnastics?"

"Yes, gymnastics!" She rubs her forehead and digs at her hair. "It was the only thing I was good at, that I liked doing, that kept me feeling good inside. Now can I please have my whiskey back?"

"You need to let me speak first."

"You're such an ass!"

"Just hear me out, and then I'll stop talking. I won't ask about your parents, gymnastics, or even how you're feeling, but I want you to listen to me. Please." I shake the bottle of whiskey, ticked that I have to bribe her with alcohol to get her to behave.

"What?" She throws her hands up. "What other shit do you wanna throw at me?"

"Remember when we talked about that Chinese proverb?"

"Not that again."

"You need to understand where I'm coming from." I sit next to her, but far enough we're nowhere near touching. "I was at zero percent. All my friends died. I went to every single funeral. I didn't cry, not one single tear. I felt absolutely nothing. And then I met you. And I began to feel something again." She turns away, annoyed by my words, but I keep going. "Maya, I feel pleasure when I'm with you. I feel happy. But I also feel sorrow when I think about you in pain. When I think about you hurting yourself. Or running away from me. I always thought sorrow was something bad. Something to avoid. But it's not. It just makes me aware of what's important. What I truly care about. You see, that proverb isn't about figuring out how to omit anything from your life; it's about letting everything in. When it happens. However it happens. Just letting life be whatever it needs to be. Even if it hurts."

She shakes her head and turns toward me. "I don't get you."

"I'm trying to tell you how I feel."

"No." She points a finger at me. "You're trying to complicate things. I told you from the start, this was going to be a pleasure ride. Not a goddamn spiritual journey or romantic cruise. If you're looking for balance or sorrow or whatever it is you're lamenting about, you need to go somewhere else."

"Fine." I stand. "But I want you to come with me."

"I'm not going anywhere. I'm happy here."

"In Fantasy Land. All by yourself?"

She stands and gets up in my face like she wants to fight physically. "I'll find someone else to be with."

"Really? That quickly? I thought you had standards."

Her nostrils flare. "Shut up."

"Does that please you? Moving on from person to person, using them for sex, and when they get too real for you, you blow them off? Is that why you broke up with

Connor? Because he cared about you too much?"

"Shut up ... shut up."

"Do you think your lifestyle is going to work out long-term? When you're thirty, and your liver is so damaged, you can't even walk? When you're out of money and whoring yourself for drugs and chips?"

"Shut the fuck up!" She grabs the nearest object, her purse, and hurls it at me. It does little damage, so she charges at me, swinging her hands left and right, beating my chest until I'm sure she's causing more harm to herself, but I can't fight back; I would never strike a girl, no matter what. My body freezes, and I take the blows until she falls back onto the couch, exhausted and rubbing her knuckles.

"You're not happy," I tell her. "You'll never be happy. And neither will I. Not unless we both allow ourselves to feel sorrow. And love."

"I have a better idea, Daniel. Go fuck yourself."

"I love you, Maya."

"No, you don't!" She half-yells, half-laughs like I'm an idiot. "You're infatuated. That's all this is. It's not *love*. It's a trick of science. Your body is charged with chemicals right now because of all the sex. Oxytocin messes with your head, making you think you're in love, but you're not."

I shake my head. "And all those drugs and alcohol in your body are making you feel and believe you're not hurting, that everything is all right when it's not. None of this is right."

"What the hell?" She paces to the balcony door and back. "What are you suggesting, Daniel? You want me to go to rehab? Church? Alcoholics Anonymous? Maybe see a shrink? Get on some prescription drugs and act like a victim? Is that what you want for me, Daniel? Cause that's what you become when you take that route.

You become a statistic—another broken human for society to cradle. And I'm telling you right now, I will not be cradled. By *anyone*."

I finally hand her back the bottle.

She takes a swig, then heads for the door.

"Where are you going?" I ask.

"Out for a while. When I return, you better be back to your normal self, or I won't be able to do this anymore. I mean that. I'll kick you out." She slams the door behind her.

I don't follow her. Continuing this fight in public would get both of us thrown out of the hotel. We need a break from each other. Maya will likely return drunk, giggling like nothing happened and wanting to have sex. And what will I do? Give in?

She's right about Oxytocin. It makes you feel good but also makes you forget what's real.

I look around the room, noting how messy everything is. I've cleaned up after her all week, yet she still causes an explosion wherever she goes. Her life is a mess, inside and out. And there's nothing I can do to change it.

Why did I tell her that I loved her? Do I love her?

Charlie had several girlfriends, but only one serious one before he died. I remember what he said the day after they broke up. *"You never really know how much you love someone until they're gone."* Is that what I need to do now? Do I need to separate myself from Maya to know whether or not I truly love her? If we separate, will I ever get her back? Or will she be gone for good?

I think about my home life. Has anything changed? When I think about the shooting and losing all my friends, do I still feel numb?

Has Maya clouded my emotions? Has she been nothing but toxic shock?

I make a decision. One that I might regret. But I knew from the beginning this was only a vacation. And vacations are temporary, for the most part.

Maya

I meet a nice guy at the bar. We throw back lots of shots. He's older than me, by a lot. He has gray hairs but a nice smile—and a good body. He asks me back to his room. I tell him I need to pee. I don't return.

Instead, I go upstairs. I'm tired. The floor dances without me. I open the door.

Daniel? Daniel, where are you?

Everything is cleaned up. Looks like room service came through, but I know it was Daniel. He's such a neat freak. I bet he's a straight A student. Teacher's pet.

His suitcase is gone. Is he playing a joke on me?

Maybe he's hiding on the balcony.

No one is there. Just the wind, hitting me like it wants me to gravitate off the ledge. The ground looks miles away. How long would it take to fall? Maybe I would float away instead. Maybe I could fly. Maybe I'm a fairy.

No. No flying. Not tonight. Where the hell is Daniel?

I stumble back inside. I'm cold. He always turns the AC too high.

He's left a sock on the bathroom vanity. A sock and a note. This has to be a joke. I try to read his overly-neat handwriting, but the words morph together. I can't make anything out. I'll have to wait. He'll come back and read it to me.

My leg throbs. It's almost like I can feel the bullet back in there. I scratch at my scar. Why does it hurt so much? Why isn't the alcohol numbing it out?

It's all Daniel's fault.

Why isn't he here?

I take a pill.

I might die tonight. Might as well get in one last ride. I'll go clubbing and ride a centaur until I collapse. That sounds like an excellent way to go out. Or maybe another fight will break out, and there'll be gunshots. While everyone cowers to the ground, I'll open my arms wide and scream, "Take me!"

Save me.

Part Three: Sorrow
Daniel

Dear Maya,

While I've enjoyed our time together, it's best for both of us I return home. Please be safe and take care of yourself. If you need to talk to me, you have all my contact information.

I meant what I said.

—Daniel

Despite my heightened anxiety level, I sleep during my two-hour flight and for some of the Uber ride home.

Night flights suck. I am exhausted beyond words. Reaching my hometown, it feels like I've been gone for months, but it's only been a week. Morville hasn't changed. It's the same old faces and buildings. At 7:30 AM, folks are already out, walking their dogs, getting coffee, and so forth. "They" say after a shooting, people are too scared to leave their homes. But eventually, they regain their faith in humanity, open the doors, and learn to live again. Slow and steady. But do they win the race? Is there any race to be won after a tragedy?

I tried the express route with Maya, thinking I'd find answers in Fantasy Land of all places. And now I feel like absolute shit. My stomach hurts, my brain pounds, almost like I'm having withdrawal from alcohol, drugs, and sex. Thoughts of impending doom and misery weigh down on me.

Dad isn't home when I walk through the door. Neither are the dogs, so I assume he took them to work today. I throw my luggage on my desk, pull down the blinds, and fall face-first onto my bed. Within seconds, I am asleep.

****

Something is burning.

Dad is at the stove, attempting to cook pasta, but he's doing a horrible job.

I step in to stir the pot before it boils over.

"I didn't know you were coming home today," Dad says.

"I decided to come home sooner than planned." I open the oven to remove the burnt garlic bread. Twenty-five percent of it is edible. But Dad doesn't seem to care as he has chips and salsa as a fallback. I think of Maya, always eating chips.

"When'd you get in?" he asks.

"Early this morning. Around seven."

"Did you sleep all day?"

"Pretty much."

"You look like you got a lot of sun."

"I did."

"How was your trip?"

"It was fine. Hey, where's Jojo?" I look across the room where her food bowl and bed usually are. None of those items are there.

Dad turns the stove off and takes a deep breath. I should have sensed something was off this morning when I came in, but I was so damn tired. I'd been worn out by my flight, Maya, everything.

"What happened to Jojo? Where is she?"

Dad raises his eyes slowly. "I'm sorry, son, but Jojo passed away a few days ago."

"What?" I bump into the refrigerator, knocking some of the magnets off. "What happened? She was fine when I left."

"Jojo was an old dog. It was just her time."

"Did you put her down?"

"She died in her sleep. Peacefully."

"Where is she?"

"She's already been buried. At the pet cemetery, down the road."

My head is doing circles. I don't know if I'll pass out or hurl. Cry or scream. In actuality, I can't do anything. I'm still frozen. Still numb. Maya woke me for pleasure. Whatever emotions I felt in Georgia are stuck there. Everything here is still the same.

"Why don't you sit down?" Dad says, pulling out a chair for me. "You don't look so good."

"Why didn't you call?"

"You said not to call unless it was an emergency."

"Jojo's my dog." *Was* my dog. She's in the past now. Just like Charlie. Just like the team. Who's going to die next? Dad looks healthy, but he could be hiding a cancer diagnosis. I would never know until he showed symptoms. Maya is a ticking time bomb, but I already said my goodbyes.

But was I ready to say goodbye?

I look across the kitchen and toward the living room where we used to celebrate Christmas mornings, huddled around the fireplace, drinking hot cocoa, and opening gifts. I was four when Mom snuck Jojo into the room, all wrapped in bows and confetti. Jojo and I immediately clicked. And after Mom left, Jojo stood by my side. Jojo was my emotional support when my father could not be.

"I'm sorry," Dad says as if that will make a difference. "But we can adopt Samantha now if that will make you feel better."

I shake my head. "That's what everyone does when their pet dies. They just get a new one. And when that one dies, they get another. What's the point in having a dog if all they're going to do is die on you one day?"

"It's the moments in between."

I finally gather all the magnets I knocked off the fridge. "I don't think there's a point in anything."

"Daniel…"

"I'll be in my room."

Cleaning or reorganizing helps me stay calm and focused, so I start unpacking. I dump everything on top of my bed. All my clothes go straight into the hamper. I put away my toiletries, plug in my phone charger, and toss aside the few souvenirs Maya bought me—a sparkly shot glass, a dragon figurine, and sunglasses. They'll likely end up in the closet next to my football trophies. Or the trash. How much of my life will be tossed away?

When I return to my bed, something glimmers between the sheets. Maya's necklace. The giant ruby one. How did it end up in my bag?

I close my eyes, trying to remember the last time she had it on. We were having sex, but the necklace kept hitting my fingers, so I took it off and tossed it across the room. It must have landed right inside my bag. In such a hurry to pack and leave, I didn't see it.

Reality is kicking me in the balls right now.

I left her a sock and took her necklace. Now would be an ideal time to get upset. To grieve. But nothing happens. After everything, I still can't cry.

But I want to. I have to.

I open my closet and dig through my things until I find a football. Then I bolt out the front door. It's near dark, but I don't need light for what I have planned. I start with a light jog and work up to a steady run, heading straight toward my high school. The fields are locked and gated, but it's not much effort to jump the fence. I run straight to the thirty-yard line. For field goals, a holder would set up the ball for me. Jeremy had that job, and he was great at it. He never fumbled. He never let me down. I trusted him.

Closing my eyes, I imagine him here with me. I imagine all my teammates. The coaches, the ref, the cheerleaders, and the crowd. I picture my dad in the stands, quiet but present. Anna is cheering with the squad, and I'm not angry with her because she hasn't cheated on me yet. This is late autumn. When we won states. When we were unstoppable. Invisible. When I had everything a guy could want—popularity, a hot girlfriend, talent, the respect of the town, and my future set in stone.

I open my eyes. With everything I have, I give the ball a good hard kick. As it soars between the goalposts, right down the middle, I wonder what would have happened if I hadn't made the state goal. We would have lost, and the town would have been devastated. I would have been blamed. It would have been a tragedy. But less severe and costly than what happened last month.

Had we lost, would Wesley still have snapped?

Am I incidentally responsible for what happened? Did my field goal push Wesley to destroy the team?

I drop to my knees. The worst feeling is knowing I still have it in me. I can be out of shape and still kick a perfect field goal. There's nothing wrong with my body other than needing to get back to healthy eating and daily exercise. I'm not damaged. I still have a future. Notre Dame won't take away my scholarship. They still want me to play. Everyone in this town wants me to play.

If Maya hadn't been shot, she'd be prepping for the Olympics. She'd push forward, all on her own, aiming for the gold. Why can't I do the same? What is holding me back?

When I return home, Dad is at the kitchen table eating chips and salsa. The house smells like burnt garlic bread, but at least he's cleaned everything up and lit a candle.

"Are you all right?" Dad asks, noting my sweaty shirt. "Did you go to the field?"

I sit with him. "Just wanted to see if it was still possible."

"To play?" He takes the ball from me.

I nod.

"And is it possible?"

"It is." I take a deep breath. "But it's not going to be the same. It's never going to be the same."

"It'll be harder."

He's right. It will be harder. Much harder. Not just the physical part. The mental.

I might as well start with being honest.

"I didn't win any raffle, Dad."

"I know."

"Wait ... what? You knew?"

He's smiling about it. "Of course. The minute after we spoke about it, I created an account and joined that online support group. Nothing was posted about a Fantasy Land trip. When I messaged the website manager, he had no idea what I was talking about."

"Why didn't you say anything?"

Dad leans forward in his chair, placing the football between us. "Because if you had to lie to me, you must have really needed to go. But I can't fathom you went alone, considering how expensive the trip would have been."

I squeeze the football with one hand. "I didn't go alone. I went with a girl."

"Not just any girl?"

"Someone I met through the support page. We clicked right away, and she invited me to go with her. So I went. And it was a lot of fun. But in the end, it just didn't work out between us. That's why I came home."

"Sounds similar to how I met your mother."

"In Fantasy Land?"

He chuckles and shakes his head. "We didn't have online dating back then or support groups or Facebook. We had good old-fashioned AOL."

"Age, sex, location?" I sigh, remembering the joke with Maya.

Dad nods. "But your mom and I talked for several months before we finally met. And when we met in person, it was instant how we clicked. She had a lot of passion, and I had much to give. But we clashed instantly too."

"What caused you to stay together then? If there were problems from the start, continuing wouldn't be worth it."

"If everyone ran away the second a flag went up, no one would fall in love. Think about how many flags the refs throw during a game. None of your teammates quit over those flags. They took the penalty and worked harder."

"Dad, I'm not saying I'm in love with this girl."

"And I'm not saying I'd call you a fool if you were. I'd say: don't give up until you're certain the game is over."

It's like he knew I'd return in pieces and would need his words of wisdom. That's how well my dad knows me. But how well do I know myself? I'm conflicted on so many levels. Maybe I should focus on one thing at a time. To tackle everything at once would be overkill. But what should I start with?

"Get some rest first," Dad says, answering the question for me. "And see how you feel in the morning."

Sounds like a plan.

Maya

Dawn meets me at the airport with a bottle of Evian and extra-strength Tylenol. She's dressed in all black like she's welcoming me to my own funeral.

I certainly don't add to the mood. I've been wearing the same outfit for over two days.

"Have you heard of deodorant?" Dawn asks, waving a hand in front of her nose. "Geez, you reek of everything."

"I know," I groan.

She grabs my carry-on and gives me the water. "Drink up. Your detox starts now." Then she puts out her hand.

"Yeah, yeah." I give her the bottle of Vicodin.

She tosses it into the nearest trash can.

That was the deal we made over the phone.

No more drugs.

We've been through this before. It's been over a year, but there was a time when I needed to get sober. Dawn was the only person I trusted to take care of me without sending me to rehab or calling for professional help, which could have gotten me into more legal trouble. She monitored me for a few days until the hardest part of the detox was over, and I showed signs of being "normal". But that only lasted a short while.

Alcohol always finds its way back in.

So far, I've survived over twenty-four hours without drinking, but half were spent in the ER being treated for alcohol poisoning. Luckily, I did not have to get my stomach pumped. Only IVs and oxygen were administered. And now I have a headache the size of a double-burrito, and the thought of eating anything, even chips, makes me want to puke.

Once we're settled in her car, Dawn rolls down all the windows and coerces me into putting on body spray so I don't stink up her seats.

"No one knows you're back home," Dawn says once we're on the highway. "What should I tell my parents?"

"Does it really matter?"

"Well, if you're going to stay with me, they need to know. And they're going to ask questions."

I rub my greasy forehead, then the space between my eyebrows. Everything feels gross and wrinkled, like I've aged a decade. I check myself in the side view mirror. Yep. I'm hideous. I'm hardly a shade darker, and I've been in the sun for a week. Maybe I'm meant to travel north. I'd probably do well in Russia. Everyone drinks there.

"I don't want to go to your parents' house," I finally say, itching the IV bruise on my hand. "They'll try to send me to rehab."

"Then back to your grandmother's?"

"I don't want her to see me like this. Let's just find a hotel."

"A hotel? Seriously?"

"Yes, seriously. Now please stop talking. My head is going to explode."

****

The nicest hotel is ten miles south of Coors, so there's little chance we'll encounter anyone from home. Having a temporary place with room service and HDTV will be easier. But this so-called 4-star hotel doesn't even come close to what I had at Fantasy Land.

What *we* had.

After I shower, Dawn brushes my hair since I'm too jittery to do it myself. I'm at the point where the withdrawal causes my body to shake. Everything hurts, and while a swig of Jack would silence the burn, it'll only cause the cycle to restart. I'm not ready for that button to be pressed again. Not when I'm at a low.

I think back to what happened at Fantasy Land. How it happened. Where it happened. Why it happened. In my mind, it plays back in little blurs, like a black and white film with poor editing and no sound. But one thing is certain: I almost died in the middle of the dance floor. And I would have been alone, surrounded by strangers.

But despite that near-death experience, I will start drinking again. It's inevitable. Detoxes are temporary, like most diets. And when you're an alcoholic, you're an alcoholic for life. Even if you go years without drinking, the cravings will always be a part of you, just like this goddamn metal rod in my leg. I'll be buried with it. If that's the case, they should bury me with a bottle of Jack too. I should write that into my Will. All my money goes to Dawn so long as I have Jack to rest eternally by my side. I always thought cremation was the way to go, but what if the metal doesn't melt?

Once I'm dressed, Dawn braids my hair while we watch an episode of House Hunters. She offers me food, but I refuse everything, even chips. Consuming water is difficult enough.

"Maybe you should cut it?" I suggest.

"Cut what?"

"My hair."

"You could use a trim. I know a stylist who does wonders with long hair. You could—"

"I want to cut it all off."

"For real? But you've been growing your hair out for years."

"I know."

"You love your hair."

"It's just hair. Look, if you don't do it, then I will."

"Maya…"

I rush to the bathroom. There's a small pair of scissors inside one of my makeup bags, but my hands convulse, and I end up spilling everything on the ground. Defeated, I sit on the toilet and stare at the wall.

Dawn stands in the doorway with her hands folded across her chest. "We need to talk about this."

"There's nothing to talk about."

She picks up everything I dropped. "You shouldn't be around sharp objects right now." She slips the scissors into her back pocket.

I roll my eyes. "I'm not suicidal."

"You got very depressed the last time you tried to detox."

"Doesn't everyone? Detoxes aren't any fun. They don't bring me any pleasure."

"No shit. But you can use this *unfun* time to your advantage. You can talk to me. And I will listen. I want to know what happened down there. Was he not a nice guy?"

"No, he was too nice."

"So nice that you had to mix alcohol with Vicodin?"

I splash my face with sink water. Then I stick my head under the faucet and chug water. First, I imagine it's whiskey filling my body, drowning out all the madness inside my head. Then it becomes Daniel, kissing me under a waterfall. My legs squeeze together; I hate how much I miss his touch.

My stomach is about to burst. I pull my head out of the sink and return to the bedroom. I turn off the TV and lay sideways on one of the beds.

Dawn leans against the wall, determined to keep

an active watch over me.

"It's probably best you sleep first, anyway," she says. "But we're going to talk tomorrow. And you are going to eat something. Even if I have to force you."

****

I don't know how long I've been asleep, but it feels like my bladder will explode. I roll out of bed and scamper for the toilet.

Dawn is up, showered, and changed, dangling food in my face—bagels and potato chips from *Panera*. Dawn holds on to the chips until I eat one of the bagels. It takes me nearly a half-hour to eat the whole thing, and now I'm too damn full for anything else.

"What time is it?" I finally ask, ready to puke from carb overload.

"Almost ten."

"How long have you been awake?"

"Since seven."

I lie back on the bed. My headache has subdued, but my body still feels weird, like at any minute it might combust. Am I that fragile without my booze?

"I got you an appointment to get your haircut," Dawn says. "At one, if you're up for it."

"I thought the plan was just to lay low for a while. Until this is over."

"The best way to detox from alcohol and bad decision-making is to start with some good decision-making. That starts with your hygiene, which we've improved drastically since yesterday, but a haircut would be the next step. Not as drastic as cutting the whole thing off because with your bone structure, you'd look horrible with anything shorter than shoulder-length hair."

"And I suppose afterward we'll get manis and pedis?"

"We can."

"Sounds boring."

"It's called taking care of yourself. It's what you should be doing with that inheritance of yours. Not blowing it on crazy vacations with crazy one-week boyfriends."

"Daniel was not crazy. And he wasn't my boyfriend."

"Ah, so Kicked123 has a name after all."

I cover my face with a pillow. I could use another twelve hours of sleep. But Dawn has opened Pandora's Box, and now that I'm sober, it's impossible to push those thoughts away. I can face reality with my cousin. Or suffer on my own.

All pride pushed aside, Dawn would likely be the safer choice.

"Let me make something straight," Dawn says, pulling the pillow off my face. "This is the last time I'm going to do this with you. If it happens again, you're on your own. You'll have to go to rehab. And that may be really hard for you to deal with, but it's hard for me too, watching my little cousin slowly kill herself."

"I'm not killing myself."

Dawn tosses the pillow on the ground rather aggressively. "You don't remember what it was like after the shooting. You didn't talk to anyone when you got out of the hospital. You didn't cry. You just went home and drank your dad's whiskey like it was medicine. You went out and got high with strangers. You even went to death metal concerts. It's like you did everything your parents would disapprove of. And nobody could do anything to stop you. Not even when you got caught and the judge sent you to counseling."

"It was either that or rehab. I chose the lesser of two evils."

"You're lucky Grams and I had your back on that

decision. We made sure you attended all those sessions. We made sure you didn't do anything stupid in public. But I could see you slipping away in private. You may have Grams fooled, but I know everything. I just don't understand why you do it. One would think it's because you lost your parents and PTSD, but when you went through your first detox with me, you confessed it was because of gymnastics, not being able to compete anymore. It surprised me you could be more upset over losing trophies than losing your own parents. But it was a real pain. A real loss to you. You talked some of it out, and things started to look up. But then you started drinking again. And all that sorrow got buried away again. Then came all these girlfriends, a new one every other month. Did you choose to only be with girls because you lost Connor?"

"I don't want to talk about Connor."

"He was your only real boyfriend, he loved you, and he died. Don't you think that warrants some attention?"

"I wish he hadn't."

"Hadn't what? Hadn't died?"

"Hadn't loved me so much." I close my eyes, remembering the last time I saw him at the concert. He kept asking if we could go outside to talk, and I kept blowing him off. I could be so cold to him.

"Do you want to expand on that thought a bit?" Dawn asks.

I shake my head and revert to her original question. "I've been with guys too. Not just girls."

"Name one besides Daniel."

"Lucas and RJ."

"I'm pretty sure Lucas was gay."

"Still counts!"

"No, it doesn't."

When I reach for another pillow, she grabs it from me.

"What's your problem? I like having sex with girls. It feels good. You should try it sometime."

"That's not it, and you know it. Why girls?"

I rub my forehead. "They're easier to control. They let me be in charge."

"But?"

"But they're too emotional. They get too attached and too needy, and I can't deal with that shit anymore."

"You can't deal with someone needing you?"

"Not like that. I don't want the responsibility."

"Of what? Of having to care about someone other than yourself?"

"Jesus, Dawn!" I grab the last pillow and throw it for her. "You're making it sound like I'm this awful, selfish person."

"That's because you never think about the rest of us. You're not the only person that lost someone that day. They were my aunt and uncle."

"They were shitty people."

"No, they weren't. Don't say that."

"They always acted so nice and loving around you. Around everyone but me."

"They gave you everything."

"Everything but their time!" I have nothing left to hurl, so I pound my hands against the bed like a mad gorilla. "Did they come to any of my gymnastic meets? Did they ever teach me anything? Other than what fork to use at a dinner party?"

"So you're mad at them?"

"Of course I am. They were workaholic assholes. They…" My whole body shakes. All the memories flood in. I take a deep breath and uncurl my fingers before the nail marks become permanent. "They didn't care about my dreams of going to the Olympics or what I did or who I hung out with. Until I started dating Connor. It's like my self-worth was determined by who I would potentially marry. And then one day, they announced we're all going to this country Christian music festival. I suffered along, not expecting much of a good time. And what do you know? The whole time, they talked to other people, ignoring me yet again. And all Connor wanted was to talk to me, and I ignored him. Maybe if I had just gone outside and talked to him, none of this crap would have happened. But we were all inside when the shots were fired. And my idiot mom ran across the floor, screaming my name, making herself the biggest target of the night. She ended up getting shot and falling on top of me. Then I got shot in the leg, and my dad got shot trying to save us both."

"So you're mad at them for trying to save you?"

"I would have made it out on my own! I didn't panic like everyone else. I knew I had to lay low and sneak out quietly if I didn't want to be hit. If my mom hadn't tried to be the town hero, she wouldn't have died. My dad wouldn't have died. Connor wouldn't have died. And I wouldn't be here with a fucking metal rod in my leg, having to second-guess if I feel any guilt or not."

"Guilt that you survived and they didn't?"

I take a deep breath, feeling razors in my throat. "I should have gone down with them."

"Don't say that. Your parents did not want you to die. Your mother shielded you. She took the death shots, not you. She wouldn't do that for anyone. She did it because she loved you."

"Showing love only during life-or-death situations is not love. I will never believe they loved me, no matter what anyone else says or thinks. Love has to be consistent. The only thing consistent about my parents was their absences."

"If that's true…"

"It is true. And if any part of me feels grief or regret, it's not telling them how I felt. I never got the chance to tell them how much it hurt not to feel loved by them. By my own parents. And if I am going to be completely honest with myself, I regret not talking to Connor that night. He died thinking I didn't give a shit about him. I did care. I just didn't want to be his girlfriend. I didn't love him. I wanted my parents to love me!"

Dawn sighs and softens her gaze. "Then I'm sorry. I'm sorry you didn't feel any love from your parents. But that doesn't mean you can't have love with someone else. It doesn't mean you can't trust people."

"I trust you. For the most part."

"It can't only be me. I'm just one person. You have to be willing to let others in. Maybe not my folks, they can be a little much, but your grandmother isn't a bad person. She loves you. She's done her best to take care of you. And you're the only family she has left."

"It's not that I think she's a bad person. She's just … you're going to think me selfish for saying this ... but she's no fun. I only want to be around people who make me laugh, who get my jokes, who want me to be happy. I don't want concerns and frowns and 'oh you shouldn't do this' crap. I get it from you in small doses, but most of the time, you're fun to be around. I can be myself and have a good time. Is that such a bad thing? That I only want to have a good time?"

"It is when you use all the good times to cover up all the bad ones."

"You sound like Daniel."

"Well, then I applaud this Daniel guy for being able to see through you in less time than most."

I scoop one of the pillows off the ground. I need something to hug. "He was ... different."

"So, are you going to tell me what happened with him?"

We're on a roll with all this honesty talk, so why not? I tell Dawn everything, from the moment Daniel and I started to chat online to when I read his goodbye note. How he was the most fun person I had ever been with. The best sex of my life. The best high of my life. And after one fight, he disappeared, and I couldn't handle it. I drank until I passed out on the dance floor and woke up in a hospital.

"It's going to be hard to find someone to replace him," I say.

"Why do you need to replace him?" Dawn asks.

"Um, he left."

"So? Why don't you call him? Why don't you reach out?"

"Because we don't have the same wants and needs. Daniel got attached just like everyone else. He wanted more. I don't."

"You really don't? That's bull. You wouldn't be here now, telling me all this if you didn't have feelings for him."

"It's just the sex I'm missing."

"It sounds like it's more than just the sex. Did you talk to him a lot? Did you share stuff?"

"Yes."

"Personal stuff?"

I swallow hard. "Yes."

She tosses me my phone. "Call him. Right now."

"It's not that easy."

"Then go to him. Go to his house."

"He lives in Pennsylvania. It's like a six-hour drive from here. Maybe even more."

"So?"

"Dawn, I'm going through a detox right now."

"Then you'll go tomorrow or in a couple of days. After we get those cuticles under control. And put some inches back on those hips of yours. You look like a cancer patient right now."

I roll my eyes. "You sound ridiculous. This isn't some cheesy movie where everyone gets a happy ending. You don't know Daniel like I do. He lives in Morville where that football team got slaughtered. Daniel was the kicker, the only one who wasn't there."

Dawn nods her head but musters a quick response. "That's horrible. And it changes things. But it doesn't change how you feel for him, right?"

"What I feel doesn't make any sense."

"Logically, it makes no sense. But if you could allow your heart to breathe a little, I'm sure you'd see that it makes a lot more sense to go to him. Tell him you're sorry, and talk to him. Be honest with him like you are with me right now, and see what happens."

I take a deep breath and glance at my cuticles. A whole week in Fantasy Land and I didn't take advantage of any of the spas.

"I want my nails black."

Daniel

Three days in. An eternity to go.

Every day, I wake up at 5:00 AM for a long run. It's the ideal time to exercise because the air is breathable, and everyone else is still asleep. I can go wherever I want without worrying about someone running into me. Once the sun rises, I lift weights at the gym, scaling some of the load until I build some decent strength. Still, not many people to worry about. Around seven, I return home for a shower and breakfast. Then the rest of the town wakes up.

Since school is out, I work at the animal hospital from 8:00 AM to 3:00 PM, making an effort to do more than just paperwork; I help Hallie with mundane tasks such as filling up the candy bowl and feeding the fish. After my shift, I go home and walk Samantha, who is with us permanently. I also try reaching out to at least three different people each day.

On the first day, I visit Jeremy's parents, who own Mary's Diner, which closed down for all the funerals but is now back up and running. I give his parents hugs and ask if there's anything I can do for them.

"Just continue to come into town more often."

"Keep the team spirit alive."

"Don't forget about us when you go to college."

The responses from the parents are mostly the same. But despite all my efforts to be kinder, I still don't feel much.

So, why am I doing all this again? I narrow it down to two explanations.

1)   This is me "dealing" with my grief and moving on.

2)   I'm depressed and still not over Maya.

No one knows about Maya other than my dad. And he doesn't know *everything* that went down between us. As chill as my dad can be about most topics, I would never feel comfortable telling him how often Maya and I had sex with one another.

Still, it doesn't make sense I would be more upset over losing her than losing my teammates and now my dog. If I allow myself to believe I care about her more, it will make everything way worse. Because I chose to give her up. I didn't choose to give up my teammates or Jojo.

With unusual energy, Dad spends most of Saturday afternoon outside, trimming all the bushes and trees around our house. I offer to help, but he insists he needs the fresh air more than I do. So I think about who's next on my list to see. I could always catch up with the junior varsity guys. But what about Gracie? If there's anyone I might be able to feel for, it's her.

After a much-needed haircut, I offer to take Gracie out for ice cream, so she can tell me about her protest trip. I listen to every part, stretching to feel and understand her passion and pain, but my head and heart draw parallel blanks. Emotionally, I'm a wall. And logically, I don't comprehend the purpose of the protest. You yell and scream, but the people in charge don't hear you. They ignore you. The only people that do hear are the people that yell with you. And no matter how many voices unite, if the person who needs to listen doesn't listen, then nothing will happen. Nothing will change.

"So, what about you?" Gracie asks after detailing every part of her trip. "How was your spiritual journey?"

"I didn't find God."

"Oh." She takes a bite of her mint ice cream to hide her disappointment.

"But I did find myself. A little."

Her face brightens. "My parents said you came to see them yesterday at their office. That was nice of you."

"I'm trying to be more supportive around here. Help out when I can. Make sure everyone is okay before I leave." But am I going to be okay?

"In July?"

I nod. "I go to training camp."

"I'm sure you'll crush it." She puts her hand on top of mine. For a second, I'm tempted to pull away, but when I allow myself to feel her skin, I am drawn back to the hotel room with Maya. Why does everything have to pull me back to Maya? Why can't I just forget about her?

Before I know what's happening, I'm kissing Gracie exactly like I kissed Maya. Full-on, with no boundaries. But Gracie isn't like Maya, so it's only natural she jolts away. "Whoa," she gasps, covering her mouth. "I, uh ... I wasn't expecting that."

"I'm sorry." I look down, realizing I have chocolate ice cream all over my white shirt from leaning across the table. "I shouldn't have done that."

"It's okay." She smiles and bites her bottom lip. Crap, she liked it. Now, she's going to think I like her now. Have I completely lost my grip?

"I'm sorry. I should get home," I say, frantically trying to wipe my shirt with a couple of paper napkins. "I forgot I need to help my dad with yardwork." I have lied way too many times to this poor girl. Why am I such an asshole?

"Oh, okay," she says, clearly disheartened.

I wait for Gracie to finish her ice cream before driving her home. We barely speak to one another. By the time I get to her house, she looks like she's going to cry. And despite my emotional imbalance, I do feel bad for her. She doesn't deserve to be lied to or misguided.

"I had a nice time today," I say.

"Yeah, me too." Her tone suggests otherwise. She unzips her seatbelt and turns toward me. "I need to know. Did it mean anything? That kiss?"

"Gracie, I ... I don't want to hurt you."

"I'm already hurt. I lost my brother. Things can't hurt worse than that. But when people lie to me..."

"It meant nothing. I just want us to be friends."

"Then why did you do it? Why did you kiss me like that? It was really intense. Like you weren't even thinking. Or were you thinking ... of someone else?"

I lower my head. I have to be honest, even if she hates me for it. "Someone else."

Gracie shakes her head. "You're still not over Anna?"

"No. It's not her."

"Then who is it?"

"Someone I lost."

"Someone around here?"

"No. She's not from around here. She's long gone."

Gracie sighs, but it sounds sincere. "Thank you for being honest with me. And if this person, whoever she is, shows up in your life again, you better kiss her like you kissed me and mean it."

"I doubt she will. But if she does, I will."

"Promise?"

"Yes."

I squeeze Gracie's hand before she gets out of the car. Today, I wanted to do something nice for her, but she did something nice for me.

She gave me hope.

Maya

This town blows.

There isn't even a liquor store. But maybe that's a good thing. I won't be tempted to buy anything while I'm here.

A lot of folks stare at me as I drive through Morville. I look out of place in my new Mustang. The people around here drive minivans and trucks, which are more sensible choices for families and farmers.

The country life must keep them busy since there isn't anything to do other than eat food or read a book. The so-called Main Street has two restaurants, one coffee shop, an ice cream parlor, and a used bookstore. Every building is unique and oddly placed, as though each came about in a different era. Dawn would call this place cute and charming, while I find it dull and boring. Daniel chose *this* over Fantasy Land?

It's a simple town, that's for sure. But not without drama, considering what happened recently. I guess Daniel thought it best to face his hometown than to ever face me again.

But the thought of seeing him makes my stomach hurt. My chest pounds so hard it feels like my lungs are compressing. Why am I so nervous to talk to a guy? Where the hell has my confidence gone?

I'm sober. I'm going through withdrawal. Therefore, I have no superpowers anymore.

I park across the street from his house. Google says I'm here, but it seems strange to believe that a superstar athlete would live in a brick rambler with a one-car garage. I'm spoiled, living in a mansion for most of my life. While alluring, a life of luxury doesn't always improve one's happiness. It's life-draining, residing in a big house with no one to talk to. At least in a small place, you have so little space the loneliness doesn't weigh down as much. Maybe that's why I always felt safe at Grams, inside my little room, getting high, never probing the depths of my own shallow world.

And now I'm panting.

I need something to calm me down. I have a plastic bag full of gum, chips, water bottles, and condoms, all bought and paid for by my dear cousin, who still believes I am capable of a fairytale ending. Seriously, she can be so naive sometimes. But she's more loving than I deserve.

After fifteen minutes of procrastination and chewing globs of bubblegum, I build up the courage to knock on the front door. No one answers. Damn. I thought for sure someone was home. There's a car in the driveway. A piece of crap Honda, probably made in the early 2000s. Daniel's? There's a football on the back seat.

I walk around to the side of the house, hoping to find an open window. Not to sneak in, just to look around, see if anyone's home. A wire fence surrounds the backyard, but the gate is locked, so I climb. As I slink over the top, my foot slips, and I fall to the ground, landing hard on my hip. It causes a spasm in my thigh, radiating pain left and right. Too bad my Vicodin is long gone. Now might be an appropriate time to take one.

After cursing a dozen times, I force myself to stand. A few leg shakes, and I'm moving. Sort of. I hobble around the house, noting the freshly trimmed bushes and new mulch. There's a swing in the middle of the yard, probably decades old and rusting. A few dog toys are scattered here and there. But there's nothing out of the ordinary. Once I make it around the whole yard, I realize I'll have to climb the fence to get out, but my leg throbs every time I try.

Does that mean I'm stuck here? Unless I want to risk hurting myself again.

Barking startles me, and I hide behind a tree. Out of the corner of my eye, I see Daniel walking some giant ass dog toward his house. He was just out for a walk. Now, what am I going to do?

There's not much I can do. Once Daniel enters the house, he opens the backdoor and lets the dog run around the yard. The beast immediately barrels at me, and before I can even scream, it knocks me flat on my back and barks in my face. I pinch my eyes shut; the slobber from its mouth flies everywhere.

"Samantha! Get off her!"

Someone, presumably Daniel, pulls the dog away. But I don't move. And I don't open my eyes because 1) I'm terrified and 2) I'm embarrassed.

"Maya?" I feel his hand on my face. I don't want it there because if I open my eyes and he pulls away in disgust, I'll hate myself for coming here.

"I got trapped in your yard," I confess.

"Okay…" Is he laughing at me? "Are you all right? Did you hurt yourself?"

"I don't know."

"Can you open your eyes?"

I open one and then the other. "You cut your hair." I immediately notice. It's back to football length.

"You cut yours." Mine is shoulder length.

"It was too long."

"Same." He moves his hand away from my face and helps me off the ground.

I stumble and hobble onto my good leg.

"Did you try jumping the fence?" he asks.

"Yeah."

"Come inside. I'll get you some ice."

He's being really nice to me after everything that's happened between us. But it's in his nature to be nice. He was raised to be a good boy, to treat women with respect and kindness. I knew that the moment I met him. And I took it all for granted.

He leads me into the kitchen and pours a glass of water from the refrigerator. I sit at the wooden table and look around, feeling out of place. Daniel's home is aged and in dire need of new furniture, but it's full of memories. There are dorky school pictures and takeout-number magnets on the fridge. Lines on the doorway mark his height growing up. My mother would never dare mark any of her walls to keep track of my height. And all our pictures had to be hung and framed, never put on the fridge with magnets. Our fridge had to be spotless.

"Thank you," I say when he hands me a bag of ice wrapped in paper towels. I place it on my thigh even though ice won't do much these days.

"No problem." He sits across from me.

His slobbering dog stands between us, staring back and forth like we're about to have a pie-eating contest.

"This is Samantha," he says, petting her brown and white head. "She's new to the family."

I try to smile, but I titter instead. "I'm not a dog person. Or a cat person. Or a pet person, really. My parents never even let me have a hermit crab."

"Wow. I had like seven growing up."

"Yeah…" I take a sip of water to avoid that topic. "So, is your dad home?" I glance out the window.

"He's at the grocery store."

"Will he mind that I'm here? Did you ... tell him about me?"

"A little. And he won't mind. He may wonder *why* you're here, though."

"You're probably wondering the same."

"I know why you're here."

"You do?" Did Dawn somehow get his number and call him? She would do something like that.

"You're here to collect your necklace."

"My necklace?" I nearly choke on the water. "What are you talking about?"

"You don't know?" He stands and motions for me to follow.

I leave the ice on the table.

His dog trails behind, sniffing my butt, clearly intrigued.

"I didn't notice it until I got home."

I linger in his doorway. His room is so neat and organized. The twin-size bed is made; even the pillows looked fluffed. His books are alphabetized, and the wooden desk looks CEO-ready. Not much happening on the walls, but there are a lot of random nails sticking out, so he must've taken down some things recently.

"You must have been in hell dealing with my messiness for a week," I say.

He smirks. "You can come in. Sit down so you can ice and rest your leg properly."

"It doesn't hurt that bad." I take a tentative step into his room.

He opens up a drawer from his desk and pulls out the necklace.

"I was going to mail it to you, but I was worried it might get stolen. Besides, I don't know your address."

"You could have messaged me."

"I could have."

"Why didn't you?"

He sets the necklace on his desk rather than hand it to me.

I take another step; the hardwood floors creak

beneath my feet.

"I would have eventually," he says. "But I needed time to get my life back in order. Running off to Fantasy Land didn't change anything for me here. So for the last few days, I've been cleaning up my act, working out, reaching out to others, and getting ready for college."

"You're definitely going then?"

"Yes, I am."

I nod my head. "That's great."

"You don't sound too thrilled."

"I, uh ... I've been…" I lower my head; fire rushes to my cheeks. How can I tell him the truth when I'm not entirely sure what the truth is? Am I upset he's moving on? Did I expect him to be miserable without me when clearly he's not?

"Are you in pain?" he asks.

"My leg is fine." It never will be, but that's my burden.

"I meant on the inside."

"I can't." I start to back away. I feel exposed, like I'm taking my clothes off for the first time, but it isn't a sexy feeling.

"Why did you come here then?" he asks. "If it wasn't for the necklace, why did you come? And why didn't you call or reach out first?"

"I wanted to see you. Face to face."

"To tell me…?"

I raise my eyes. He's not mad at me. He just wants the truth; I owe him that much. "I'm sorry," I say. "I'm sorry for how I treated you. I was pretty selfish, and I should have been better. I should have been more open with you, but I was scared. And I'm still scared. But I'm sober now, so that helps."

"Sober? For how long?"

"Since the morning after you left."

"Me leaving made you stop drinking?"

"No. You leaving made me almost drink myself to death. But your leaving also made me realize I would end up dead if I didn't get out of there. So I flew home and SOSed my cousin. She got me through a little detox. And look, now I have nice nails and hair." My sarcasm comes out just in the nick of time. I relax just a little.

But Daniel appears horrified. He overlooks the nails and gapes at the purple bruise on my hand from the IV. Why is it taking so long to turn green? "You almost ... died?" His voice cracks.

"I wasn't thinking straight. I got confused. And I couldn't find you. And I was in so much pain that I..."

"You took a Vicodin, didn't you?"

I nod. "My cousin confiscated the rest."

Daniel scrapes his fingers through his short hair. "Damn," he says, shaking his head. "I shouldn't have left you like that. I should have waited."

"Don't blame yourself. It was my fault. And I'm fine now." Not really. "I'm doing much better." I feel like stabbing myself.

"Are you really fine?"

I shake my head. "I want to be."

He blows air like he's trying to cool a bowl of soup. Then he smiles and says, "Me too."

We're alike in so many ways. Dawn could see that without even meeting Daniel face-to-face. We hide and lie, but deep down, we're in hell. There's no way to escape the torment if we keep lying to one another. But maybe if we're honest, we can help each other out.

"Anyway," I say, trying to move things forward. "That's what happened. And I'm still kind of dealing with some of the withdrawal stuff. But I'm hoping it all works so I can get on with my life."

"You're going to stay sober?"

"I honestly don't know. I don't know what to do with myself now. My cousin thinks I should take a college course or learn to play an instrument or build a birdhouse. Something artsy and creative, but I'm an athlete. I don't create anything. I do things that make me feel good physically."

"You could do anything. You could travel the world if you wanted to."

"Not by myself."

"Well, if you're looking for another *friend* to tag along with you, I'm not game for that anymore."

"I'm not asking that."

"Then what do you want?"

I want you to hold me in your arms and never let go. I want you to look at me like I'm the only person in the world who needs you. I want you to tell me that everything that happened in Fantasy Land was real between us, that it was more than an infatuation, that I was wrong and you were right. You were always right.

But instead, I squeak out, "I just want to spend some time with you."

He nods. "And?"

"And get to know you. For real this time."

"Maya." He rubs the back of his neck and heaves a sigh. "Maya, I don't know…"

"You said in your note that you meant what you said. Did you mean all of it or just some parts? Because if you didn't mean all of it, then I shouldn't be here."

I wait patiently for his response but am met with heart-wrenching silence.

I should have known better than to think he would take me back with open arms. He poured his heart and soul out to me in Fantasy Land, and now he's home, working toward this amazing college-football life, maybe even the NFL. And now I'm here with black fingernails and no plans, asking him for a second chance. He'd be a moron to say yes.

"I should go." I try to turn around, but that gigantic dog is right in my path, causing me to trip and bump into Daniel's dresser, knocking over pictures, cologne, and God knows what. I immediately fall to my knees in a desperate attempt to pick everything up, hoping I didn't break anything. "I'm sorry. I'm so sorry." One of the pictures is Daniel when he was a little boy and an older woman, presumably his mom, dressed up for Halloween. She's holding him so tight and smiling so much. You can feel the love spilling out of the photo. How could she leave him? How could anyone leave him?

Daniel is on his knees next to me. "It's okay," he says, pushing the photo away. "It's okay, Maya."

My hands are shaking now. He slides one arm around my shoulder. Immediately, my head cradles against his chest, and I feel dampness. Is he sweating? No, it's me. I'm crying! Showing emotion in front of someone. What do I do? This is so unnatural to me—I'm literally freaking out. Maybe if I don't move, he won't notice. But I'm making a mess of his shirt.

"Maya, are you crying?" he asks.

"No." I cover my face with one hand.

I sniffle in an attempt to pull myself together. But he moves my hand away and lifts my chin with the tip of his finger, and there I am, red-eyed and exposed. A part of me wants to pull away, too ashamed to allow him to see me like this. But a bigger part of me wants him to see all of me, even my shame.

And then he kisses me. My hands no longer shake because they're all over him. Pulling, grabbing, taking whatever I can get. I may not know what the hell I'm doing with my life anymore, but one thing is certain.

I need him in it.

When I try to take his shirt off, he pulls away, and for a moment, I'm convinced he'll change his mind and tell me to leave. That I'm not worth the trouble. That I'm a crazy alcoholic who isn't capable of having a normal life or even a normal relationship.

But I speak first.

"You said that you loved me, Daniel. That's why I'm here. Please don't tell me I was wrong to believe that. Please don't tell me it was all just an infatuation. Because it wasn't for me. It was real."

Daniel

The second we kissed, I told myself it would just be a kiss. Let's face it, can I really trust her? What if she has sex with me and runs away? What if this is all just a pleasure trip? What if the whole detox story is a bunch of bull, and she left Fantasy Land because she couldn't find anyone else to be with?

Or she's here because she wants to be with me, for real this time. And I would be an idiot not to give this another try.

Still, neither of us can deny our physical need for one another. And while it would be smart to talk everything out, I wouldn't have anything to say because I'd be too distracted by her brown eyes, the way she bites her lip, and how she pushes her whole body into me whenever we kiss.

I want her. I want all of her.

So, it's on.

From the ground, I stand with Maya wrapped around me. Samantha barks and growls when I push her out the door; I can't have a giant dog in the room, staring and slobbering. It's just too creepy.

Once the door is shut and locked, I carry Maya to the bed and lay her down.

She pulls off her shirt while I take off her shorts and underwear. She attempts to sit up to undress me, but I put my arm out. Despite my impending need, I have to make sure this is more than just a hookup. What am I to her? A boy toy or a boyfriend?

"Do you want to be with me?" I ask. "For real be with me?"

"Yes."

"Say that we're together." I cup my hands around her face.

"We're together, Daniel." She kisses me. "We're together."

Finally.

It's like we're back in the hotel, only this time I'm pleasuring my girlfriend, not my vacation buddy. My confidence restored and emotional needs met, I touch her without fear or hesitation.

I remove my shirt before I sweat through it. Maya feverishly goes after my pants, and at last, we're skin to skin. She doesn't object when I put a condom on, but when we connect, her mouth opens, and out comes this tiny little cry.

At first, I take it as enjoyment. But then her lips tremble, and giant tears plummet from her eyes. I panic for a second, not knowing what to do. Do I stop? Do I continue? Is crying normal? Am I hurting her?

"Hey, hey," I say, kissing her cheeks. "It's okay, baby. I'm here."

"I know," she says, quickly wiping her face. "I just don't want you to leave again. I'm scared…"

"Don't be scared. I'm here. I'm not going anywhere."

She buries her head on my shoulder and pushes her hips up, encouraging me to continue.

I go slowly, kissing her gently, whispering sweet words. The tears subdue, and she's smiling and rocking her body in tune with mine. We're no longer screwing each other. We're making love.

She cries again when we finish. I don't know what to say, so I wrap her in my arms and hold her like I'll never let go. Eventually, she falls asleep. And even though it's still daylight and I have no idea when my dad will be home, I sleep too. Because I know when I wake up, she'll be with me.

****

It's evening. Maya isn't with me.

In a panic, I throw on shorts and bolt out the door. I check the bathroom then the kitchen. I hear voices from the living room. Dad's. Then Maya's. I panic even more.

I steady my breathing before making my presence known.

Dad is relaxing in his lounge chair.

Maya sits on the adjacent sofa with Samantha by her feet. Thank God she is fully dressed, her hair brushed, and from the fruity aroma in the air, it smells like she showered.

"Hey, son," Dad says, waving as though nothing were out of the ordinary. "I met your Fantasy Land friend. What a surprise!"

"Oh. That's, uh, great." And awkward.

"Your dad is a vet. That's cool," Maya says as she woodenly pets Samantha's furry head. Even Samantha seems chill about everything.

What the hell is going on?

"Maya said she's going to be in town for a while," Dad says. "She said she was going to check into a hotel, but I told her we had a perfectly fine guest room in the basement she's welcome to stay in."

"If that's cool?" Maya asks.

"That's very cool," I say.

Dad stands. "Good. Then it's settled. Now, if you'll excuse me, I have some reading to do." He heads for his bedroom. What reading? He winks at me when he passes by.

"So, are you hungry?" I ask Maya.

"I guess so."

"Has your diet changed at all?"

"No. But I'll try to be more open-minded."

****

Maya lets me drive her new Mustang, which is probably the nicest car I've ever been in, let alone gotten to drive. I take her to The Eagle's Wing, a diner run by a local couple and their grown son. They serve anything from hamburgers to fish tacos to margherita pizza, but I'm mostly a fan of their cobb salad. And since I'm back to eating healthy, it's the only place I can think of with healthy and delicious options.

What I don't anticipate is how many people would be out eating dinner at 9:00 PM. It almost feels like the old days, minus my teammates not being around. Just their jerseys and photos on all the walls.

I ask for a seat in the far back and keep my head low while we pass through the diner.

Maya looks around, noting the decor. "Ooh, you're famous," she says, pointing at my picture. My teammates hold me up after I just kicked the winning field goal of the state championship. For a second, I'm drawn to that moment I had on the field the other night. When I thought of Wesley and if my field goal had fueled his decision to massacre the team. Will I ever know? Is it worth it to even wonder?

"Famous?" I say, sliding into the booth. "It doesn't feel that way anymore."

She sits across from me. "What does it feel like?"

"It feels like everyone is waiting for me to crack."

Maya turns around, finally taking in all the eyes. "Maybe they're wondering who I am."

"That too."

"So, ignore them." She brushes her foot against mine. "They can worry about themselves."

"It's not that easy. This is a close-knit town. When somebody gets sick or dies, everyone hears about it and passes condolences. When somebody gets engaged or married or has a baby, everyone celebrates. It's always been that way."

"Must have been a big deal when you got your scholarship."

"Even more now." I finally open a menu even though I already know what I want. "But you're here now, and I don't wanna spoil the mood."

"What mood? I'm not a bundle of joy right now." She tries to smile, but her bottom lip trembles. Is it the withdrawal or something else?

"Is there anything I could do to help?" I ask.

"A drink would help, but I see nothing but soda and juice on the menu." Her smirk reveals her sarcasm.

"It's a dry town."

"For real?" She laughs now. "Guess I was meant to come here."

"It doesn't mean people don't drink. They just have to drive a bit to get their booze. But you're not thinking...?" Of drinking?

"I'm *always* thinking."

Just when I'm about to ask about the withdrawal, the waitress comes to take our order. As predicted, Maya orders French fries. I'm starving, so I add a side of crab soup to my Cobb salad. We both ask for water.

"It's not that easy." She echoes what I said earlier.

"What isn't?"

"Everything."

Her hands are shaking. I wrap my hands around hers in an attempt to keep them still. Her skin is cold against mine. I wish I could numb out all the pain she must be feeling, but then again, pain is a part of life, and Maya has been avoiding it for too long.

"I'm sorry, Maya."

She smiles, though her eyes are watering. "You still want to do this?"

"Have dinner with you?"

"No, I mean *everything* involving me. You're on track to go to college, play football, and get a degree. I'm a spoiled, rich alcoholic with zero plans. Do you not see a problem with that?"

"I only see a problem if we're not together."

The waitress returns with our drinks and my soup. I offer Maya my crackers, but she shakes her head. It's not just the alcohol she's fighting. It's food. Her injury. Her past. The load she carries is heavy. And while I want to help, I'm not sure how it'll all play out in the long run. What will happen in July when I go away to college? I'll have practices, games, classes, and homework. How will Maya fit into my schedule? Where will she even live? What will she do with her time?

"Tell me," I say. "Tell me what life would have been like had none of the bad stuff happened."

She sighs but doesn't seem reluctant to share. "I had a really big tournament scheduled the day after the concert. And had I gone, I likely would have won, which would have gotten me one step closer to the Olympics. Most Olympic gymnasts are between the ages of sixteen and twenty, so it would have been my only chance, unless I did exceptionally well the first time, I could have qualified again." She sighs again, this time with a smile. "I was so happy whenever I did gymnastics. I loved the competition. I loved the praise. I loved to fly and feel weightless. I would have continued it for the rest of my life. And if or when I got too old to compete, I'd probably have switched to another sport like CrossFit, something to keep me moving. Something to keep me feeling high."

"It was all you had?"

"It was everything."

"What about your parents?"

She sighs and circles her straw around her glass

several times. Her shoulders tense. I'm sure she'll pass on the question, but then it all spills out without a shred of hesitation. "They weren't like your dad. They didn't talk to me unless it was to criticize me. I never felt any love from them, so I didn't feel any sadness or sorrow when they died. All I felt was myself dying. It's like I didn't exist anymore after that. I couldn't move my body the way I used to, and my brain didn't process things the same way. Maybe I would have been more normal if I hadn't been shot. I would have grieved for them. But I'm just not the same. It's like the metal has made me a part robot."

"I don't think you're a robot. I think you feel lots of things."

"Yes, but I'm not always sure what I'm feeling. Or if it's just a need."

"Feelings are needs. You feel something for me. And you need me."

She nods. I see a full smile now.

The waitress arrives with our food. We talk a little more as we eat. I encourage Maya to eat the whole plate of fries and to try a bite of my salad. Maybe one day, I'll be able to take her out for ice cream.

As we're leaving, we bump into a group of high schoolers, one of them being Anna. They smell like beer and probably just came from a party. I recognize a few of the guys from the JV team. They crowd around us like we're VIPs, while Anna stands eight feet away with a sneer so wide she could pass for The Joker. I bet she's still pissed at me for pushing her out of my car.

"Daniel, what's going on?" Travis asks, high-fiving me.

"Nothing much," I say. "Just grabbing a bite to eat with my girlfriend, Maya." It seems weird to say that out loud, but when I see the dumbfounded expression on

Anna's face, I feel like a million bucks.

"Hey, Maya," Travis says. "Are you from around here?"

"I'm from Fantasy Land," Maya says, causing everyone to laugh.

Sensing everyone's curiosity, I grab Maya's hand and pull her from the small crowd. "Sorry, guys, we have to get going."

"There's a party going on at Justin's house. Do you want to come?"

Maya squeezes my hand. "That sounds like fun."

"You guys should come," Travis says.

"Maybe," I call over my shoulder, but my answer will be no. A party will only bring trouble. Maya will be tempted to drink. Everyone will want to know where she really comes from and how/why I suddenly have a new girlfriend. Do I want to be put in that situation? Besides, I'm not super close with any of these people.

I have to consider what's best for Maya.

But from what I'm sensing, Maya still wants to have fun.

Maya

"We don't have to go," I tell Daniel once we're in the car. "I just thought it'd be nice to get to know some of your friends."

"That's just the problem," Daniel says, gripping the steering wheel like he means to break it. "They're not my real friends. All my real friends are dead."

"Oh." I didn't think about that. "Then maybe we should just go back to your house."

"I'm sorry," he says, easing his tension on the wheel. "A party isn't the best place for either of us to be right now. There will be alcohol. And people prying, wanting to know all about you, where you're from, how you know me, and everything in between."

"We can just lie."

"I don't want to lie anymore."

"Then tell people to mind their own business."

"But I am their business. Football is life here. And I'm the only one on the team who survived. You don't get it. It's like being royalty and having obligations to your people."

"That's bull. You don't owe anyone shit."

"I owe this town everything."

He feels obligated to care, but I know deep down he doesn't want to. He wants to get away from it all. He wants a new life somewhere else. And knowing him, he won't admit to any of that because he'll feel guilty about such thoughts. But it's not a crime to want to do things and be in places that make you happy.

"Are you happy in this town?" I ask as he pulls out of the parking lot.

"I was. But it's not the same anymore. It'll never be the same, and there's nothing I can do to change that."

"If it makes you that miserable to be here, why do you stay?"

"I'm leaving for college in July. It's not like I'm staying here forever."

"But you'll come back for holidays and breaks."

"My dad lives here."

"I know. I just thought…"

"What are you suggesting I do, Maya? Go on another vacation?"

He sounds bitter and annoyed. Like how dare I suggest he go somewhere fun? I don't know what to say at this point. All I know is how to have a good time. What else could I offer Daniel? Other than my company, which is drifting between lame and lamer.

What is Daniel to me? The term boyfriend doesn't sit right with my brain. It makes me think of high schoolers and cliché things like prom and weddings. I'd rather think of him as my lover. An *important* lover I can't let go of.

Is it because I love him or because I'm afraid to be alone? Could it be both? Or could it be something else entirely? If I processed human emotion like everyone else, I might have a clearer understanding of our relationship.

He parks my car in his driveway alongside his charming Honda. All the house lights are off except for the front porch, so his dad must be asleep. Daniel takes his seatbelt off, but I don't. I'm not ready to go inside yet.

"You okay?" he asks.

"Daniel, what if I'm not capable of love?"

"What ... what do you mean? You said you wanted to be with me. You said…" He shakes his head, the nervous sweat visible on his forehead. "Why would you say that?"

"I do care about you. And I feel something for

you. And I want to be with you. But I don't know if I love you."

He releases a held breath. "It takes time, Maya."

"Then why did you feel it so fast for me?"

"I don't know. I didn't plan on falling in love with you. I didn't even plan on falling *for* you. It just happened. And when I knew, I had to say something, even if it meant knowing you wouldn't feel the same way."

Tears prickle at my eyes. I appreciate and dread his honesty because it opens so many doors. But rather than get too caught up in the moment, I take off my seatbelt. "I'm not tired. Should we watch a movie?"

He smiles. "Sure."

****

I convince Daniel to watch some of Star Wars, which he reluctantly enjoys. We fall asleep in the basement, but when I wake up in the morning, he is gone. He left a note letting me know he's out for a run and will be back by seven. I rub my eyes to check the time. It's 6:30 AM. Who in their right mind is up this early on a Sunday? Obviously not Samantha, who fell asleep with us and is snoring into next Tuesday.

After a quick shower, I throw on some clothes and drink a tall glass of water. I answer some of Dawn's texts, email the realtor who has a new lead on my parents' house, and even play with Samantha in the backyard. This is probably the most productive morning I've had in years, but I'm missing Daniel, and it's well past seven now. And for the first time in forever, my stomach growls. But not for chips, I want real food. I want to go to a diner and eat breakfast.

I try calling him. No answer. He probably has it on silent mode while he's running. I linger in bed, wondering what to do. Should I go upstairs? See what his

dad is up to? Or just keep waiting?
But what exactly am I waiting for?

Daniel

I've been running since five-thirty this morning, and I've been up since four-thirty. After sleeping so much the afternoon before, I still don't feel revived. Instead, I feel stressed and uncertain about a lot of things. Running usually makes me feel better, but it's nearing 7:00 AM, and I don't want to stop.

I'm glad Maya is with me. I just wish it were under different circumstances. I wish we were both regular high school graduates, attending the same college in the fall with all our family members alive or in the picture. With Maya on a gymnastics scholarship, we'd both have our passions to follow. That timeline could have existed had we not lost so much of our lives from gun violence.

Gun violence. Gracie's protest makes sense to me now. If Wesley hadn't been able to buy an assault rifle so easily... If our government did a better job regulating such purchases... The Texan who sold the gun to Wesley admitted he didn't ask a reason for Wesley's purchase. Wesley was of age and had a valid license. That's all the guy asked for. But he was at fault for not knowing or caring about Pennsylvania firearm rules, which would have required Wesley to have a permit before buying any weapon. Likely, Wesley researched where it'd be easiest to secure a weapon without the permit part or any legit questioning.

So many pieces to put together. And his mother had no idea what he was planning or what was happening behind closed doors?

Wesley's mom lives in one of the poorer areas of Morville. A little road behind Main Street hosts a couple of small apartment buildings and tiny old houses, probably made in the forties, rented out to low-income families. I never run through that part of town. The road is in poor condition, so I'd be more susceptible to twisting an ankle. But today, I take that risk. I want to see where Wesley grew up.

I don't have to know his address to know which house was his. The white picket fence, barely holding any ground, is covered in graffiti.

Devil! Murderer! Burn in hell!

No one made any effort to clean it up. If Wesley's mom still has to work two jobs, I doubt she has the time to deal with vandalism. Has anyone shown her sympathy? Or do they just see her as the faulted mom? Do they blame her for Wesley's downfall?

I halt my run to take a closer look at the single-story home with one door and one window on the front side. It's about half the size of my house, with many roof shingles missing, an overgrown yard, and a busted car in the ramshackle driveway.

Suddenly, the front door opens, and a woman with near-white hair comes storming out like she means to fight me. "Don't you be doing any more damage to my property!" she yells, waving a fist.

I put my hands up in defense. "I'm just passing by."

Her green eyes narrow, but she loses the angry tone. "I know your face. You were in the paper. You're that kicker."

"I am."

"Are you really just passing by? Or do you want to cuss me out for birthing the evil boy who killed all your friends?"

"I don't want to do that. I just want..." I want people to leave this poor woman alone. Let her live her life in peace. But instead, I say, "I'm sorry for your loss."

The woman takes a step back, one hand over her chest like she's having a heart attack. "You're…" She gasps to get the words out. "You're the first person to say that to me. And yet, the last person I'd expect to hear it from."

"I am sorry. Truly."

The woman sniffles, trying to stay composed. "Since you seem a little more humane than the other folks around here, I'll have you know Wesley was a good boy. Always did his homework and worked hard. But something broke his soul when he started high school. Something or *someone* hurt him real bad, and he never was the same after that."

"He never told you what happened?"

"The school said he was bullied for quitting football. Wesley never wanted to talk about that, and I never had enough time to be with him to force anything out. That's what happens when your husband walks out on you."

"My mother walked out on me."

She nods. "Folks may think mothers are more important, but the father sets the path for that child's future. Every boy needs a father. Otherwise, they spend the rest of their lives looking for something or someone to fill the gap. Wesley just got lost along the way. If I could go back, I'd push harder to figure out what broke him. But something tells me now the person truly responsible for breaking him is the one person no one would suspect had done anything wrong."

"Who might that be?"

"You seem like a smart boy. Who did Wesley fire at first?"

I close my eyes, trying to remember the detailed report of the massacre. It happened so fast; most people don't recall who went down first. It would make sense that the person closest to Wesley would be shot first, but Wesley started at the podium and worked his way down. So who was at the podium?

Colebrook.

If I had been there, I would have been at the podium accepting *Player of the Year Award*. Was I the original first target?

Or was it always Colebrook?

"I have to go," I tell her. "I meant what I said. Goodbye." I don't wait for a response. I sprint out of that sad little neighborhood and head back to Main Street. My head is spinning. I keep thinking about all the times Colebrook squeezed my shoulder and how it didn't start to feel weird until he came to my house to give me my plaque.

I know where Colebrook lives. That's the perk and downfall of living in a small town. It's easy to find people. But what if those people don't want to be found?

What time is it? I check my phone. I have several missed calls and messages from Maya, asking me where I am to then telling me she's starving and wants to go into town to get breakfast. Maya wants to eat? That's a surprise.

The only place that serves breakfast this early on a Sunday is the cafe. Their choices are limited, but they have a pretty decent breakfast sandwich. I'd love to meet Maya there, but I'm covered in sweat and preoccupied with Colebrook. What if he knows something about Wesley? After all the years of trust put into him, I can't even fathom how I would feel if it turned out Colebrook knew something. Or worse, did something to antagonize Wesley.

I text Maya we can go in an hour, that I have to take care of something first. My legs start cramping, but I run the extra mile to reach Colebrook's house. He's a porch-kind-of-guy, so it's not surprising to see him sitting in his rocking chair with his iPad and a glass of orange juice. I slow in front of his mailbox to stretch.

"Daniel!" he calls.

"Oh, hey, Coach! How's it going?"

"Fine. Just fine." He rushes over with a long, eerie grin. "It's good to see you out running. Getting excited for Notre Dame?"

"Yeah. Definitely."

"Always smart to run in the morning. Gets too hot during the day. Are you going to the track or just around town?"

"All over. I explored some different areas today. Kind of shocking, but I ran past Wesley Dover's house."

"Oh." Colebrook's smile takes a U-turn. "That's not the safest place to be right now."

"Why isn't it safe? Because poor people live there?"

"No, it's just..." He scratches the back of his glabrous head. "There's been a lot of negative attention on that house."

"The vandalism?"

"I wouldn't want someone of your potential to be exposed to such horrors."

I'm taken aback by that word *potential* again. Colebrook said Wesley showed potential. Potential for what? And what horrors am I being exposed to? Poverty isn't a crime.

"What was Wesley like in school?" I ask.

Colebrook blinks several times as though stunned by my question. He composes himself and answers, "He was an outcast. Never spoke much. Kept to himself."

I know all that. "What about before he quit football? What was he like before that?"

"I never spoke to the kid. He was on JV. I saw

him play, and that's about it."

"Do you know why he quit?"

Colebrook sneers. "Why the sudden interest in the person who murdered our team? Why do you care what he was like? He slaughtered nineteen innocent boys."

"I just want a clearer picture of what happened to him. I think if I understood Wesley's past and his motive, it would give me a sense of peace. Wouldn't you want that too? I mean, he did shoot at you first."

"I am a pretty big target." Colebrook tries to laugh it off, but I can tell he's disturbed by my inquiry.

"I just don't understand why no one knows why Wesley quit football. None of his teammates knew. None of the coaches. Not even his own mother."

"And you think I would know something?" Colebrook folds his arms across his chest. "What are you trying to say, Daniel?"

"I'm just asking questions. If that's not okay, I'll be on my way."

"No, it's fine to ask questions, but I'm unsure what answers you're looking for."

"So am I. That's why I'm asking."

"And are you asking anyone else?"

"Not at the moment."

"Hmph." Colebrook looks left and right as if I might have a camera crew hiding. His behavior is off.

"I don't want to take up your time. I have to—"

"There is something I could tell you," Colebrook interrupts. "But not outside. We'd have to go somewhere private. Would you come inside?"

Why does that sound like a terrible idea?

"I would like to hear what you have to say, but I need to go home and shower first."

"Then stop by later today. I'll be home all day."

"Okay. Definitely. Thanks, Coach."

He smiles, but his eyes seem sinister. It's obvious Colebrook knows something about Wesley and blatantly lied when he said he never spoke to the kid. What's the big secret? What is Colebrook hiding?

I'm incapable of running at this point. The cramping intensifies; I hobble through my neighborhood. Maya's car isn't in the driveway. Did she leave without me?

"Maya said she was heading into town," Dad calls from inside the garage. He's filling the lawnmower up with gas. He has been quite the yardwork man these days.

"How long ago?"

"About ten minutes."

"Damn. I just missed her."

"You better go shower if you want to catch up to her. She said she was starving."

So am I. But I'm starving for information more than a breakfast sandwich.

Maya

If I'm not careful, food will become my next pleasure ride. How have I lasted two years without pancakes and syrup? Without scrambled eggs and bacon? This is probably the biggest meal I've ever consumed. While I wanted Daniel to witness my gorging, he obviously had more important things to do this morning.

"Can I get you anything else?" the waitress asks as she refills my orange juice.

"I'm good. Do you mind if I sit here for a while? I'm kind of too full to move yet." I hand her my credit card.

"No problem. It doesn't get busy in here until after church lets out."

The front door swings open, and four teens parade in, smelling like cheap beer and dirty sheets. I recognize the group immediately. They spoke to us at the diner last night. Too loud to be completely sober, they squeeze into the largest booth by the window. The lone blonde girl moans and rubs her forehead, lamenting about tequila shots.

The waitress returns with my card before greeting the new arrivals.

"Coffee, pronto," the blonde snaps. What a bitch.

I listen in on their conversation. Blondie is pissed about being hungover. The two white boys are debating how many pancakes to order. And the overly-tired or still-drunk Asian chick is barely able to keep her head up. They must've stayed up all night partying, crashed together in someone's nasty basement, and now they're out for recovery food.

Daniel texts me.

Daniel: **Are you still at the cafe?**

Maya: **yeah do u want me to order u something?**

Daniel: **Breakfast sandwich with bacon. I'll be there in five.**

After the waitress serves the hangover club their coffee, I wave a hand to grab her attention. "I have a friend joining me soon. Could I get a breakfast sandwich with bacon for him?"

"Sure, no problem."

When the waitress returns to the kitchen, one of the boys waves at me. "Hey! Aren't you Daniel's girlfriend? Maya, right?"

"Uh, yeah. Travis, right?"

"Yeah. Do you wanna sit with us?"

Blondie elbows Travis in the stomach. Is she that threatened by outsiders or just a nasty person?

"I'm waiting for Daniel. He was running all morning."

"Why didn't you run with him?" Blondie snaps, glaring at me like I'm Satan's whore.

"I prefer REM cycles."

The boys laugh. Blondie continues to lour. Is she cursed with a resting bitch face? No, there is definite animosity coming from this chick, almost like she means to get up and challenge me.

"Don't pay any attention to Anna," Travis chuckles. "She's just jealous."

Blondie, aka Anna, elbows the guy again. Jesus, he must be wearing armor underneath his beer-stained clothes not to feel any pain.

"Anna and Daniel used to date," the other guy chimes in. He's too far away to be elbowed, but Anna sends him the death glare.

"Oh, I see," I say. "So, are you the cheating whore

or the one who got freaked out by sex?"

I probably should have omitted the word "whore" because now Blondie is up and livid, heading in my direction. But I anticipate her attack and throw my orange juice in her face.

"You bitch!" she screams.

She raises a hand as a means to slap me, but someone grabs her. And it's not one of the two boys laughing hysterically over our brawl. It's Daniel, who must've made one hell of an entrance for no one to notice.

"That's enough, Anna. Settle down." He lets her go and hands her a napkin.

The juice mingles with her smeared makeup. She looks like a Picasso painting now. "Your girlfriend called me a whore." She rubs her wrist as though Daniel bruised her.

"Well, that doesn't sound too far from the truth." He turns to the waitress, who is too nervous to speak. "I'm sorry about the mess these ladies made. Do you have a mop they could use to clean it up?"

These ladies? As in, he's blaming both of us? Clearly, my move was in self-defense. Shouldn't Anna be the responsible party?

Biting my tongue, I mop up the OJ so the crazy ex can wash her hair in the bathroom.

"Do you still want that breakfast sandwich?" the waitress asks.

"We'll get it to go," Daniel says.

****

"Why are you so pissed?" I ask as soon as we're outside the cafe. "She came after me first."

"Why'd you antagonize her like that?"

"Technically, I didn't call her a whore. I *asked* if she was the cheating whore or the one who got freaked out by sex."

"What?" Daniel's eyes blink a mile a minute. "Why would you ask her that? That's also revealing personal stuff about Monica and me. They all know I dated Monica too."

"Oh, well, I didn't—"

"This is a small town, Maya. If you let one thing spill, everyone finds out."

"Okay, but it's not a big deal."

"It is a big deal. You don't get it because you severed yourself from your community. I didn't. I'm still a part of this place."

"That could change one day. You might find your life more enjoyable, living somewhere else."

"It's not about enjoyment. It's about doing what's right!"

He's yelling now, so clearly, something is bothering him beyond the orange juice. I look around for his car. Did he run here too?

"Did your dad drive you?" I ask.

"Yes, but now I'm wishing I'd driven myself."

"So you could ride home by yourself? Seriously, Daniel, what gives? Are you that pissed off by what just happened, or is something else going on?" I unlock the Mustang, but he doesn't seem inclined to get in. "Are you having second thoughts about us?"

"It's not that. It's just…" He takes a deep breath and lowers his volume by half. "There's a lot I'm still dealing with. And I don't know if you being here is helping."

And there you have it. I figured he would realize what a disaster I am and end things before I got too caught up in his personal life. I just wasn't expecting it to happen this soon. Does everything in my life have to be so short-lived? Does anything last forever?

"I have a lot I'm dealing with," I remind him. "But if you need space to figure things out, you can have it. I don't fit in with this town anyway."

"You don't fit in," Daniel says. "You stand out. But that's not a bad thing, Maya. It's what makes you special to me. But it doesn't help solve my problems."

"What problems? If you could just be a little more specific, maybe I could help? Maybe I would know not to talk to the crazy ex-girlfriend, which you could have pointed out last night when she walked by us. I just think you don't trust me around anyone except yourself, which is pretty selfish of you."

"Selfish? Maya, you almost drank yourself to death, not even a week ago. I'm terrified of what you might do all on your own."

"Oh, I see. So, you don't want me around because I'm not helping to solve problems. But you don't want me to leave because you're scared I'll do something reckless like break my sober streak? That doesn't sound like a viable relationship to me. That makes me sound more like a burden than someone you're with romantically. So what am I to you?"

"I can't put a label on this when I have no idea what possible future I have with you."

"You said you wanted to be with me. You even called me your girlfriend in front of people. Was that just an act?"

"No, it was real. All of it was real. I just ... I'm stuck, okay? I can't see the picture ahead of me."

"Then to hell with that picture. Just focus on the now. What can we do right now to make things better?"

Daniel closes his eyes and rubs his forehead. I miss how his hair used to fall across his face, just enough to shield his eyebrows but not his eyes. I miss holding his hand in Fantasy Land. I miss *being* with him. Since arriving in Morville, it doesn't feel like I'm really with him. Even though I've let my guard down, several times now, there's still tension. There's still so much we have to fix.

"Let me help," I say. "With whatever's going on. If it's the future you're so worried about, we can talk it out, if that'll help focus you."

"No, it's the now. I need help now." He opens his eyes and looks at me, almost terrified. "I learned something today about Wesley Dover."

"The guy who killed everyone?"

Daniel nods. "I don't know the whole truth. But I need to find out. I just…" He takes a deep breath. "I'm scared to do this all on my own."

I smile. Only because I'm relieved that his behavior was merely his inability to admit he needs help. "It's all right to be scared."

"It's more than that. I'm not good at investigating things or asking questions or starting something all on my own. I observe and watch; I let others lead. But this time, I'm alone and could really use some backup."

"So, you need a sidekick?"

"Something like that."

I take a moment to consider what he is asking. Two years ago, when I woke up in the hospital and saw my leg all bandaged up, my first instinct was to stand. To walk away. But I had to wait. I had to "heal." Weeks later, when I could get up, every step shot stabbing pains up my leg and into my lower back. I was angry, scared, and confused, but not once did I think about the person who had done this to me. In my mind, my shooter was as real as the shooters in a James Bond movie. The rod in my leg *was* real, and I did everything I could to not feel it.

"Allen Timberlee," I say.

"What about him?" Daniel asks.

"He's dead. But what he did to me still hurts." I lay my hand against my scar. "Even if I discovered something new about him, it wouldn't change anything. The people he killed are still dead."

For a second, Daniel looks pacific enough to let it go. But then his face twists up like he bit into a lemon, and he shouts back, "This is personal for me! Wesley grew up in this town. He went to my high school."

"Okay."

"Okay, what?"

"I'll be your sidekick."

I choose to be kind. Because there's no way to reason with Daniel when he's still a newbie to death. He needs time to be out of control and figure out what path to take. I hope it isn't the route of sorrow and despair. That's not a place I'm willing to go. Not when I'm already at a low from the withdrawal.

So I imagine we're superheroes fighting crime together. We're strong and powerful, and we have no weaknesses.

Except for each other.

Daniel

Now that I've caught Maya up on everything, she's more than willing to help. Help as in come with me to Colebrook's house to gather as much of the truth as possible. She and I both agree Colebrook is hiding a secret. One that could shed some much-needed clarity over Wesley Dover's motive for slaughtering the team. You can't just blame video games and bad parenting. The fact that he targeted the varsity team after their first state victory since his time as a player speaks more than enough. It's just a matter of getting Colebrook to reveal the truth and be willing to share it with others.

I've never been inside his house, but with Maya by my side, I'm not as nervous to knock, talk, or investigate. I am surprised to get a whiff of coconut when the door opens. It smells like a Yankee Candle store inside.

"Daniel, I'm glad you came back," Colebrook says with a warm smile. Then he notices Maya. "And who is this?" His eyebrows arch.

"This is Maya, my girlfriend," I say, wrapping my arm around her waist.

"Are you from around here, Maya?" Colebrook asks.

"I'm from Fantasy Land," Maya says.

Colebrook doesn't laugh. He smirks and focuses his attention back on me. "I thought it would just be you coming over. I don't feel comfortable having a stranger listen in on such personal matters."

"Maya can hang out in a separate room if that would be better."

"I'm not all that familiar with the town yet," Maya adds. "So far, everyone has been really nice and welcoming." Minus Anna.

Colebrook finally smiles at her. "Of course, you can come in. I just made some lemonade." Colebrook drinks lemonade? It seems like a strange choice for a man who can outlift the whole town. But who am I to generalize?

We follow him inside. His house is also a rambler, probably built in the seventies but completely updated. He has stainless steel appliances throughout the kitchen, polished hardwood floors, exotic lighting fixtures, and a giant fish tank in the middle of his dining room. He pours Maya a glass of lemonade and offers her a chair, though I'm sure the living room leather sofa would be more comfortable.

"We'll talk downstairs, Daniel," Colebrook says. "Maya, if you need to use the restroom, there's one just down this hall. We shouldn't be too long."

Maya waves her phone. "I've got plenty of YouTube videos to watch."

I figured the coach would suggest another room nearby, but if he wants the utmost privacy, the basement is the best choice. The coconut aroma follows us down the stairs; it must be the house fragrance.

Colebrook hasn't gotten around to updating the basement. Like ours, the walls are wooden panels, the carpet is old and worn, and all the light switches are yellow. But it's not like he uses the space for any company. Dozens of filing boxes circle a wooden desk and chair. The lone window is covered by a black curtain. It's a tad creepy, but I don't think he's keeping any bodies around. He's just your average hoarder.

"Take a seat, son," Colebrook says, pointing to the swivel chair.

"I'm fine standing."

"Very well." Colebrook opens up one of the

boxes and pulls out a manila folder. "What I'm about to tell you has to be kept between you and me. It's not because I'm trying to withhold information from the police or community. It's because I'm trying to respect Wesley's wishes."

"His wishes?" Why would he be concerned with a *murderer's* wishes?

Colebrook opens the folder to reveal a photo. It's the junior varsity team celebrating a win. Wesley's red hair is quite visible. He looks happy, healthy, and proud. He has his arms around two other teammates.

"What do you see?" Colebrook asks, handing me the photo to study more closely.

"A team celebrating their win?"

"Look at Wesley's eyes. Who is he looking at?"

"At the guy next to him?"

"His name was Matthew Sanders. He moved to California after playing a year on JV. And sadly, he died a few months ago. Suicide."

"What does this have to do with Wesley?"

"Can't you see it in his eyes?"

"I'm not sure what you're asking me to see." I hand him back the photo. "Everyone in the picture looks happy."

Colebrook returns the photo to its envelope and box. "I lied when I said I never spoke to Wesley. I spoke with him once. He came to me one day after practice, wanting to know how he could improve his game to make varsity the next school year. We talked openly for a while. The boy never had a father growing up, so he needed someone to confide in. Someone he could trust with an important secret."

"Which was?"

Colebrook sighs. "You can't tell anyone. Wesley made me promise to keep this information private. He was ashamed and yearning to figure out a way to solve his problem. But it was destroying him."

"How does this connect to Matthew Sanders?"

"Wesley confessed he had romantic feelings for his teammate, Matthew. But he knew there was nothing he could do about it, considering how conservative the town is. His teammates would never accept a homosexual on their team."

That's not true. "You don't know that. I don't think any of the guys I've ever played with would be that prejudiced. Is that what you told Wesley? That he would be outcasted if he came out?"

"No, of course not. I listened to Wesley and encouraged him to stay focused on the game. It was his choice to quit. Which was a terrible choice. It tormented him even more, being separated from Matthew. And then after hearing of Matthew's passing, it could have contributed to the shooting."

So Wesley murdered the team out of grief? That doesn't make sense. I'd rather go with the video games and bullying analogy.

"Did you ever speak to Wesley after he quit?" I ask instead.

"Not directly. He wrote me a letter requesting that I never speak to him again and to refrain from ever telling anyone what he confided in me. Even though what he did to our town is unforgivable, I've kept my word until now."

"You don't think his mother should know? Or his old teammates who bullied him for quitting? If they knew how much pain he was in…" I can't understand how Colebrook thinks it was okay to keep Wesley's secret when it clearly caused Wesley continual damage. Isn't there a rule that if a child's secret harms them, the adult has a legal obligation to tell someone?

Colebrook clears his throat with a loud cough. "Daniel, I'm sensing some hostility. Now I told you the truth. In return, I ask that you respect my wish and Wesley's wish for privacy."

"But Wesley is dead. And the whole town thinks his soul is damned anyway, so what's the harm in letting them know now? At least let his mother know so she can stop being blamed for what happened."

"It's not that simple, Daniel."

It's simple for him. He's protecting his ass. If he reveals information now, he'd be scrutinized and face possible legal consequences for withholding details from the investigation and the school. He had a moral duty to protect his athletes. And it's obvious he failed Wesley.

But more importantly, what is my moral duty? Do I keep the secret to protect Colebrook? Or do I risk the repercussions if I reveal it? Colebrook could deny what he said. That I made the whole thing up. And really, it's his word against mine. I didn't think to record the conversation.

My phone vibrates inside my pocket. It's Maya texting me.

Maya: **your coach is gay**

What?

"Is something wrong, Daniel?" Colebrook asks.

The life drains from my face, but I make a quick comeback. "My, uh, dad was just checking in on me. We just got this new dog, and she's very needy. She needs to be walked a lot, or she goes nuts."

"Hence why I've never had any pet but a fish all my life. I couldn't stand having to clean up after an animal's drool."

"Yeah…"

"Daniel, I know you need to leave, but can we come to an agreement? Don't tell anyone that poor

239

Wesley was gay. Just think about what that would do to this town. And how it would open more prejudice against homosexuals. Do we really want that?"

"I won't tell anyone." But I definitely won't keep my mouth shut about Maya's comment. Just what the hell is she doing up there?

"Do you feel a sense of peace knowing the truth about him?"

"I just wish someone could have done something for him."

Like you, Colebrook!

"Some people just can't be helped."

I nod my head and start moving toward the stairs. If I leave right now, this is the last time I'll ever speak to Colebrook, mainly because of how disappointed I am. So if anything needs to be said, I need to say it now.

"Just one more question," I say. "You promised to keep Wesley's secret?"

"Yes."

"And he knew that you kept it all these years?"

"I would think so."

"Then why did he shoot at you first?"

Colebrook's deadpan face wrings the moisture right out of my mouth. Suddenly, the basement feels too crowded, hot, dusty, and downright unsafe. I find myself backing away, almost like I might sprint up the stairs, grab Maya, and never look back. But I can't run away from this. There is some truth in what Colebrook told me. But it's twisted and morphed into something else. Something that protects Colebrook and vilifies Wesley.

Is that what I'm searching for? A way to make Wesley a victim instead of a murderer? Would that make the loss of my team easier to bear? Would I move on in peace, knowing it wasn't my kick that triggered Wesley but something from his days on the field?

"You've asked enough questions," Colebrook says, all emotions set aside. "I don't want you coming around here anymore."

"I wasn't planning on it."

"I don't want you asking anyone else these questions either. You need to let the past go and move on with your life. You owe it to your teammates. You should focus on your future at Notre Dame. Not on murderers like Wesley."

"I owe my teammates the truth."

"You just got the truth, and you're the only teammate left. That should suffice."

"Should it?"

"Worry about your future, Daniel. And maybe keep an eye on that girlfriend of yours. I'd hate for anything to happen to her."

"Is that a threat?"

Colebrook chuckles. "Of course not. She just seems like a wild little thing. No wonder you don't want to leave her all alone."

But leaving her alone this time did me some good should her text message merit some truth.

Maya

I wasn't going to stay in that kitchen forever. I did have to use the restroom shortly after Daniel and Mr. Clean went downstairs. Too much orange juice from the cafe. But I couldn't help taking a peek inside the coach's bedroom. Silk sheets, memory foam pillows, polished furniture, and the most bizarre artwork covering the walls. It didn't scream football coach. More like an eccentric theatre professor.

I only searched through a few of his dresser drawers. Typical men's clothing, all folded nice and neat, categorized by color. But digging a little deeper, between those ankle-high socks, I found the secrets. Immediately, I snapped a picture of my findings, put everything back, and returned to the kitchen to dump my overly sweetened lemonade and text Daniel.

Now I'm wondering if I made the right choice.

He doesn't come upstairs for another five minutes, but I wait by the front door, ready to leave. The coach fast on his heels, Daniel gives me a look that means don't say anything, just get out. So I follow him out the door. We don't speak until we're back in the Mustang and away from Colebrook's house.

"Did you find something?" Daniel asks.

I take a deep breath. "He has a brown jewelry box in his sock drawer. And there are pictures inside."

"Of?"

"You're not going to like this." I show him my phone.

Daniel nearly swerves off the road. He hits the brakes and grabs the phone to take a safer look.

"These are from the locker room," Daniel says. "He ... oh my God." His eyes grow wide. Shallow breaths. Panicked voice. Will he lose it this time?

"I'm sorry."

"Where ... where did you find these again?"

"In his sock drawer."

"And you're sure you put everything back the way you found it?"

"Yeah, I—"

"God, Maya, you told me he was gay in your text. Not that he's a *pedophile!*"

"I didn't want to freak you out. I just wanted to get you out of there. Besides, I thought it was obvious he was gay from the moment we walked in the door. Single, decent-looking guy, making lemonade and color-coding his drawers? Plus, he seemed threatened by me. It's like he wanted you all to himself. And now we know why."

Daniel rubs his forehead as though pined with a sudden headache. "This is so ... fucked up."

"Look, we have baggage on the guy now. This is a huge lead for us."

Daniel shakes his head. "He told me Wesley was gay. And that Wesley quit football because he was too afraid to come out. Fuck!" He bangs his fists against the dashboard. "I'm not sure if I should believe anything Colebrook told me."

"He had to cover up for something."

"He knew I wouldn't stop searching for the truth. He thought whatever he said would satisfy my curiosity. But it doesn't. Not with this added in." He hands me back my phone. "If Colebrook finds out you were in his bedroom, I don't know what he'll do, but it won't be good."

"Well, no shit. If this gets out, he risks losing his job, his reputation. He'd go to prison."

"Were there any pictures of Wesley in there?"

"There were like 30 pictures total. I only took five

shots. I figured that was enough."

"It's hard to tell who is who in the photos. But we could look up jersey numbers. We could figure something out."

"Or we could just hand it over to the police." Wouldn't that make the most sense?

"But then you'll have to admit you snuck into his bedroom."

"Big fucking deal! He'll have to admit he took pictures of naked underage boys without their permission. Daniel, do you realize there could be photos of you in there? Do you want Colebrook to get away with this?"

"I don't want to risk anything happening to us, especially you. Let's just say if we go to the police, and they decide to arrest Colebrook, and Colebrook runs, don't you think he'd come after us first?"

"If you are that scared of one person—"

"It only took *one* person to kill all nineteen of my friends!"

With an untamed roar, Daniel beats his hands against the steering wheel. One ... two... I cease counting after ten. Tears spill down his face. He turns away from me. I wish he wouldn't. He shouldn't feel ashamed to cry in front of me. But at least he's letting some of his pain out.

I didn't cry or scream when I found out my femur was shattered, and I had two choices: amputation or the rod. I didn't cry or scream when Grams told me my parents and Connor were dead. I just asked for more Vicodin. Then it was alcohol. Weed. Sex. Loud music and good times. All cover-ups. A way to hide.

Is it too late to cry?

"We just need time," Daniel says, pulling me from my thoughts. He sounds much calmer. He's no longer shouting. "We need time to sort through everything." He wipes his face on his sleeve. "Figure out facts from lies. And then we'll go to the police."

I put my hand on his shoulder and again choose to be kind. "Okay."

But eventually, he's going to have to face the truth.

And so will I.

****

Daniel is stressed. Big time.

He's been at his laptop for an hour, doing extensive research on Wesley, Colebrook, and this Matthew Sanders guy. He tries identifying the boys in the five photos, but so far, the only clear one is a ninth-grader from the 2008 team. This means Colebrook has been photographing for as long as he's been coaching, if not longer. This could also mean he has more than just photos in his house. Videos, perhaps? How could this guy go years without anyone discovering his perverted pastimes?

I have the power to turn the pictures over to the police myself. But Daniel is convinced he'll be able to sort through everything on his own. Why take that burden? Why not let the police handle it?

As the seconds tick by, I grow restless and bored. There's nothing to do in this town that I haven't done already. Even if I wanted to venture out by myself, Daniel is too afraid I'll run into Anna again. Or worse, Colebrook.

"Why don't we take a break and go for a walk?" I glance at Samantha, who looks anxious for some exercise.

"Later," Daniel says, not taking his eyes off the screen.

"Well, do you mind if I go for a walk? I can't be cooped up all day, doing absolutely nothing."

"You brought your laptop with you. You could be helping me."

"Daniel, you're not going to find anything online. You need the police to search Colebrook's house if you want information."

"Maybe we could do it."

"Are you nuts?"

"We'll just wait for him to leave and then sneak in somehow. He has dozens of boxes in his basement. There could be more information on Wesley down there."

He must be losing it. Only idiots in a horror movie would do something like that. Why risk antagonizing Colebrook even more? Why give him the chance to retaliate?

"Daniel, you sound crazy now. For your own good, please just give up on this. Let the police handle it."

"I can't!" Daniel pounds his hands against his desk, startling Samantha to bark.

"Why?"

Daniel pinches the bridge of his nose. His eyes start to water. "Because they're going to worry way more about the kids in the photos than Wesley. They don't care about him."

"And you do?"

"If something horrific happened to Wesley, then I need to know. Otherwise, I'm always going to blame myself."

"Blame yourself for what?"

"For what happened to my team."

"You had nothing to do with that. You were sick that night."

"Wesley snapped because we won states, and I'm the reason we won."

"That's ridiculous. You didn't even know the guy.

You didn't help him buy a gun. You didn't tell him to slaughter the team. That was his choice. It doesn't matter what sort of tragic childhood he may have had; it doesn't excuse him from murdering a bunch of innocent people. And let's just say you do uncover some truth about him. Maybe he found out Colebrook was snapping photos, and Colebrook did something to make him quit the team. Do you really think people are going to stop seeing Wesley as a villain? Wesley could have been gang-raped by every boy on the team; the people who lost their sons are not going to forgive him."

"I would. I would forgive him."

"Some people don't deserve forgiveness. Some things just aren't forgivable. But you will be miserable if you continue to blame yourself for this. You didn't do anything wrong."

"I did indirectly."

"Then so did I! I'm the reason my parents are dead. I didn't want to go to that concert, but I did. If I had stood my ground and stayed home, my mother and father would likely still be alive because there wouldn't have been anyone they needed to save. I'd have two working legs, and I'd be going to the Olympics in two years. And Connor…" I bite my lip, hating how my stomach twists whenever I mention my ex.

"Connor would still be alive," Daniel says.

I nod. "But he's not. He's gone. There's no way to fix what's been broken or get back what was stolen. Life now is just learning to exist with what you have left and trying to find some happiness. You still have the chance to do that. You can still play football. I have nothing. Other than a ridiculous amount of cash and the naive hope that you and I will somehow make it through all of this and still be together. But that's a fairytale ending I'm not counting on, so the best-case scenario is it lasts as long as it's going to last, and then I move on."

I'm surprised I said all that, but it needed to be said. I'm just wondering how much Daniel processed and how much went out the door. Can he focus on anything right now when he's so wrapped up in his guilt? All while trying to dig up answers impossible to find on his own? There's a reason why certain mysteries remain unsolved. The truth would cause greater harm.

I head for the door. I need air.

"Where are you going?" Daniel asks.

"Out for a walk. Don't worry. I don't plan on running into anyone who may want to throw orange juice at me or take pictures of me naked."

****

Now I'm pissed. I opened up to Daniel and tried shedding light on his dead-end situation, yet he still can't let go. What will it take to get through to him? He seemed more chill and confident at Fantasy Land. Since returning home, he's regressed. If he wants to bury himself in a grave, then power to him. I can't be a part of that. Not when I have my own demons to contend with.

I could use a drink.

But to hell with this dry town. I can't even get a beer!

Nixing the walk, I drive fifteen miles to the nearest non-dry town. My views along the way are cows, crops, and the occasional windmill. Google Maps lead me to a run-down liquor store next to a gun shop. Now that I'm eighteen, maybe I should consider owning a weapon. Would I find pleasure in firing a gun? What do mass murderers feel when they fire their assault rifles? Do they feel anything? Do you become inhuman, incapable of emotions, when you stoop to killing that many people all at once?

I'm in and out of the liquor store in three minutes.

The ancient old clerk doesn't even ask for ID. Once inside the Mustang, my body breaks into a sweat as it feverishly yearns for a swig of sweet Jack. One burn to silence all the other burns.

My hands start shaking. It hasn't even been a week since I was at the hospital for alcohol poisoning. I went through a detox. I even regained some of my taste buds and ate real food. But more importantly, I got Daniel back. If I drink now, it would all be for nothing.

How did I get myself into this mess?

Unable to think on my own, I call Dawn.

"You have to be patient," she says after I tell her everything, minus the whole confidential crap with Colebrook. "It hasn't even been a month since all his friends died. He needs time to process his emotions. Feeling guilt and coming up with irrational ideas is totally normal after someone dies. And it'll pass. You have to give it time."

"It was just so different for me."

"That's because you skipped the grieving period and headed straight for the pleasure zone. You never allowed yourself to feel guilt or denial or any of the other things people normally feel."

"Not everyone has to go through the fifty stages of grief to get over something."

"Maybe not. But it definitely helps. Perhaps one day, you'll allow yourself to go through the stages. And it's only five stages, not fifty."

"It's too late for me."

"It's not. And you know it."

I sigh and glance at the beautiful bottle of poison I just bought. How can such a small substance feel so heavy and have so much control over my life? If I can let down my guard for Daniel, I can say no to a stupid bottle. I was destined for the Olympics, not Alcoholics

Anonymous.

I can help Daniel. And myself.

I toss the bottle across the backseat. "I need to go, Dawn. Daniel will think I took off for good if I don't get back soon."

****

When I return, Daniel is in bed, curled in the fetal position. Sleeping? Not even close. He's bawling his eyes out.

A week ago, I would have told him to suck it up, stop crying, and get back to the fun zone. But things have changed. I no longer see crying as this forbidden thing but as a way to let some baggage go. It feels good if the tears bring you relief or joy. In my case, my tears gave me Daniel.

But from the amount of weeping from Daniel, he must have discovered something horrific while I was gone.

"Hey," I say, sitting down on the bed. "That bad, eh?"

He wipes his face with a pillow. "I thought you had left for good."

"Is that why you're crying? Because you thought I was leaving?"

He nods and reaches for my hand.

I curl up next to him and rest my forehead against his chest. "It's nice to know you'd miss me if I left," I say.

"I don't want to lose anyone else," he says, rubbing my back. "Especially you. I'm sorry for being a dick this morning. I'm sorry if I pushed you away."

"It's okay." I keep saying that. Okay ... okay ... okay ... is it okay?

We should talk about it, but my body takes control. My fingers sneak under his shirt to feel the warmth of his skin. It doesn't take long for his lips to find mine. I love how solid and snug his body is. He'd be the perfect mate should we ever travel north. Maybe to Alaska. Or across the ocean to Iceland. We could watch the Northern Lights and make love in the snow. Is there any place we couldn't go to?

Daniel

We stay in bed the rest of the afternoon. By evening, I feel bad for neglecting my dad all weekend, so I cook lasagna for everyone. We have a satisfying evening with no awkwardness or burnt garlic bread.

Dad seems taken by Maya, so at least I have that going for me.

Maya and I finally walk Samantha. My legs still throb from my marathon run, but with Maya, it's not too much to keep moving.

And all the while, I've managed not to obsess over Wesley or Colebrook. At least not vocally. The investigation is on hold until morning. I don't want Colebrook to do anything hostile should we go to the police too soon.

As the opening credits roll for Star Wars: Episode V, Gracie texts me.

Gracie: **Got too wasted at the barn. Could you give me a ride home?**

It's not even eight o'clock. And who the hell throws a party on a Sunday night? Are the parents really okay with this much partying? Are they even aware?

"What's wrong?" Maya asks.

"A friend of mine needs a ride home. She's drunk. I can go get her and be back in a half-hour."

"Or I could come with you?"

"I don't know." Alcohol is always a temptation for Maya.

She squeezes my thigh. "I'll let you drive the Mustang again."

****

It's one thing to throw a party once a week, get drunk, and spend the next day with a miserable hangover.

But now the parties are becoming more frequent, and it's not like Gracie to be a part of such gatherings. I'm nervous to see her again, especially with Maya in the car. By now the whole town probably knows about my new relationship status. I hope Anna hasn't poisoned everyone against Maya. Then again, people know what kind of tramp Anna is. Would they believe her?

I park away from the bonfire and kegs, not wanting to tempt Maya out of the car. "I'll be right back."

I try texting and calling Gracie, but she doesn't answer, so I'll have to search for her. What if she's passed out somewhere?

Every kid is drunk and out of control. My eyes and nose tell me it's not just beer on the menu; an orange Gatorade cooler is filled with a mixed drink. A scantily dressed girl falls into me and compliments my biceps. I gently push her aside and keep searching for Gracie. Eventually, I ask around.

It takes me a while to find someone not entirely wasted. One of the cheerleaders tells me, "Gracie was over by the horses the last time I saw her."

I hope she's not trying to ride them.

By the time I reach the fence, I'm far enough away from the bonfire to hear the crickets. For a second, I'm taken back to the time Charlie and I drew away from a party and had a long talk about the future. Charlie spoke about getting married and how many kids he wanted. Whereas, I deliberated what my major should be. Charlie always looked deep into the future, fearlessly. He had confidence everything would sort itself out. Whatever problems lay ahead, he would get past them.

The crickets were so loud that night they almost overpowered his voice. And Charlie was anything but quiet.

I close my eyes, taking in all the sounds, feeling

all the memories. I allow the pain to take over, and I cry for Charlie. He was my best friend. I would have gone to his wedding and met his kids. Hell, maybe our kids would have grown up together and played football. That's if I ever planned on having kids. I never thought much about becoming a dad. Does Maya ever think about having kids? What kind of mother would she be? Hopefully, a better one than hers and mine.

I think about all the moms and dads in Morville, passing by their son's empty rooms every night before bed. What would they think of me if they knew I had evidence against Coach Colebrook, a man they trusted just as much as their sons did and hadn't shared it yet? Would they see me as a villain too?

Do I want people to hate me? Do I want to be blamed? Is that what I'm searching for? A way to take responsibility for it all? Why would I do that to myself?

Suddenly, I hear a faint cry.

"Gracie?"

She's sitting against the fence about twenty yards away. I never would have seen her if I hadn't heard her first.

"Gracie, are you all right?" I run to her side, my calves pinching with every step. "Gracie?"

She's conscious but a crying mess. Black eyeliner drips down her brown cheeks. One of her spaghetti straps falls off her shoulder as she cradles a near-empty cup of what smells like vodka and Kool-Aid.

"How much of this have you had?" I ask, taking the cup from her then emptying it onto the grass.

"Oh, you know, like a few." She smiles and tosses her hands like she's lost control of her joints.

"Do you need me to carry you? My car's not too far away. Well, it's not my car. It's too nice to be mine."

"I know it's a nice car," Gracie says. "Everyone

has been talking about your new girlfriend's Mustang."

I swallow hard. "She's here with me."

"The girl you were thinking about when you kissed me."

"Gracie, I…"

She tosses her other hand, almost slapping herself in the face. "I wish you hadn't done that. I don't need that kind of false hope right now. I'm already so hopeless."

"But you just did that big protest. You should be feeling good about yourself. And hopeful things will change."

Gracie snorts, trying to laugh it off. "Nothing is going to change. There will be another shooting next week, somewhere else. Cause there will always be guns. And they'll always be assholes. You can't get rid of both." She tries to stand but falls onto her knees. She immediately tries again, but this time I catch her and hold her up. I feel her heart beating against my own. She wraps her arms around me and cries.

"I miss him so much. I just want him to come home."

"I know, Gracie. I miss him too. I wish he was here right now."

"It's not fair." Her body convulses against mine as she weeps. "Why did this have to happen? Why did he have to kill them all? I don't understand what made him do it. It doesn't make any sense."

I hold her tight. I know exactly how she feels. Except I know more than she does. I wonder how Gracie would feel if she knew about Colebrook. Or would it make things worse? Knowing Colebrook might have snapped photos of her deceased brother? Maybe Maya is right. Maybe I should stop digging for answers before I cause people like Gracie any more pain.

"I think you'd feel better with a good night's rest

and some water," I finally say. "Come on. Let me take you home."

She wipes her nose against her upper arm and unlatches her hands from my waist. Even though she's wobbly, she can walk on her own. As we reach the Mustang, I hold my breath, panicked Maya will be gone, but she's still in the passenger seat, on her phone, and seemingly sober.

"Wow, this is the nicest car I've ever been in," Gracie says as I open the back door. Maya was smart to buy a four-door model.

Maya turns around and waves. "I'm Maya. You must be Gracie?"

"Wow. You're really pretty," Gracie says.

"Thanks. So are you. Don't forget to buckle up."

"Daniel, you lied to me." Gracie taps the back of my seat.

Oh no...

"You said you didn't find God," Gracie continues. "But you did. You did indeed."

I have no idea what that means, but Gracie seems pleased with Maya. I get in and start the car. A quick drive to Gracie's house and things should be back to normal. For now, at least. I wonder if Gracie's mom and dad know how much she's been drinking lately. Some parents don't care, so long as no one gets behind the wheel. But mixed with grief, it's a recipe for dependence. Maya is living proof.

Surprisingly, Maya and Gracie start a conversation almost immediately. Maya asks about high school and competition cheerleading. Gracie laughs over how bad the team placed this year because they all suck at gymnastics. Even with hard feelings over her old sport, Maya doesn't seem to mind listening to Gracie's archive. She seems intrigued.

As we pull into Gracie's driveway, Gracie stumbles over something on the floor. "Ew, which one of you drinks Jack Daniels?" She holds up the bottle.

I'm stunned, shocked, and mortified. But for Gracie's sake, I react as calmly as possible. "I'll take that," I say. "Gracie, do you need help getting inside?"

"I'm good. Thanks for the ride, Daniel. And it was nice meeting you, Maya. Thank you for bringing Daniel to God."

"No problem." Maya laughs, probably thinking Gracie made a joke when Gracie might be convinced that I met Maya during my "spiritual retreat".

But I don't care about any of that when there's a bottle of liquor to be dealt with first.

I keep my cool until Gracie has made it inside the house. "What the hell is this?" I ask, shaking the bottle in front of Maya.

"It hasn't even been opened, so don't get upset," Maya says, clearly annoyed by my query.

"Why is it in your car?"

"Because I bought it."

"And do you plan to drink it?"

"No."

"Then why did you buy it? When did you buy it?"

Maya rubs her forehead. "Let's just go back to your house. I don't want to have this conversation."

"Why not? It's important."

"Because I'm tired, and I want to go to bed. And tomorrow, get out of this town."

"This place dissatisfies you that much?"

"No, just you."

I'm stunned. She was on my side earlier. Now she's turning? "I can't ask questions? I can't be concerned?"

"Not when you have your own shit to deal with. I

tried to be supportive. Tried not to be too overbearing or selfish. But I don't think I can anymore. Not when every little choice I make is going to be scrutinized."

"What are you saying?"

"Can you please drive us back? Or do I need to drive?"

"No, I can drive." I place the Jack between us and put the car in reverse. My head spirals with thoughts, wondering if she was planning to drink but denied it once I found out. Will I always have to worry about her addiction? Will I always have to fear a relapse?

I can't hold back my feelings. "This is a mess. This whole thing is a mess."

She nearly laughs. "Why do you think I never wanted this to go beyond a physical relationship?"

"Well, it did go past that point. For both of us. You came here to prove that, and now you just want to leave?" She couldn't have picked a worse time.

"I didn't agree to move in with you, Daniel. I agreed to be with you. I even agreed to help you. I thought I could get you to let go of all of this, but I was wrong."

"I said I'd deal with Colebrook in the morning."

"And go to the police like you should have done earlier?" She shakes her head. "You're going to bail."

"Why would you say that? You don't believe in me?"

"I believe in the Daniel I met in Fantasy Land. The Daniel who took a leap of faith for me. Who put his heart on the line for me. And now all I see is a Daniel who wants to put his heart through a blender for a murderer and a pedophile."

"You just want me to leave my home and forget about all this, but I can't ignore this part of my life. I have to deal with this, and you may disagree with my methods, but they're a lot better than yours!"

"Really? Now you're going to try to compare what I went through to what you're going through? I was *shot*, Daniel! They had to rip me open and remove splintered bones out of my thigh. I guarantee if you had to feel any ounce of the pain I went through, you'd be begging for a drink or pill, anything to numb it out."

"You could have gone to therapy."

"Well, fuck, so could you! But you chose to reach out to a stranger online. You chose to get away with me. I didn't force you. Every decision you have made has been for yourself. You may think you're doing your town this big favor by taking on the burden of Wesley and your sick coach, but you're just making everything worse."

"I'm making everything worse? Things were fine until you decided to sneak off to buy alcohol. Rather than tell me how you really felt about all this, you chose to run away."

She takes a deep breath and no longer shouts. "I was doing you a favor. You were just too caught up in your guilt to see."

We're in my driveway now. I don't know whether to cry, scream, or sit in silence until I calm down. I'm hurt by what she said, but to be fair, can I blame her for wanting to get away from a broken town she has no place in? Can I be angry with her for not wanting to deal with my trauma when she has her own problems to contend with? Why the hell did I criticize her so much? And to compare my suffering to hers? I am selfish.

But before I can apologize, she opens the bottle of Jack. "Don't!" I yell, trying to grab it from her.

As though anticipating my reaction, she storms out of the car and leaps onto the grass. I halt when she empties the bottle, every last drop. I stand three feet away, watching in disbelief. Why is she pouring it all out? To prove something?

To prove she was telling the truth the first time I asked her.

With deadpan eyes, she smashes the empty bottle against a tree, shattering the glass until it's no longer recognizable except for the smell. She winces and opens her hand. Crimson liquid seeps from her palm.

"Maya…"

"Don't come near me." She squeezes her hand into a fist, allowing the blood to spill.

"You're bleeding."

"We all bleed, Daniel. Some of us more than others."

What is that supposed to mean? Those words sound far too morbid to unfold from Maya. Why is she putting herself through more pain? To show me she can handle it better than I can? Or just to show me how vulnerable we all are?

I take a deep breath and open my arms. "Please, let me help you."

She closes her eyes and nods her head once. I remove my shirt and wrap it around her hand. She doesn't muster a sound, but her body shakes. I guide her into the house and down to the basement, where the carpet is so old a drop of blood wouldn't make much of a difference in its color. In the bathroom, I run cold water over her hand. It's not that deep of a cut, but her silence and resilience are a bit concerning. No tears. No signs of distress or pain. I wonder what she was like when she got shot in the leg. Did she scream? Did she cry? Did she feel anything? Or was it complete shock? I think of what she said earlier about the doctors having to remove pieces of bone from her body. It's one thing to break a bone, but to have it shatter? I should be thankful I never had to go through that. But I wish Colebrook had. He lucked out;

the bullet went straight through muscle, dodging all bones and joints.

"Do you want to go to the ER?" I ask as I wrap the wound in gauze and a bandage.

"What for?" she asks.

"In case you need stitches."

She shakes her head. "I just want to go to bed."

Despite having our own rooms, we've been inseparable in terms of actual sleep. She pushes me back when I try to get into bed with her. I don't argue, don't say anything. I know I messed up and need to make things right, but now is not the time.

As I clean up the broken glass outside, I plan out tomorrow morning in my head. I'll make her breakfast and then drive straight to the police station. I'll confess I found the photos so Maya doesn't have to be involved, and then I'll sit back and let the police handle the investigation.

More importantly, I'll make the day about her. I'll let go of my sorrows and worries and be present with her. I'll show her that I still care. That I love her. Now and forever.

But as I lie awake in bed, I have an awful feeling that my plan won't work out. Because I'm not sure I have the confidence to hand over my guilt to a bunch of officers who have no idea what I'm going through. If I bail, I will lose Maya forever. Because the Daniel she met in Fantasy Land will be gone, and in its place will be the villain Daniel who lets murderers and pedophiles win.

Part Four: Love
Maya

When I couldn't get out of bed on my own, Grams would help me. She would hand me my crutches, put my socks on for me, and even braid my hair. When I couldn't walk straight after getting too drunk at a club, Dawn would rescue me, put me to bed, and leave a glass of water on my nightstand. When I got caught drinking at sixteen and had to go to court, Grams vouched for me, promising the judge I would attend counseling and stay sober. When my aunt and uncle fought to take custody, Dawn stood up for me and told them to back off.

Countless acts of kindness, and I've done nothing for them in return. But they don't expect much from me. I once asked Grams why she put up with my crap, day after day, and it was a one-word answer.

Love.

When I look at Daniel, I see the beginnings of a dark and endless road. I'm not sure if anyone else sees what I see, considering how well he masks his pain. At least I made it clear I was suffering through my umpteen acts of underage indulgences. I didn't realize how much I suffered until I met Daniel, until the wounds reopened and I allowed myself to feel again.

Abandoning Daniel in his time of need wouldn't be atypical of me. But doing something in secret to push him out of his guilt? If I am capable of love, this may be the only way to show it.

Nearly all police stations have an online option where a person can anonymously report a crime or send in evidence. I don't know if Daniel knows this, but I don't wake him to find out. Without hesitation, I send a short message with the photos attached.

These photos were found inside Hank Colebrook's dresser drawer. There are about 30 photos in total.

That's all they need to know.

Then I quietly pack my things and leave town for good.

****

I'm only ten miles away when my phone rings. I left when it was dark, but Daniel wakes early to run. Of course, he would check on me first and find my bed empty.

I left a note this time. Much longer than the one he left me in the hotel room. I could have waited for him to wake up, to talk this out face to face, but it would have ended with us naked in bed together, and we can't keep relying on sex to "fix" all our problems. As much as I enjoy Daniel, I need a break from him. I have to go home and face my own truth. I'm hoping my absence will allow him to move on. If you love someone, you'll let them go, right? Or did some loser make that saying to cover up why he couldn't keep a girlfriend?

Daniel continues to call.

I turn the radio on.

It's just me and the open road now.

Daniel

I knew she was going to leave. And yet, I didn't do much to stop it other than call her eight times and leave a bunch of voicemails.

In my boxers, I sit on the front porch with Samantha. The sky is dark blue with streaks of orange across the horizon. I don't want this day to begin. Or the next. Instead, I want to go back and relive other days. I want to climb Mount Doom with Maya. I want to eat pizza with my teammates. I want to take Jojo for a walk. I want my mother to hold me. I want to witness my parents kiss and hold hands.

For all the bad that's happened, there has been a lot of good. Yet, when I reflect on the good memories, I feel anger and despair. What if there's no happiness in my future? What if I'm condemned to be miserable for the rest of my life?

Is this what depression is like? Just a never-ending feeling of menacing doom?

I scroll through the photos Maya sent to me yesterday afternoon. Why am I not more disgusted? My coach is a sick man. What's worse, he's gotten away with his crimes for years, and it had to take a mass shooting for just *part* of his secret life to be revealed. I hold the key to unlocking the rest. Maybe I'm hesitant to go to the police because it'll put me in the spotlight again. Not only will I be known as the one who got away but also as the one who discovered the morbid truth about his football coach.

The front door opens, startling me from my thoughts.

Dad steps out in his blue bathrobe. "You might

want to put on some clothes before you go running," he says.

"Not today." Even if I wanted to run, I destroyed my legs yesterday and need a day to recover.

He looks at the driveway. "Where's Maya?"

"She went back home."

"Oh." Dad sits next to me. Samantha rests her chin on his lap, and he pets her. "Was Maya planning on leaving today?"

"Not really. But I didn't expect her to stay here forever."

Dad nods his head. "It takes a certain kind of person to want to live in a small town. Maya seems like the kind of girl who wants a life bigger than this."

"I can't give her that."

"Not when you don't know what kind of life you want for yourself."

"My life is pretty planned out for the next four years. College and football. If I do well in both, then the next part of my life will go smoothly."

"You can't count on life to go smoothly, even when you have everything planned out. You need to be flexible. I wanted your mom to stay with us, for us to be a family, but it didn't happen. She left, and I had to adjust my attitude and my way of life."

"But you didn't even try to get her back."

"I did try. For years, we struggled and fought. We held on as long as we could, but in the end, she chose to leave. I could have followed her, packed us all up, and taken you to Puerto Rico. But I had made my own life here, and it wasn't something I wanted to give up. You see, I'm happy living here. I've always been happy here. Everything about this town makes me happy, from the cows to the ice cream shop. I love that I know every single person who brings their animal into my office. I love receiving Christmas cards every year. I love the parades and fireworks. I love everything."

If only he knew about Coach Colebrook's secret life. Would he still love *everything*?

"You have no concerns or issues with this town?" I ask. "No one has ever rubbed you the wrong way?"

"Every town has its eggs, but in terms of legit concerns, I've only ever had one. Whether or not this town makes *you* happy."

That is a legit concern. But one I know the answer to.

"It used to make me happy."

"And it doesn't anymore. That's okay. A bad thing happened here. You don't have to come up with a reason to stay. You don't owe it to me. And you don't owe it to anyone else in this town. I know you still have a month or so before you leave for school, but if you wanted to leave right now, I wouldn't try to stop you."

"Where would I go?"

"Isn't it obvious?"

"Dad…" Maybe I should finally tell him some of the truth. "Maya isn't well."

"Neither are you." He puts his hand on my shoulder. I think of Coach Colebrook, squeezing my shoulder. How many times did I let him do that? Why don't I have the guts to go to his house right now and kick his teeth in?

"There's so much you don't know," I finally say, trying not to tense up, but it's useless. I can't hold back in front of my dad. "And I don't know how much to tell you or how much to keep inside. But it hurts." My throat tightens, and my eyes burn with the onset of tears. "It's like a mass growing inside my chest. And I don't know how to make it go away. I feel so hopeless right now. And I miss Maya. I don't care how crazy she is or how many problems she has. I freaking love that girl."

"Then perhaps the way to let that mass go is through love."

I shake my head and wipe my nose against my forearm. "I don't know how to help her. I can't even help myself. I don't even have the courage to…" Sirens in the distance compel me to stand. "I wonder what that is."

"That's an ambulance siren," Dad says, since I don't know the difference between the three.

Closing my eyes, I try to imagine where they're going. In such a small town, everyone finds out by the end of the day, if not sooner, especially if a person got hurt or died. Log onto Facebook, and someone will have posted the news.

I don't want to find out that way. It's easier to disconnect from something when you read about it online. Like #thoughtsandprayers. But if you witness it for yourself, it's a part of you forever.

****

The doorbell rings an hour later. I'm dressed at least, but I could use a shower before I head to work with Dad. The sheriff is at the door with his hat off, which means he's here to deliver bad news. My dad holds Samantha by the collar. She barks only a few times before settling down.

"I'm sorry to bother you," the sheriff says, keeping close to the doorway, "but I felt it was my personal obligation to let you know that Hank Colebrook died by suicide earlier this morning. Before that, we received an anonymous message with some shocking evidence against Colebrook. When we arrived at his house to investigate, Colebrook locked himself in his bedroom and shot himself in the head."

I don't know how to process anything said. What anonymous message? Who else would know except for…?

Maya.

The sheriff continues without delay. "I know this may come as a shock to you both, but Hank Colebrook may have committed many crimes against his athletes over his coaching career. The investigation is still underway, but we will be releasing a public statement later this evening." He clears his throat with a gentle a-hem before speaking again. "Daniel, were you at all aware or suspicious of your coach's behavior?"

I try to speak, but I'm lost for words. I can't even swallow, let alone get out much air. Do I need a lawyer for this?

Dad steps in for me. "This is a lot for him to handle right now," Dad says.

"I understand, but Daniel is the only one left that could shed some light on this matter."

I'm the only one left. There it is again.

Can I be alone and still be strong? Can I find a way to rise?

"I believe Coach Colebrook did something to Wesley Dover," I say, loud and bold. "I believe whatever he did to Wesley caused Wesley to retaliate against the team when we won states this year. I hope you find the answers to that."

"We will, son, we will. But what makes you suspect he did something to Wesley?"

I swallow the growing lump in my throat. The sheriff doesn't know half of what I know, but I'm sure once Colebrook's house is thoroughly searched, he'll know more. But for now, I go with what Maya suggested earlier. That I only share what I want to share.

"It's the way he squeezes shoulders."

****

The sheriff's statement causes an uproar among

the parents. Now they have to wonder if any of their dead sons were photographed (or worse) by their coach. Everyone threatens to sue the school, the principal, the athletic department, even the marching band director. Anyone who ever worked alongside Colebrook is a target. But not me. For once, I am left alone.

In addition to the thirty photos found in Colebrook's bedroom, numerous videos are discovered in his basement. The police don't have the authority to release the children's names in the photos or videos. Still, the revelation is enough to motivate past victims of Colebrook to speak up. The first is a boy from California who never even knew Colebrook but knew the deceased Matthew Sanders. The boy reveals that Matthew was molested by Colebrook during his sophomore year of high school. Matthew never told anyone because he was afraid he'd be labeled a homosexual and banned from the team, which was complete bullshit fueled by Colebrook who always made a boy question his sexuality before abusing him. In actuality, Colebrook had issues with his own orientation, likely triggered by military trauma.

I wait patiently for the news of Wesley. For anyone to speak up for him. For more evidence to be found against Colebrook. But Colebrook must have done away with all his footage of Wesley. Maybe the only photo left is the one of Wesley smiling at his teammates. This is how I want to remember Wesley. As a happy, innocent young man, full of potential. But I know deep down, his story bears a fate similar to Matthew's and many other boys who were too ashamed or scared to speak up. And that is why I must forgive Wesley for what he did.

But I will never forgive Coach Colebrook. He can rot in hell.

****

Two days go by without a sound from Maya. When I'm not staring at my phone or laptop, waiting for more news, I lie awake in bed, stroking my fingers against the unwashed sheets. When the loneliness becomes unbearable, I call and leave another message, begging to hear her voice again.

Finally, after one louder-than-usual call, my dad barges into my room without knocking and slams my keys on my desk. "Get your ass up, and go after her! There's nothing left for you to do here besides wallowing up like a dead leaf."

"Dad, I can't just–"

"Yes, you can. Maya came to you. Now it's your turn to go to her."

"I didn't ask her to come here."

"But you were glad that she did."

"Yes, I was. I was ... happy."

When I saw her lying in the backyard with Samantha barking in her face, my whole body filled with warmth. Just like it did when I first laid eyes on her in Fantasy Land, her hair long and wild, the sun shining across her face. And all the moments in between. The feel of her skin against mine, our hearts in sync, sharing memories I'll never let go of.

She brings me to such incredible highs but also horrific lows. The thought of her dying from alcohol poisoning still haunts me. But even without her dependence issues, how can we be together when our lives are steering in opposite directions? I'm moving away, and she has no idea what to do with her inheritance. Is college even an option for her? She mentioned earning her GED but also how much she loathed the process. I can't imagine she'd be into furthering her education.

And yet, we've suffered similar tragedies. We've

lost loved ones, and we've survived. Maya chose a dangerous path at first, but she's trying to improve. She could have drunk the whiskey in secret or in front of me, but she poured it out. She made the hard choice. And an even harder one by leaving me behind. But she saved me from my despair by turning in the photos herself. She gave me the chance to move on.

But I don't want to move on without her.

I rub my forehead, suddenly tortured with a headache. "I don't even know where she lives."

"You could find out," Dad says.

"How?"

"You have social media, a phone, and a brain. Use all three, and I'm sure you'll figure it out."

"And what if I don't come back?"

"As long as you're happy, wherever you end up, I'll be happy for you."

I have nothing to lose at this point if I go after her. If I stay, I have nothing to gain but regret. I don't want to end up like one of Colebrook's victims, waiting years to finally speak up. It will take more than a phone call to get Maya back. It'll take everything I am and more.

Maya

"Hello, my name is Maya, and I'm an alcoholic."

I've said it thirteen times to Dawn, but the idea of saying it in front of a bunch of people, who may or may not know me, terrifies me. The pamphlet says I'm not required to speak or say anything about myself. I could use the entire time to listen to others, as hearing their struggles and insecurities might help me with my own.

Nothing about AA sounds helpful. It's an hour of torture, sitting in uncomfortable chairs surrounded by weirdos. I'd much rather light up a joint and dance at a nightclub. Exercise away my so-called struggles and insecurities.

"It starts in five minutes. Do you want me to go in with you?" Dawn, my support guru, asks.

I unbuckle my seatbelt, but I still feel glued to the car. "This isn't going to solve anything," I say. "No one gets cured of alcoholism by attending a meeting."

"It's not meant to be a cure. It's a way to help you to stay sober."

"I can stay sober on my own. It's just not enjoyable."

"That's why I suggested you come to yoga with me."

"Yoga is so boring."

"All other high-endorphin activities are not on your safe list."

I sigh and rub my forehead. "I want to go back to Fantasy Land."

Dawn huffs, clearly annoyed by my excuses. "Are you going to do this or what? Do you want me to walk you in?"

"No. I can do it myself."

"All right. I'm going to get my nails done. I'll be back in an hour. Please don't laugh or say anything sarcastic to anyone."

"Are you worried I'll get kicked out?"

"Just be sensitive to the people who actually take AA seriously."

I bet they take all the free cookies and milk seriously.

With some effort, I get out of the car, put on sunglasses, and walk toward the front door, the entrance to a Baptist church. Two overly perfumed ladies walk past me, chatting loudly about their ex-husbands refusing to pay alimony. If I have to mingle with people like that, shoot me in the foot. I'll likely be the youngest person in the group. If I say anything, all the old people will lecture me and share stories of "when I was your age…"

I wait for Dawn to drive away before continuing down the sidewalk. I'm not ready to go in, not yet, or maybe not ever. I need fresh air and exercise first.

The bizarre thing about this church is that it's only a two-minute walk from the gymnastics center I used to train at, a place I haven't set foot in since before the shooting. I didn't even go back to clear out my locker. It's been two years. I wonder who's taken the top spot on the team since my departure.

Even though my brain is telling me to retreat, my feet keep pushing me toward the gym. It's Wednesday. If the schedule has stayed the same, the preschoolers train now. I see a dozen or so minivans in the parking lot. Most of the moms watch from the bleachers. Some entitled ones try to sneak onto the floor but are usually shooed away by coaches. I don't remember my mom being the sneaky kind or the bleacher kind. She was the no-show mom who dropped me off so she could take a long phone call or get her hair done. I was always angry she never stayed around to watch me, but that anger pushed me to be more aggressive on the floor. I wanted all the other moms to see how much better I was than their daughters. I made sure to jump higher, stretch farther, and run faster. So if one day my mom did decide to stay and watch, I'd say, "Look what I did all on my own." Just in case she tried to take any credit for my success.

"Maya?"

A voice startles me as I peer through one of the windows. Holy crap. It's my old coach. She looks the same. Except now she has her eyebrows tattooed in addition to her lips.

"Miss Betty?" I take off my sunglasses to make sure it's her.

She holds the door open for me. "It's nice to see you. I always wondered if you'd ever come to visit us again."

"I was just passing through. I'm actually on my way to, uh, a meeting." Dare I tell her what it's for?

"Do you have a few minutes? Come see some of the girls."

"I really can't…"

"You're still the best gymnast we ever had. They would be thrilled to meet you."

What could be worse? An AA meeting or talking to a bunch of adorable four-year-olds? I'm sure the kids would be a lot less judgmental than the old people.

Miss Betty guides me inside. The place hasn't changed much in two years. The lobby walls are covered with photos and newspaper clippings. I notice myself in many of the pictures, holding up trophies bigger than the podium. I should have returned my trophies to the studio rather than trash them all.

The four-year-olds are on the balance beam when Miss Betty and I walk onto the main floor. I don't recognize their coach, a young woman with strawberry blonde hair and amazing thighs, but she smiles as though she recognizes me.

"Girls, we have a guest athlete," Miss Betty announces.

"Retired athlete," I correct.

The girls hop off the beam and gather around like I'm a celebrity about to show them a double backflip while blindfolded.

"Girls, this is Maya Floros," Miss Betty says. "You may have seen her picture in the lobby. She used to compete on the elite team."

"Did you go to the Olympics?" one girl immediately asks.

"No," I say.

"Are you going to go to the Olympics?" another girl asks.

"Probably not." Unless I go as an audience member.

"Can you flip in the air?"

"Ooh, watch me!" One kid does a cartwheel with bent legs and unpointed feet.

"No, watch me!" Another girl does a more graceful cartwheel.

"Girls, girls, settle down. Miss Maya can only stay for a few minutes."

"I'm not dressed to show off any tricks," I say, not that I'd be able to do much beyond hang from a bar uselessly.

"Aw, and you got a boo-boo." One of the girls notices the bandage around my hand.

"Yes, I got a boo-boo."

After much persuasion, the girls return to their class. I linger in the corner with Miss Betty, watching their tiny feet stretch and move across the beam. When I was four, I had little trouble finding my balance as I would imagine myself high in the air with no safety net to fall into. A thought like that would make any kid nervous, but it calmed me and made me work harder. Every step I took was a life-or-death step. So it had to be perfect. I could not afford a single error.

"You know, we have an opening for a coaching position if you're interested," Miss Betty tells me. "It's part-time, just a couple of morning classes we could use help with right now."

"I'm really in no shape to be coaching," I say.

"You don't need to be in shape to coach four-year-olds."

"I'm not sure…"

"If you change your mind, the door is always open."

And now that I've walked through the door, there's no real excuse why I couldn't take on the challenge. It's not like I have a jam-packed schedule or anyone other than my cousin to hang with. Maybe coaching little kids would be fun.

Or it could be torture. Wanting to flip for them and not being able to.

****

I return to the church just as Dawn pulls into the parking lot. I grab a flyer from one of the information bins, so it looks like I went in and showed some interest in rehab programs.

"How was it?" she asks as I buckle my seat belt.

"Very boring."

"I figured you'd say that."

"What's next on the checklist?"

"Nothing. You accomplished your goal of the day. Attend an AA meeting. Should we celebrate?"

"Fantasy Land?"

"No, thank you. Fantasy Land in the scorching heat is not my idea of a fun vacation. Speaking of which, I received a Facebook friend request and several messages from loverboy. I thought you two broke it off."

I groan and crumble up the unread flyer. "What does he want?"

"He wants to see you again."

"I told him I needed space. It hasn't even been a week!"

"You barely survived three days before you went to see him."

"That was different."

"I don't understand why you guys can't just work out some kind of long-distance relationship."

"Because Daniel won't have time to see me once college begins. Football is going to take over his life."

"He would still make time for you."

"You don't know him. How can you make that assumption?"

"Because he's reaching out even when you pushed him back. And he's not angry about it and cursing your name like Nicole did. Which shows he's willing to compromise and make things work."

"You're still counting on that fairytale ending?"

"Of course!"

I shake my head. "Can we focus on something else today? You made a list. What's the plan for tomorrow? Let's start on that. In fact, I want to know everything on the list."

She pulls out her phone. "Visit parents' graves."

"No."

"Visit Connor's grave."

"*No.*"

"Start physical therapy again."

"I went through that already. It didn't work."

"You gave up too easily. They have methods for helping former athletes to regain some of their former glory and strength. You'll never be able to vault or do floor, but you could do the uneven bars again, just without the hard landing. You could even do the balance beam."

"What's the point in doing any of that when I'm going to wake up feeling just as alone as I did the day before?"

"Then we can add Daniel to the list to help with that part. Have him go with you to the cemetery. Maybe you'll do it. And maybe you'll *actually* go to an AA meeting if he was with you instead."

"What?"

She wiggles her fingers at me. "You didn't notice my nails are still the same color as before? And that we just got our nails done last week? Why would I need them done again so soon?"

She must have hung low and spied on me. Clever cousin. I'm only mad for a split second because I no longer have to lie. And should anyone really trust me to attend an AA meeting? You'd have to give out free sex toys and chips if you wanted to ensure my participation.

"What made you go back?" Dawn asks after I tell her about Miss Betty.

"It just happened."

"Man, I didn't even think to add gymnastics to the list. That would have been a good one."

"Well, it's done and over with. Nothing has changed except…"

"Except?"

"I got offered a job."

"For real?" Dawn's freckled face blossoms like a rose. "Yay! That's so exciting!"

"It's whatever."

"Maya, you should feel good about this!"

"It's only part-time, and it's teaching little kids. I don't need the money, so there's no point in pursuing it."

"Oh, yes, there is a point. You could end up *enjoying* it!"

"No, it's just going to make me even more pissed off about my injury than I already am."

"Maybe it'll be the motivation you need to get back into physical therapy. Come on, Maya. You should consider doing this."

"I thought it was more important to rectify my relationship with Daniel?"

"I never said that. But it's something you need to consider as well."

"Along with attending AA meetings and visiting gravestones? This is too much. I need a simpler plan."

"No, it's not too much, and screw simplicity." Her happy manner takes a hard turn back to castigation. "You're lucky you're financially set and don't have to worry about needing an actual income to survive. You can afford any necessity or luxury right now. You could go to college, travel, support a charity, anything. If you would just get out of your limited head and see the possibilities!"

"All right! I see the possibilities!" I feel like I'm talking to my eighth-grade guidance counselor. My phone rings again. Daniel has slowed to calling me only once an hour instead of every four seconds. I'm about to block his number when Dawn shows me his latest Facebook message.

Daniel: **I am on my way to Coors right now. Where can I find Maya?**

"He's coming for ya!" Dawn exclaims.

Seriously, how can she be this excited and overworked? Then again, she hasn't had near the amount of drama when it comes to men as I have.

"Don't tell him where I'm staying."

"You don't think he'll figure it out? There's only one nice hotel in the whole area."

"Then it looks like I'll be checking out today."

Daniel

I don't know if my car will make it to Coors. I'm overdue for new tires, and it takes several attempts to start the engine. I could have asked to borrow Dad's more reliable car, but I didn't want to leave him the crappy Honda, not knowing when I'll return.

Fortunately, Maya's cousin, Dawn, whom I easily found on Facebook, is more than willing to help me reconnect with Maya, who is not keen on seeing me right now. I can't wait for Maya's attitude to change; I need to fix things now before she slips away for good.

Three hours into my trip, I stop at a gas station to pee and fill the tank. I re-read Maya's letter for the eight millionth time. It's hard to believe it was Maya's writing because she used punctuation. I guess she wanted to make her intentions clear.

Daniel,

It's not going to work. Even if you move on from your grief and guilt, I don't want to keep you from your goals. You deserve a clean streak at college where you can make new friends and find someone who will complement your life rather than weigh it down. Please don't call or follow me. I need space right now.

Maya

She'd signed it with a heart before her name. That's how friends sign letters and cards, not people in committed relationships. It hurts, but it's my fault. I should have tried harder. She made an effort to see me, to confess how she felt. She gave up the party life. She even came with me to see Colebrook and turned in the photos anonymously so neither of us would be legally involved. What did I give her in return? A bunch of excuses and a bad attitude.

But what finally pushed her to leave?

I didn't believe her about the alcohol. She needed someone to believe in her, to have faith in her, and I turned my back.

Karma must be out to get me. Because now my car won't start. I'm at the mid-way point between Morville and Coors, so towing in either direction would cost a fortune. I have no idea where the nearest mechanic is. Google points me toward a garage fifteen miles north, but I'd still need a tow to get there.

Maybe I can fix the problem myself. I pop the hood and take a look. I know the basics of a car. I can pinpoint where the engine is, where the oil goes, and some of the belts and screws. But I can't tell what's wrong just by looking. My car has over a hundred and fifty thousand miles. It was bound to die at some point. But why did it have to be today?

First my teammates, then my dog, and now my car. What next?

"Do you need a jolt?"

I turn around. An older woman approaches from the convenience store. After a brief conversation, ending with me telling her my romantic purpose for traveling to Coors, the woman pulls her car in front of mine and attaches our batteries with jumper cables. My car starts up on the next try.

"Probably just a bad battery," the woman says. "You could probably get it over to a mechanic and have it changed. Just don't make any stops along the way."

"Thanks a bunch."

"And good luck on your quest. I hope she takes you back."

"Thanks."

I got the support of a stranger, so karma can suck it. I won't get to Coors anytime soon, but at least I'll get there with a working car.

****

It's near dark by the time I'm on the highway again. I had to wait several hours for a new battery, but luckily it didn't cost me an arm and a leg. My car starts up without issue, and I make the final punch to Coors.

Coors is a much bigger town than Morville, but I don't think it's big enough to be a city. It's hard to see everything now that it's dark, but I'm sure it's more entertaining than Morville. Mom and pop shops take up Main Street, but just around the corner, there are plenty of mainstream places like Walmart and Applebee's. There's even a Chick-fil-A! Back home, my teammates and I would drive an hour to reach the closest one, but it was always worth it for their dipping sauce. Funny how every place in America can remind you of home.

At the first red light, I message Dawn to let her know I'm here. Instantly, I'm plagued with bad news.

Dawn: **Maya checked out of the hotel.**

Me: **Do you know where she went?**

Dawn: **No clue. She says she wants to be alone.**

Me: **Where does she usually go when she wants to be alone?**

Dawn: **A bar.**

Me: **She's eighteen.**

Dawn: **Maya has her ways.**

Me: **Would she actually?**

Dawn: **I honestly don't know**.

Maybe I shouldn't have reached out to Dawn. She obviously told Maya I was on my way, giving Maya plenty of time to think about my arrival and figure out how best to avoid me. Now here I am with an ugly car, little cash, and no idea what to do.

Relying on Google again, I calculate sixteen places that serve alcohol in the area. I could try every single one until I find her, but something tells me Maya isn't there. What would be her next outlet, if she couldn't drink?

Sex.

I swallow hard. Awful images parade through my head. Have I ever really thought about the number of people Maya has had sex with? I can use one hand to count the number of girls I've been with. How many hands would Maya need?

She only needs one hand, and that's mine. We can't change the past, but I'll be damned if I can't make a better future for her. I just wish I knew how to find her.

My phone buzzes, saving me from despair.

Dawn: **She just updated her Facebook status. Says she's staring at stone.**

Staring at stone? What the hell could that mean? Several things are made out of stone. Churches, statues, tools, gravestones…

Me: **I know where she is.**

Maya

I thought about getting a drink (I'm always thinking about it) but settle for a cigarette. It gives me the minimal high required to endure this trip down memory lane. I haven't been to a graveyard since my parents met the ground. I was supposed to stand in the front row with my family, but because I was in a wheelchair, I asked to be in the back so people wouldn't stare at me. Still, they stared. Always staring, wondering when I was going to crack.

I smoked a cigarette during my parents' funeral. Afterward, I got drunk off wine at the gathering at my aunt and uncle's. Dawn did her best to cover for me, blaming the Vicodin for my slurring behavior. Really, I just wanted to disappear from existence. I wanted to close my eyes, find a rainbow, and slide on down until I found gold or something better than what life was giving me. But I was in that wheelchair for weeks before I could move on to crutches. And once I managed to walk, I didn't care how much it hurt; I was getting out and having fun.

Closing my eyes, I inhale the nicotine and imagine that rainbow, taking me far away. But no matter where I land, even if it's Fantasy Land, I can't have fun anymore.

Because I'm alone.

I sit between my parents' gravestones. Just like bathrooms, they each had to have their own stone. Beautifully engraved, always surrounded by flowers. Who knew you could prepay for a service that puts fresh flowers on your grave every week? Were my parents that self-conscious, or did they worry no one in the family would bring flowers? I certainly haven't paid such respects, but I'm sure Dawn has. *They were my aunt and uncle too...*

My hands are empty besides the cigarette, which is almost out. I take the final inhale and throw the bud across the field. I don't know what I expected to feel or find by coming here, but it was on Dawn's checklist. Until I figure my life out, I might as well follow her advice. She told me I should speak to my parents while I'm here. Seems pointless since they're in the ground, and I don't believe in heaven or hell. I can't imagine them in either place. I only see them in their coffins, rotting away.

"You can't hear me, but if you could, I want you guys to know a few things." I take a deep breath; my chest burns from the smoke. "I'm mad at you for not coming to my gymnastic meets. I'm mad at you for always working and taking vacations without me. I'm mad..." My heart ossifies with some kind of emotion, but I can't distinguish if it's rage or sadness, guilt or despair, or maybe just cigarette tar. So I take another deep breath and allow the emotion to fill my body. I hope for tears, anything to clarify what I'm feeling, but nothing happens.

Maybe I'll have a different reaction at Connor's grave.

I start cigarette number two and make my way across the field, using my phone flashlight since it's pitch black. Technically, I shouldn't be here after the sun sets, but screw the rules. The dead don't care what time you visit.

Connor's grave is less flamboyant and decorated with hand-picked daisies. His parents were well off, but they lived in a ranch-style home and expected Connor to work hard to match their wealth. Sophomore year, Connor took on a part-time job, scooping ice cream. He always insisted on paying for everything when we went out, even though my weekly allowance could cover dinner and movies for a month. He was always polite and generous, but just so-so in personality. But that wasn't why I broke up with him.

The night before an important meet, my parents insisted on having Connor and his parents over for dinner. Everyone had someone to talk to, except for me. The conversation lingered on politics and religion, so I excused myself to use the bathroom, when really I snuck into the wine room to drink a glass of merlot, anything to mellow out how annoyed I was feeling. Not only did I have to endure another awful dinner, but Connor had made plans to golf with our dads the next day rather than attend my meet. He didn't understand my "obsession", as they all called it.

Rather than cause a scene, I went to bed, complaining of a headache and needing to rest. The next day at my meet, I stuck every single landing. And then, trophy at hand, I called Connor, while he was not making any hole-in-ones, and dumped him. But my exact words were: "We need to go on a break. I need to focus on my obsession."

His response: "I know you're mad I missed your meet today. Let me make it up to you."

Mine: "You can still hang out with my dad. I think he likes you more than he likes me."

Then I hung up.

A few weeks later, Connor died.

He hated country music too.

I'm caught off guard by the tears spilling out of my eyes. If there's any regret I have in my life besides telling my parents how I truly felt, it's not telling Connor what a great guy he was. The letter I wrote Daniel, I should have given to Connor. But instead, I acted like a child and used condescending words, giving that boy false hope instead of the truth.

It's harder now, ending things with Daniel, because at least with Connor I had drugs and alcohol, and later sex, to get me through the lows. Now it's just me and myself. And we don't make a winning team.

Since I don't have any flowers for Connor, I leave the unfinished pack of cigarettes next to his grave. He never smoked, but he had an unusual fascination with the movie Grease, so here's a tribute to that. *Hope they're playing Grease Lightning wherever you are, Connor.*

I wipe my face dry, exhausted by everything. I need to get out of here before I relapse.

What's next on Dawn's list? Can't do physical therapy this late at night, so I'll have to postpone that one. I've already missed AA. Looks like I've achieved everything I can for one day. Now I need to figure out where to sleep tonight since Dawn has ruined my stay at the hotel. Why the hell would she help Daniel, the one person I'm trying to avoid right now?

Technically, I have a house I could stay at. A very large house. A mansion, actually. It's under contract, but it's mine for a few more weeks. Unless I want to sleep in my car or drive even farther to find a decent hotel, I'm left with no other options.

When I reach the parking lot, there's a car next to mine. I freeze, panicked the cops are here to arrest me for trespassing. I quickly formulate an excuse. *Sorry, officer. I was here earlier and lost my phone. Had to come back to find it.*

Squinting my eyes, I see it's not a cop car. It could be a creeper. Which is worse because I can't defend myself. I back away until I'm out of the car's light and dig around for something sharp or heavy. I find a jagged rock about the size of a baseball.

Finally, the headlights turn off, and the person

exits the car. I maneuver behind a tree and wait. Whoever it is, they're carrying a bundle of flowers.

I release a held breath and drop the rock. They're just coming to pay their respects to someone. I guess I'm not the only one who sneaks into graveyards after hours.

Once the person is far enough away, I tip-toe back to my car. Just as I'm about to get in, I look at the car next to mine. Is that...?

My stomach leaps into my throat.

How the hell did he find me?

I'm mad enough to break his windshield, but his car already looks pathetic as is. I just wanted some space. Why couldn't he give me that? How dare he come to my hometown? To my parents' gravesite! With *flowers*? Who does he think he is?

If he thinks I'll turn around and chase after him, he's dead wrong. He can spend all night trying to find me. I hope a zombie eats him.

But he must've seen me or heard me moving because now he's coming back to the parking lot. I leap inside my car, turn it on, and go in reverse, squealing the wheels like a getaway van. When I move the car forward, Daniel screams, *"Stop!"* and belly-flops onto the hood.

Panicked, stunned, and mortified, I hit the brakes.

He rolls off the car, landing several feet away.

My heart hammers against my chest. I wait for him to get up, but nothing happens. If he's faking it, I *will* kill him.

What if he's already dead?

"Daniel!" I run to his side. He's sprawled out like a murder victim, but I don't see any blood or injury. Just dozens of white flower petals covering his body like a macabre work of art. His eyes are shut, but he's breathing. "Daniel, wake up!" I try shaking him.

He coughs once and then slowly opens his eyes.

"Getting tackled without any padding ... is rough."

I'd hit him if he wasn't in pain already. "Are you all right? What the hell were you thinking, jumping on my car like that? I could have killed you."

He sits up, dusting himself of the flowers. "I didn't want to lose you."

I do not need this. "You shouldn't have come here. Didn't you read my letter?"

"I read it a million times. I don't care. I'm not leaving you again."

"You must've hit your head. Get up. I'll drop you off at the ER for a CAT scan."

When I put my arms around him in an attempt to lift him, he grabs me by the waist and buries his face in my chest. He's either delusional from his fall or desperate to win me back. I can't handle either case, so I might as well give in until I can get him out of my hair for good. I will not have a repeat of Connor.

"All right, nice and slow," I say as he gets to his feet.

"I can walk," he says. "I'm fine."

"Then you can let go of me."

"I don't want to."

I squirm my way free. "So, you want me back? What's your plan? Give up your scholarship and football career to be with me?"

"I don't have a plan."

"Yes, you do. It's all laid out for you, the next four years. I don't belong in the mix."

"You belong wherever you want to belong, Maya. If you want to travel the world and I want to be a pro football player, we can still be together. Maybe not physically every day, but every chance I get, I'll be with you."

It's precisely as Dawn suggested. A long-distance

relationship. But just how many of those last?

"It won't work," I say. "You can try all you want, but until you let go of—"

"Colebrook is dead," Daniel says.

That escalated quickly. "Did he try to run?" I ask, thinking the police must have gunned him down.

Daniel shakes his head. "The police had a warrant to search his house. I guess he couldn't handle anyone finding out about his private life, so he shot himself." Daniel sort of smirks. "I think I may finally be getting used to death."

"No one gets used to it. According to Google, you just develop new defense mechanisms."

"Like sarcasm?"

I nod. "Like sarcasm."

We both smirk, and I feel that connection, that burning desire to reach out and touch him, but I have to remember why he's here. He wants me back, and I'm determined not to lead him on.

"So did the police search his house?" I ask.

"They found photos and videos. Now former athletes are starting to speak up. The guy was a monster."

"And you're not mad at me for turning in the photos?" He has to know it was me.

"I'm thankful. Without your help, I wouldn't be here right now, able to leave my town to go after the one thing I want."

He's making me out to be his saving grace, but I'm as faulty as the next drug addict down the street.

"You shouldn't want someone like me," I say.

"Why?"

"Because I'll mess up. I'll miss you too much. I'll start drinking again. I could cheat on you."

"No, you won't. We can do this." He grabs my hands. "Please, just give it a chance. A real chance this time."

"I did give it a chance. It didn't work."

"That's because I was stuck in a shithole situation back home. And now that everything's out in the open, we don't need to go back."

"What about Wesley? Did the police find anything on him?"

He sighs heavily. "Not officially, but it's implied."

"It won't drive you mad not knowing the absolute truth?"

"Not when I have you."

"Don't put it all on me!" Seriously, I'm trying to move on with my life, not get caught up in more drama.

"I'm not. I'm just telling you how I feel and what I want, Maya. You told me I shouldn't be ashamed of my wants and needs. That I shouldn't deny myself something because I feel like I don't deserve it. Because I do deserve it. And so do you."

I shake my head. This is too much for one day.

"I should've held on to the cigarettes," I say.

"I thought I smelled something."

"Yep, I'm smoking again. Doesn't that piss you off?"

"You leaving pisses me off."

"You *being* here pisses me off!" I twist away from him. "If you're really okay, you can drive yourself. I'm leaving."

He jumps ahead of me. "I'm here, telling you I'm willing to do whatever it takes to be with you, and you're mad at me?"

"Ah!" I throw my hands up. "I'm not mad at you. I'm mad at ... myself!"

"Why?"

This is killing me. "Because I fucked up my life,

and there's still so much I have to do to recover. And I'm scared that I'll fuck this up too. And then my life will be doubly ruined, and I just don't want to have to fix anything else. I'm tired of being broken. I know I preached nonstop about how unbroken I was at Fantasy Land, but it was all just a cover. I am broken. And it sucks!"

"So am I!" he exclaims, as though that will magically cure everything. "I'm broken, and there's still a lot I have to do to get better, but that doesn't mean I'm going to let you go. I won't. Even if you walk away right now, I will keep fighting for you. I'll do anything. I'll find a goddamn magic carpet and take you on a ride across the sky. I'll grow my hair out again. I'll—"

"You do not need to do all that." It sounds ridiculous. Though if Dawn were here, she'd think it the most romantic thing ever said.

"Then I won't. Because I can't have long hair when I play football. I sweat too much. And that's something I can't change. I'm a sweaty guy."

"I don't care that you sweat a lot. You don't smell bad when you do. You smell…" Like a wild demigod.

"I smell amazing, right?"

I don't want to laugh, but I do. "You're good with words. But don't think that's going to change anything."

"Nothing needs to be changed, Maya. I still love you. And I think you love me too. If you would just allow yourself to feel it."

"I feel plenty right now."

"But love is the one thing you said you would omit, remember? For me, I chose sorrow. And really, I don't want to have to choose anything anymore. I want to feel everything, even the bad stuff. Yours and mine."

"You're talking about things you don't understand. You're still new to all this. You think it's so easy to be normal after you go through something so horrific?"

"It's not easy. It's hard. All of it. But I don't care. Because I want you. All of you."

Why does he have to tempt me with such words?

"It's hard to be with someone," Daniel says, his voice so soft and gentle he could make demons cry. "But it's even harder to be alone."

There's no way to escape the hard. Everything I've done and everything I will do is hard. The alcohol withdrawal, coming to terms with my past, taking the next step, whether traveling the world or coaching a bunch of four-year-olds. I have no set plan. I have no idea how any of it will turn out. I might return to my old, destructive self by the end of next week. And if I turn down that path, I won't have anyone to bail me out again.

I'm more afraid of failing Daniel. Losing him permanently scares the hell out of me. I could see myself hurting him like I hurt Connor.

Do I trust myself at all?

No wonder I'm so scared. I actually love this guy. I'm a zillion times more vulnerable than I've ever been with anyone. Potentially, I could go a hundred steps forward with Daniel.

Or a thousand steps back if I screw everything up.

My legs are shaking. I wish we were somewhere less creepy with blankets, TVs, and potato chips. But that would warrant an invite on my part. Am I willing to give Daniel a chance? Am I willing to give *myself* a chance?

"You can follow me to my house," I finally say. "It'll give me some time to think things over. But if I change my mind once we get there, you'll need to go, okay?"

Daniel

It's legally her house for a few more weeks. By house, I mean mansion. It has a five-car garage, pillars in the front, statues, perfect grass, fountains, and a driveway longer than two football fields. But I don't care about any of that. I care about the girl sitting in the car ahead of me, debating her future and mine.

Should I get out? Wait? I've never felt more nervous before in my life. Has she had enough time to think? Will she tell me to leave?

Finally, she turns the car off and gets out.

Immediately, I do the same.

Her deadpan face doesn't leave me with much hope, but she nods at the white stone walking path and motions for me to follow. I grab my bag, hoping this means I can spend the night.

Through double doors, we enter a foyer twice the size of my living room. There are a few pieces of furniture in various rooms, all for selling purposes, I'm sure, but nothing on the walls minus a few mirrors and generic paintings. Everything is polished, shined, and perfectly arranged. No one would ever imagine a little girl grew up here.

In silence, Maya leads me up the circular staircase to a long hallway with four doors. She opens the last one, a white bedroom with a queen-sized bed and nightstand.

"It's changed a lot," she finally says.

"This was your room?"

She nods. "It was dark purple before with posters of all my favorite gymnasts over here. And I had my trophies here. And I even had my balance beam next to the window to practice on my own." She opens the window and runs her fingers against a protruding tree branch. "When I was a kid, I snuck out a lot. I didn't go anywhere. Just around the yard, down the driveway. Sometimes I'd sit outside for hours, wondering if my parents would ever go into my room to check on me and what they would do if they found me gone. I did this for years, but they never came in. Not once."

"I'm sorry."

"I figured if they didn't notice me sneaking out, then they wouldn't notice the bottles of wine missing from their basement."

"When was this?"

"It started when I was fourteen. A glass of wine now and then, just like my mom."

"And once she was gone…"

Maya shrugs her shoulders and laughs it off. "I'm not going to miss this place. It's being sold to another rich couple with a neglected son. Maybe he'll get this room and sneak out like I did."

"Where are you going to live?"

"I thought about buying a condo in Georgia to be close to Fantasy Land. I'm also thinking of getting a place somewhere around Coors so I can still see Dawn and my grandmother. I just haven't decided where."

"That sounds like a good plan."

"It's not a plan. It's just an idea."

"It sounds like a great idea."

"You think?"

"If you went through with that idea, I'd spend all my breaks and holidays in Fantasy Land with you."

"You wouldn't get tired of that? You wouldn't want to go home and visit your dad?"

"My dad plans to drive up for most of my home games. I'll see him lots. I was hoping you'd come up too. If you were free and wanted to."

"Indiana is cold."

"I'd keep you warm."

"With your sweat?" Her lips curve to one side, suggesting a smile.

"You could keep my dad company while he watches the game."

"I like your dad. He's nice."

"Then it's a perfect *idea*. Yours and mine."

"I wouldn't call it perfect, but it sounds ... nice." She looks out the window again. The wind blows the branch against the glass. For how well the house has been kept, why has no one thought to have that tree trimmed? I would fear someone was trying to break in every time the branch struck the window.

I've been in the doorway the whole time, but I make my way across the room and push back the invasive branch, silently promising to trim it should she allow me to stay. Maya closes the window. She shivers and rubs her bare arms.

"I feel dirty after being in that graveyard," she says.

"I feel dirty after being hit by your car."

She smiles again. "You can take a shower. Every bedroom has a bathroom."

"Okay."

"I'll order some food. Are you hungry?"

"For chips?"

She laughs. "For pizza?"

"Sure."

****

Maya's shower is probably one of the nicest showers I've ever been in. I spend the first five minutes soaking under the warm water, thinking about Maya's idea combined with my own. We'd spend most of our time apart, but our time together would be fun and meaningful. She'd watch me play football, and we'd spend quality time in Fantasy Land. And when football season ended, I'd visit her in Coors or wherever she chose to live. I'd go back to Morville from time to time but not for any extended period. Our lives would finally be balanced. We'd have everything and more.

But all that could go sideways. Maya could relapse. College could overwhelm me, and visits could become scarce. My dad might need me back home during breaks to help at the animal hospital. The police could ask for my help again should more evidence turn up against Colebrook. Will the investigation ever end? *Not until every child has been accounted for*, the sheriff said during his last public statement.

My eyes are closed, so it startles me when I feel her arms wrap around my waist.

"Maya?"

She buries her head against my chest and presses her cold, shivering body against mine. I hold her for the longest time, rubbing her back, restoring the warmth, washing, and gently kissing her. She cries but doesn't say anything. I don't need to hear words to know what she's trying to tell me. Finally, she takes my hand and places it directly on her scar. I feel so much pain, I cry with her.

After our long shower, we dress and eat pizza in the barren kitchen. Maya opens up about the coaching opportunity and how it might be good for her to return to physical therapy. She even mentions AA meetings. All the stuff she would have scuffed her nose at had we been having this conversation only weeks ago.

Things can change in a heartbeat. One minute you have nineteen friends and a safe community, the next, your friends are gone, and you feel like a stranger in your hometown. One minute you're convinced you have everything figured out, and then life throws you a curveball and you feel like you have to start over.

Sometimes you feel so alone and hopeless, and then someone walks into your life, pushing you not to give up.

I could have turned my back when Maya and I first connected online. I could have seen her as an out-of-control, emotionless person, not worthy of my time. But she ended up being so much more. She didn't save me from myself; she showed me *how* to save myself. By finding happiness and love, even in the darkest of places.

I won't bury myself anymore.

"Do you love me?" I ask.

She sets down her pizza slice and opens a bag of chips. "I love chips," she says. "But I love you more."

"More than Jack Daniels?"

"More than anything."

Even though my hands are greasy from the pizza and we both have pepperoni breath, I take her into my arms and kiss her. I have no idea what the future holds for us, but I'm holding on to her. I'm holding on and not letting go.

The End

NATALIE BLANK

Evernight Teen ®

www.evernightteen.com